AN EROTIC REIMAGINING
OF THE CLASSIC STORY

HER
SECRET
GARDEN

paige press

AN EROTIC REIMAGINING
OF THE CLASSIC STORY

HER
SECRET
GARDEN

RAVEN JAYNE

Paige Press
Leander, TX 78641

Ebook:
ISBN: 978-1-957647-02-9

Print:
ISBN: 978-1-957647-03-6

ALSO BY RAVEN JAYNE

PROLOGUE

MORNINGS ARE my favorite time of day because I have them all to myself. Some on the commune find it difficult to wake early, to leave their warm beds for the cold outdoors, but I've never minded. The light is gray and then blue, and the crisp air tickles my ankles and calves under the swirl of my skirts. I get to watch the sun rise as I collect eggs from the chicken coops, each one promising the yield of a fat orange yolk; next I milk the cows, always scooping a cupful out of the bucket for myself when I'm finished. The cream is sweet on my tongue, and it fills my empty belly and prepares me for the day ahead.

Best of all, though, since no one else is awake, there is no one to scold me for closing my eyes in bliss as I sip, or pausing to admire the way daybreak turns the pastures pink and gold. My mother was a painter once, and surely these were the colors of her palette. The elders built this community in order to withdraw from the world and abstain from its pleasures, but I can't help seeking them out anyway, these small, simple delights: the caress of a cool breeze on my sweat-damp face, or the grass glistening with dew in that first light. I know it's wicked to want luxury; I know that I risk my place in heaven for every one of these indulgences. But then God made them, I think—how can loving them be wicked?

But then again, God made *me*. And I want wickedness so much more than I should.

This morning, after I tend to the animals, I head to the kitchens for breakfast. Usually we eat as a community, but today it's a meeting day, so I'm all alone. Despite having reached legal majority, the elders won't let me take part in community meetings, and I can't pretend it doesn't sting. As they age and their bodies begin to quit on them, I've taken on more and more of the work of keeping the farm running, my strong young back shouldering some of its heaviest burdens. They need me to keep this place functioning, so why won't they let me have a say in how it's run?

At least I can take advantage of the solitude to raid the larder. I open the cupboard doors, but am faced with disappointment: there's nothing exciting in there, no butter to fatten my bowl of thin, tasteless porridge, or even sugar to sweeten it. In fact, there's almost nothing in there at all: just a brick of moldy cheese and a few onions starting to sprout stalks in the darkness.

That's when I hear the shouting. For a moment I think I've been caught and I freeze, terrified, even though there was nothing for me to find.

Then I realize the noise was coming from the meeting house. I shouldn't be able to hear them all the way over here—they must be arguing something fierce. And maybe that's no surprise, I think, closing the door on the bare shelves. We had a bad season this summer, our crops getting washed away by too much rain, and the winter was a long, hard, and hungry one. The elders took a vow of poverty when they established the commune, but I've lived my whole life here, and I've never seen our storehouses this brutally bare before.

I don't have time to think about it for too long. I always have the most chores, but on meeting days, I take on everyone's work: I am expected to weed the fields and to till them, to water what needs watering and make sure the cows move pastures. To bring sandwiches into the meeting hall when they break for lunch and to start cooking dinner as soon as the midday meal is eaten.

My good mood from the dawn evaporates as I go to one of the sheds to get a bucket of manure. It stinks of sulfur and ferment in there, and as I spread it over a newly empty field, it's hard not to feel hopeless. Our soil is and always has been rocky and thin; years of trying to improve it have been a dismal failure. There wasn't much porridge left by the time I got to the kitchens, and my stomach is grumbling with hunger again despite having just eaten. My arms ache from carrying the bucket, heavy with its fragrant load. I hear more shouting from the meeting hall. It sounds like the thunder that heralds a big, big storm.

I put the bucket down. They'll be at it for hours yet. So I decide to give myself a small gift—something much more indulgent and dangerous than admiring a sunrise or sneaking a little syrup into my porridge. I go to the orchards and sink down under one of the apple trees, which is just starting to sprout leaves again, little buds of green appearing on its stark bare branches. Its trunk can take my weight, and I close my eyes and let my limbs go loose, soaking up as much of the pale early spring sun on my face as I can.

There's nothing like these moments when there's no one around to keep me on task, to remind me to be good and be grateful. I breathe in the scent of decayed apple blossoms and, after a while, I let my hand wander under my skirts to the place between my legs, my deepest pleasure and most carefully guarded secret. Even more than luxury, we aren't supposed to have secrets on the commune—*don't be selfish* has been the soundtrack of my life since I was old enough to understand it.

But I *need* this. I need it to get by, to withstand cold mornings and late nights and the knowledge that despite the work I put into this place—despite the fact that it's the only home I've ever known—the elders will never respect me as an equal. So I let my fingers stroke the soft folds of my opening, where it's wet and hot and warm. I tease myself for a while, carefully avoiding my favorite spot until I can't wait any longer, and I have to press my fingers to that little nub, the sensation so shocking that I let out a gasp when I do it. My eyes fly open, praying no one was around to hear me, knowing no one ever is.

But for once, I'm wrong. In front of me stands a boy, maybe a few years older than I am. His hair is a mess of sandy curls, and he's broad shouldered, with the kind of strong, stocky body you get from working outside every day. He's looking at me and smiling.

As soon as my shock clears, I realize who it is: that's Mr. Petersen's son. Mr. Petersen runs a small general store nearby, and he buys honey from us once a week. I've met his son a few times in passing, but we've barely spoken before.

"Hi," the boy says. "I'm sorry to bother you. My father broke his leg, so he missed this week's pickup. He sent me in his place, but I must have gotten the day wrong. No one was at the honey sheds when I arrived, so I went looking and...can you help me?"

I rise to my feet, knowing my face must be pink with leftover heat and fresh shame. I almost never speak to boys, especially not by myself; we aren't allowed to spend unsupervised time with the opposite sex, so the adults try to keep us separate as much as possible. What did he see? Will he tell anyone what I was doing with my hand in my skirts, rubbing on myself like a cat in heat?

I try to remember myself. I am Mary Lennox, a daughter of the commune. I know how to behave, even if I don't always do it. "Of course," I say, keeping my gaze trained on the ground between us. "Come with me."

He keeps a respectful distance between us as we walk through the empty grounds to the sheds where the honey is processed and jarred. The day is already starting to grow colder, the sun slipping west in the sky, and I can feel my nipples prickling against the coarse fabric of my undergarments, straining against the front of my dress.

When we step into the shed together, the door swings closed behind us. In the quiet that follows, I hear the sound of his breath—the straw crunching underfoot as he shifts his weight—and realize I am truly alone with a boy for the first time in my life.

As I look around for the box with his father's name on it, I let myself sneak another peek at him, this time noticing his stark blue eyes and crooked smile. I'm not supposed to think about earthly beauty, but it makes me feel something when I see him dip a hand into his pocket, pull out a flask, and take a swig. His mouth is wet with the liquid. He licks his lips.

"Do you want some?" he asks.

"What is it?"

"Helps keep you warm on cold days," he says. His eyes skim my chest and I know he can't see my nipples beneath the coarse fabric of my dress, but still, it feels like he can sense them there, straining for someone's touch.

"Thank you," I say. The flask is cold against my lips, but whatever's in it stings like fire going down my throat. I cough once, twice, my cheeks heating all over again with shame. But he just draws closer. When he takes the flask back from me, his fingers brush gently against mine.

"There," he says. "It's getting so chilly outside. You'll start feeling warmer in a minute or two."

I do: a fire blooms in my belly, sending sparks all over my body. The shadows in the shed seem to deepen and dance, the warmth of all of it making me a little woozy, especially after having been out in the chill all morning. I reach out a hand and steady myself against the boy's shoulder.

"I saw what you were doing back there," he confides. "Exploring yourself."

"It's a secret." Whatever was in the flask makes me bold enough to meet his gaze at last, and his eyes are smoldering with heat.

"Of course it is," he says. "Everybody has one. Do you want to see my secret?"

Fear rises in my throat, but along with it, something else. Something hot and sweet and sharp, an ache that rushes through my body and makes my head nod *yes*.

The boy puts the flask back in his pocket before reaching into his pants and drawing out his penis.

I've seen them before, of course, but only ever on animals. You don't grow up on a farm without learning the plain facts of biology, so I've seen the cocks of cows and horses, but they were nothing like his, which is large and handsome and strange. His long, smooth shaft is as thick as the rest of him, and it's topped by a soft, round head with the wink of a slit in the middle. It's nestled in a dark thatch of hair, and it makes something inside of me twitch awake.

So this is why the men bathe alone. This is what they keep between their legs, in their pants. What they've been hiding from me all my life. I bend a little closer, unable to help myself, and it jumps in his palm, like it wants to touch me as much as I want to touch it.

The suddenness of the movement startles me, though, and I flinch back in surprise. The boy's hand touches my shoulder, and I can feel his warmth through all my layers. "Don't be shy," he says. "That's a good thing, when it does that. It means it likes you."

There's something happening between my legs again, like when I was touching myself but even more powerful, a pulsing like a heartbeat. I'm wet there, still, again, my slickness almost dripping through my undergarments now.

"You can hold it if you want," he offers.

I drop to my knees eagerly, my palm reaching out to replace his. He's heavy against my skin, so warm, and it jumps again, getting even fatter and thicker under my gaze. My mouth waters, getting wet just like my secret spot. I am certain what I'm doing is wrong.

Yet, I can't bring myself to stop.

"Does it feel good when you touch yourself?" he asks.

"Yes," I whisper.

"That's how it feels when you touch me," he says. "Just like that, when your fingers play with your sweet little clit. You don't even know what you're doing down there, do you?"

I look up at him, feeling trapped and ashamed and like I'm on fire with wanting something I don't understand, and can't name. A wicked need beyond anything I've ever known. *Clit*, I repeat to myself. A secret name for the hidden place.

A shaft of light falls across our bodies, and for a moment I'm grateful because now I have a much better view of his cock, pink and pretty, and how it's starting to rise up hungrily from the dark place between his legs.

Then I hear Sister Rachel's voice. "Mary," she's saying. "Mary, what have you done?"

It's not a question. It's a cry of horror.

And just like that, my world smears, and blurs, and falls apart. Did I misjudge the time? Did I fall asleep too long under the apple tree? How could I have let this happen?

My mind stays fixed on these questions through all that follows. I barely register what's happening as Sister Rachel drags me out to the border of our property, just inside the high walls of the Kingdom of Love, and instructs me to stay where she leaves me. I can't recall who comes next, or what they say. All I know is that I have committed a mortal sin, one that could infect every other girl in the commune. There is no forgiveness. There can be no appeals. I am handed a small bag of my belongings and ordered to leave the only life I've ever known.

I can never, ever come back.

The sun is setting in earnest by the time I start walking down the road, shaking with cold and shock, my feet numb in my shoes. I have complaints about the commune, of course, but I never expected to be cast out like this. Where will I live? What will become of me? The only stories I've heard about life outside are of its decadence, and how that decadence poisons the soul and keeps people from the paradise of the hereafter. I already gave into so much temptation within the commune—what will become of my soul outside of it?

I want to stop and weep, but I know that if I do, I might lie down in the road and never get up. I cling to the strength of will that's pulled me out of my bed on every cold morning, through endless chores—and *how* are they going to manage without me? Will they starve? Who will push the wheelbarrows, spread the manure, muck out the horse's barns?

I'm so consumed with questions that I barely hear the boy from the shed until he's right next to me, begging me to stop and talk to him.

"Mary," he says. "Mary, please—it's going to be okay, it is, I swear it."

"No!" I round on him, and now my cheeks are hot with fury. He seems surprised to see me go from meek to bold. I'm surprised, too. I've certainly never spoken to a boy like *this* before. "Don't you dare. Did they banish you? Are you never allowed to return?"

His stupid crooked mouth gapes open like a fish flopping. "You sinned the same as I," I cry. "Why are you allowed to go home when I am not?"

He shakes his head and reaches into his pocket mutely, pulling out a wad of crumpled bills and a few coins. I've learned to count money in order to sell our farm's products, but I don't know the value of what he's handing me—is it enough for a meal? Someplace to stay? Where might that be? I'm so ill-equipped for the world outside our walls. I don't know the first thing about how to survive on my own.

Somewhere in the depths of my mind, a memory stirs and sprouts.

"That's all I have," he says. "I'm sorry. I am. I wasn't—I didn't—"

I'm still staring at the money. I have no idea what to do with it.

It's worth a lot of money, Mary.

My mother's voice; it's her memory that begins to surface. She used to tell me about money before she died.

"You—" he starts. "You're very pretty, Mary. You could use that money to stay somewhere tonight. Maybe someone else would think you are pretty enough to share a room with you."

Your uncle Arch...you understand this is a last resort, only if you have nowhere else. No one else.

The boy continues talking, making me a plan. "I bet lots of men have never seen a girl as pretty as you. I could tell them, if you want. You could get plenty of money from them. Enough to stay in any room you wanted, and never wake in a cold bed again."

My mind is a tornado, a spinning mass of panic and fear. Still, though, I can grab onto one thing through the madness. If I had enough money, I could save the farm. I could go home again, if I could show them that I had the answer to the question they fought over even today—how to afford what we need to ensure good crops.

He will give you the painting, and you can sell it.

"I could bring you lots of this." He pulls out his flask, though I flinch at the memory of the taste now. "You'll feel so good, all the time. I can take care of everything for you."

There was something else, something important that she'd told me.

"Don't you want me to take care of you, Mary?"

If you must go to Misselthwaite Manor, remember one thing. Promise me.

The boy is right: I do need money. And I can get it. I have an uncle, and he has a painting I can sell. I can buy back my old life, maybe even have a dowry to make a proper match with an elder. Misselthwaite Manor isn't so far from here that I can't walk for a few days, or perhaps use this money for a ride. As long as I remember my mother's warning.

"Mary?"

You can never, ever trust Archibald Craven.

1

"Whore!"

That was the last word I heard before the gate closed.

Whore.

I hear it as I ride in the cab Mr. Petersen's son helped me get, despite being disappointed I would only allow him to take care of me like this. I've never ridden in a car before, and though my head is still aching with fear and grief, I appreciate how warm it is in here as I watch the still-thawing countryside speed by.

I was afraid the driver would talk to me the way the boy had—give me more of that drink, ask me to show him my secret, too, and again, I would say yes, again, I would want to, again, I would prove my wicked unworthiness—but he's silent as we wind our way through the last of the winter wheat fields towards Misselthwaite Manor.

It appears on the horizon like a dream. Its dark, sprawling face is lit up by the last rays of the setting sun. We pass through the front gate and drive twice what feels like the length of Kingdom of Love's farmlands to reach the front door. My home is a place of grays and browns, simple cotton, rough wool, thin soil, and stacked stone; here the land is covered in glossy green grass, and thick with trees and hedges. The house is grander and larger than anything I've ever seen; even the thick-paned glass in the windows seems luxurious to me.

How could my mother ever have walked away from all of this?

The sun sinks another few inches below the horizon, the world turning a shade darker, and I can't help shivering. *It's for the best that she did*, I remind myself. *She made an incredible sacrifice to ensure my ticket to heaven. She abandoned everything she had here so that I could grow up simply and devote myself to God.*

The driver stops the car and opens my door for me. I get out on shaky legs, feeling like a new lamb. There's a quiet about this place that seems supernatural, like a spell's been cast. The air is just as cold as it was at the commune, but I can smell something sweet on it, laurel or maybe sage. *There's a secret here that's bigger than my secret*, I think. An enchantment that has nothing to do with the cruel, invisible God I've worshipped since I was born.

But none of that matters, I remind myself. *I'm not*

here to stay. I'm here because this is my only hope, and the home of the only person I know on the outside.

Well, I don't exactly *know* Uncle Arch. Not really. He isn't even my uncle, biologically speaking. Before my mother came to the commune, he married her best friend, my aunt Lily; the three of them used to live together here before my mother got pregnant with me and renounced the wicked world for my sake.

She rarely spoke of that part of her life, but she would use it as a threat against me sometimes: when she'd find me dawdling over my chores or sneaking extra clementines into my pockets to snack on while I did my afternoon tasks. "If you prefer to be wicked, you can always go live in the filth and sin outside, if that's what you really want," she'd say. "A one-way ticket to hell, wrapped in your selfishness. It already has your name on it."

It wasn't what I wanted then, though, and it isn't now. My preference for wickedness came at too high a cost. I'm just here to earn my way home again.

I'll get the painting, sell it, and return to the Kingdom of Love a lost daughter, found. They won't be able to turn away the cash in such a desperate hour of need. And they need my labor, too. I can make things right again, I know I can.

I have to.

My return will prove that I am not selfish. I can pay back what they've spent on me over the years, and hopefully that dowry besides. If I can bring enough, marry a godly man, it will wash all my sin away. I'll become what I am meant to be: a worker, a mother, a wife. A good girl, on her way to heaven again. As I once was and can be again.

As long as you remember your promise. I silently promise again that I won't forget the dangers of trust.

The driver gets my bag out of the trunk and hands it to me, along with a card bearing his name and phone number. He's younger than the commune elders, but his hair and beard are shot through with the silver strands. I wonder if being out here in the world ages you prematurely—if by the time I return home, it will be with a wrinkled face and stooped back.

"Be careful," the driver says gruffly.

"Of what?" I ask, but he's already getting back into his car, the slam of the door shutting echoing into the thick quiet around us. He turns over the engine and glides down the drive, and then I'm alone with the house.

His warning feels ominous, but I don't need to worry, I remind myself. I'm only here to get the painting. I could be back at the commune in just a few days, before whatever trouble lives here has a chance to find me, or at least to sink its claws in too deep.

"Are you lost, little girl?" The sound of someone else's voice makes me jump, and I whirl around to see a woman standing behind me, one hand on her cocked hip, looking for all the world like she appeared out of the fog that's starting to creep along the grounds with nightfall. I glance back at the house and see lights coming on in its many rooms, though I can't see who's doing the lighting.

The woman standing in front of me is wearing a short red dress, its silk clinging to her body and making it clear that she doesn't have a single undergarment on. I've never seen anything so indecent before, and I'm shocked by the brazenness of her bare legs, the peaks of her nipples, and the curves of her breasts, which are barely contained by the shimmering fabric.

It should be repellant, I think, repulsive, to see a woman garb herself like a harlot, but instead it makes her look...bold, and even powerful. Like she's in control. The queen of this place, surely, carrying herself with such confidence. I've always been taught to hide my body, from others as well as myself; no one needed extra temptations from the flesh. But not only is this woman exposing herself, she seems shameless about it, like she doesn't care what the sight of her is doing to God...or to me.

My voice comes out with a slight quaver. "I'm looking for my uncle, Arch Craven. Does he still live here?" I ask.

The woman smirks and doesn't answer right away. Instead, she slinks in closer to me, coming so near that I can smell the sweet green of her fresh floral perfume. She smells like the height of spring, like a garden in its lushest bloom. The silk swishes against her legs and I want to touch that fine fabric, just to feel it between my fingertips. I don't react to her the way I did to the boy, exactly, but I feel a similar sense of alertness, like my skin is prickling, like I'm hungry all over.

"Your uncle?" the woman says, her voice as rich as satin in my ear. "Hmmm. I've never heard of any stray nieces. What's your name?" She sounds like music when she talks.

"Mary Lennox."

"Mary, Mary, quite contrary." She touches me, then, brushing a lock of hair from my face. It only lasts a few seconds, but I feel the contact of her skin on mine like a brand, searing me from the inside out. I'm wet between my legs again, my body rising like that boy's cock, coveting this woman's freedom and the way she makes me feel. At the same time, my heart beats faster, too, in fear, a gathering tightness in my chest.

Is sin stuck inside of me now? Will I be this help-less, this lustful, this stupid, forever?

"Does Archibald Craven live here?" I repeat, clinging to the only thing I know for sure right now: I need to find my uncle.

The woman shakes her head. Her lips are painted to match her dress, and it makes her smile so beauti-ful. "How does your garden grow, Mary?" she asks, and I suddenly understand Eve's temptation.

Yet this is a question I know the answer to. Maybe they want me to work for my supper here? "It wasn't a good harvest. All that seemed to thrive this year were the wildflowers—"

But she isn't really interested in the answer. Instead, she giggles and runs away, disappearing into the mist.

For a moment, I think about chasing her, but the darkness is closing in around me, and so is the cold. Is this how it's going to be on the outside, I wonder? Will everyone be so brazen, and strange, and rude? Will they make me feel this way every time we meet? Will I be able to resist all these glimpses of worldli-ness and leave with my soul intact?

I take comfort in knowing I won't be here for long. I pick up my bag and push through the unlocked gate, up the steps, each one a decision to risk everything. I walk across the wide porch to the front door. The brass knocker is too big and heavy to make a sound that doesn't wake heaven and earth. I steel my hand into a fist and pick up my hand to knock.

Before I can, though, the door swings open in front of me, and I catch my first glimpse inside of Misselthwaite Manor.

2

THE WOMAN who greets me is much less confusing than that creature in red was. She's older than I am, probably in her mid-forties. I'm pleased to see that, whatever sins have found her in here, she doesn't look too ravaged by them. In fact, she looks nice: her dress is far more carefully made than my rough, homespun garments, and it covers her from neck to ankles. Her hair is pulled back from her face in a plain bun, and she smiles warmly.

"Mary," she says, clapping her hands.

"How did you know?"

"You look just like Grace—your mother, I mean. I was sorry to hear of her passing." She talks too quickly for me to get a word in. "Your uncle isn't here, unfortunately." She ushers me inside, shutting the door behind me. "Business travels—you know how it is. His successes are coming fast and thick, and we are proud, but it's hard to have him away for such long periods. Of course, I can run the household myself for as long as I need to, but it feels different when he's home, I always say." She pauses briefly and laughs at herself. "Sorry, I got ahead of myself. I'm Mrs. Medlock."

"Pleased to meet you." I don't know what I'm supposed to say next; whether I'm supposed to shake hands, as the men in the community do, or maybe if I should bend my knees, the way we do when we greet God in the chapel. Surely that's too much, but I don't know what her people's rituals might be. Luckily, Mrs. Medlock seems satisfied by my response. She's already busy, anyway, walking me through the endless, maze-like halls of the house and talking up a storm about both it and the man who lives here.

"It's particularly hard since the Master of the house was widowed," she says, shaking her head. When we pivot from the hallways, it's to pass through one grand room after another, all of them high-ceilinged and wood-paneled, with more of those enormous windows. I could stop and stare in each one for days, taking in all the details and luxuries, but she passes through them without a second glance. I am happy to be kept moving, I think: there's a fire roaring in every hearth, but they aren't enough to heat so much space, and the air in here feels as cold and still as a tomb.

In one, I spy an oversized painting of a young man. His face, rendered in oil, looks morose. I wonder if it's Uncle Arch, if he was melancholy even in youth, before meeting his wife. Was their time together only a brief happiness for him? I rush to catch up to Mrs. Medlock to ask, but I'm distracted by her words.

"And of course, your aunt Lily's death was really the end of any happiness for him," she is saying. "He could never get over losing her, and we doubt he ever will."

She turns to me as she leads me briskly down a hallway illuminated by glowing brass sconces. I have to hold myself back from touching a fingertip to their frosted glass. I've never seen so much wealth so casually displayed. "That's why so much of this place is locked up," she continues, her tone softer now, confidential. "It reminds him of her, and the life they had together. Before. He thought ridding the place of her memory would help. It didn't."

This story seems as potent and magical as the house itself does: my uncle's tragic loss, and the way he's mostly shut himself away from the world. No wonder the grounds feel haunted.

We start up a flight of stairs, and Mrs. Medlock's monologue finally has to pause so she can catch her breath on the climb. I take advantage to cut in with a question. "I met a woman before, when I was outside. I thought she might be Uncle Arch's new wife. But if that isn't so…is she another servant?" I can't imagine anyone who wasn't the lady of this manor being so bold.

"Oh, no, I'm the only one working today. It's

Sunday!" Mrs. Medlock tells me cheerfully. I'm not sure she answered my question.

"Are you sure? Do you know her? She was wearing the most scandalous—"

"People do get lost around here," Mrs. Medlock says. "Perhaps she was at a party at one of the other houses nearby and wandered away. I wouldn't worry about it, dear."

I recall the drive up to Misselthwaite: there were no other houses anywhere close to this one, certainly not close enough that anyone would wander over by accident. And *especially* not in that scrap of silk, in the cool of swiftly falling night. But I don't want to push my luck with Mrs. Medlock, especially on our first meeting, so I keep my mouth shut and follow her through what feels like a dozen more halls and up three more flights of stairs, each one narrower and creakier than the last.

Finally, she draws a key from the ring she wears at her waist and unlocks the door to a room at the end of a hallway. "This is where you'll be staying," she announces.

I should have been prepared by the grandeur of the house, but still, I had somehow assumed they'd find somewhere smaller to put me. This room isn't as large or well-appointed as some I've seen on our walk, but it's much bigger than the dormitories where I've slept my whole life—and that room housed eight of the Kingdom's women.

This place would make every elder in the

commune scowl. Dormer windows keep it airy, and the furniture, though simple, is beautifully made. In addition to the bed, which is thick with quilts, there's a single straight-backed chair and a three-drawer dresser with a lamp on top of it. It's too dark to see much out the windows, but it looks like I'll be able to see for miles from here. I do hope there are gardens.

I should rather be hoping it doesn't spoil me, I quickly correct. Should I ask if there's anything smaller? I don't want to trouble Mrs. Medlock, but—

"There's a bathroom down the hall," Mrs. Medlock says, and I don't tell her that though I recognize the word, I've never used anything fancier than an outdoor privy before. "You've likely had an exhausting day, so I'll leave you to settle in." She smiles at me fondly before bustling out of the room, leaving me alone with my small rucksack of possessions and no idea what to do with myself.

She's right, though. I am tired. I walk over to the bed and crumble into it, facedown, but it's too soft: I sink into its surface so easily I'm worried that it will swallow me up. I flip onto my back and stare up at the ceiling, my thoughts running wild as I try to adjust to all that's just happened. I'm here, but my uncle isn't. It'll be some time before he's back, which means I don't know how long I'll have to wait to ask him about the painting. I don't know how long I'll have to resist enjoying this respite from my real life.

Though it isn't all luxury: the fireplace in my room isn't lit and Mrs. Medlock didn't think to leave me any wood; the chill is sneaking in through the cracks around the windows, frigid and damp. I haven't eaten since my too-small breakfast. I have no chores to take my mind off of any of these things. I'm alone in the world, and I am frightened by my helplessness.

There is one thing, I think, that I could do to make myself feel better. Now that I'm alone in a mostly-empty house with no one to spy on me, I take off my skirts and slide under the covers, my fingers finding my spot again easily. What did the boy in the shed call it? My clit? It wants attention, and though I try not to think about anything—especially not that boy, with his thick cock, or how my mouth watered when I knelt before him—the image of the woman in red keeps coming back to me. I imagine her touching me: taking off all of my rough wool and sliding her silks against my skin.

I can't imagine anything, even the sensation I'm chasing, that would feel better than to wear a garment like that: to be brave and free like she is.

Already I'm succumbing to the wickedness that creeps into my heart like the cold night air.

3

I WAKE in the morning to the sound of my bedroom door being opened, and then shut again. I've twisted off the covers in my sleep—they were warmer than any I'd ever slept under, and they made me sweat— but now I realize my nakedness is on display to my visitor.

Yanking my shirt down to cover as much as I can, I look up to see who's come. It's a girl, probably a few years older than I am. She's very pretty, dressed in sleek black with her hair pulled up into a mass of curls, and the look on her face is one of patient amusement. I can tell already she knows heaps of things that I don't, and probably never will. "Come on, you little bag lady," she says. "Up with you, now."

I have no idea what she means by that. "What's a bag lady?" I ask, trying to reach for my skirt on the floor without exposing any more of myself to her.

"A bag lady," she says carefully, like maybe I'm slow, "is someone who needs to bathe. Come on. The shower is complicated, but I'll show you. I'm Martha, and you're Mary, or so I hear."

I finally get a hold of my skirt and slide it up around my waist, grateful that Martha isn't close enough to smell the rich scent of what I was doing last night wafting out from where it was trapped under the covers. Then I follow the clack of her heeled shoes down the hall trying to make sense of this latest mystery—how can a bath be complicated?

The bathroom has a toilet, a sink, and a free-standing bathtub as large as a horse's trough. I'm headed toward it when Martha walks over to a spigot on the wall. When she turns it, water starts to rain from a piece of metal toward a small drain on the tiled floor. "You have to push this one all the way this way for full pressure, these two are for temperature, and this one changes the rhythm of the flow," she says, gesturing to the other handles, glancing back at me to make sure I'm following. "Understand?"

Not at all, but she's already moved on to the next thing. "Come on, now. Undress. We have plenty to do, and it all starts with getting you fresh as a daisy," she instructs, her voice as businesslike as ever.

I don't hesitate in undressing. I do it quickly, making a neat pile of my clothes and stepping closer to the spray of the water, but then I do pause, waiting for Martha to instruct me in what to do next. Do I get…under it?

"It's handheld," she says, pulling the faucet from the wall and demonstrating how it moves around thanks to a long flexible metal pipe. I've never seen anything like it before. A complicated bath, after all. "You can do whatever you want with it. Reach any place," she continues. Her gaze drifts over my naked body, and I feel my skin prickle under her attention. I'm used to being naked in front of the other women, but we never looked at each other's bodies. Is that gaze what's making my nipples so hard, or is it the cold? I think guiltily of how long I touched myself in bed last night. I thought I'd be satisfied by it, but I want a hand between my legs again already.

"Is this too hot?" Martha asks. She takes my hand and guides it to the steaming spray, and the feeling of her skin on mine is so good that I let her. Then the water hits me and I jump back, unable to help myself. I've never felt anything like that before, that warm, steady spray.

Martha looks at me warily.

"We usually bathe with a bucket," I confess, my head hanging low. I hate feeling so out of place here. "So, I'm not quite sure—"

Martha doesn't laugh, though. "Oh my God. I heard about this," she says, shaking her head. "Okay. Let's get you in here and review the basics."

She has me hold the sprayer, as she calls it, and teaches me how to wet my body so that I'm warm and glistening everywhere. Then she has me hang it back on the wall and watches approvingly while I soap myself, even leaning in, sometimes, to rub some suds into a place I might have missed. Her touch is light but tender, and the soap smells like roses. I've never felt so good in my life before.

The steam thickens the air in the room, making everything warm and wet. "Look at you, so pink and white," she murmurs as she strokes a hand down my arm. "And such a nice firm bum." Her eyes trace the curve of my ass, and I feel like I'm glowing under her gaze.

"This is a funny place, but you'll do all right if you pay attention," she continues, taking the soap out of my hands and putting it back in its place in a wire rack attached to the wall. Then she takes the sprayer and rinses me carefully and thoroughly.

Her voice becomes just another lapping wave of sensation on my body. She sprays my collarbones, and then my breasts; she has me lift up my arms and rinses my underarms before gently scraping a razor along them. I'm still marveling at the sensation when she moves around to the back of my body. She let me wash back there myself, but now she parts my cheeks gently in order to let the water fall between them, rushing down to tease my special spot before dripping down my legs.

That wetness mingles with my own, and the needy place between my legs pulses harder every minute. Martha uses her razor on them too, but all I can concentrate on is how, between rinses, she brings the sprayer up so that the water hits my clit full-on and makes my knees buckle with sensation. She must know what she's doing, because she lingers there as I tremble, sparks shooting through my body like shocks. It's only after the wave of pleasure passes that guilt creeps in. My neediness is the reason I'm here in the first place.

I can't keep sinning like this.

I step away from Martha, and even though it's cold away from the spray and steam, I make myself hold my ground. I close my eyes against the sight of her, with her rich garments, her worldly smile. When I get back to the commune, I will be pure. "I really *must* return to my room until I can speak with Uncle Arch!" I insist.

But when I open my eyes, Martha is still smiling gently at me, only now there's a man in the room. He's slim, with a square jaw and a narrow, Roman nose. His hair is dark and neatly parted at the side.

Is this him? Uncle Arch, home already? And is this how I meet him, naked and wet, with my pleasure still pulsing weakly between my legs? I'm humiliated.

Martha shuts off the water and places the sprayer back on the wall. "My brother, Dickon Sowersby, this is Mary Lennox," she says. Then, to me, she continues, "Dickon's a marvelous tailor, and you certainly can't wear your old clothes. Step out here, drop your arms, let him look at you."

Ah. Not Uncle Arch after all. This is all still very

strange, but I do need clothes to wear, and maybe this is how they do things out here? Mother always said the world was full of wicked temptations. But that's fine. I know how to be a good and obedient girl. I step away from the lingering heat of the shower and allow Martha to dry me briskly with a towel so thick it could absorb an entire river.

Dickon smiles at me, and something in my heart lightens. It's impossible to be scared in front of someone whose face is so open and kind. "So *this* is the daughter of the storied Grace Lennox?" he says. "Maybe her greatest work of art."

What does he know about my mother? I open my mouth to ask him about her—what she was like here, and if *he* knows anything about my painting—but then there's something cold circling my waist, making my nipples harder than ever. I realize he's wrapping a measuring tape around me, his fingers nimble and quick on my bare skin. He's *touching* me. I've never been touched like this by a man before, on skin that's usually under my clothes, and the sensation is so overwhelming that it almost blots out everything else in the room.

Still, I hear Martha saying, "Dickon's always had a thing for wild animals." She swats him with the towel, which he doesn't seem to mind. "I'm not surprised he likes you."

I'm not wild, I want to tell them. In fact, I'm very tame. As good as can be. Pure as milk. But I can't quite get the words out with Dickon moving the tape from my waist to the inside of my thigh, stroking the tender skin there. Can he smell it on me, what I was just doing, I wonder? Or did the shower water wash it away? Martha runs a finger over the curve of one buttock, stroking me up and down, and now there are so many hands on me, so much touching making my head light and dizzy. "You'll want to emphasize this," she says. "For a girl as young as she is, she has all of a woman's curves."

"She does," Dickon agrees. The measuring tape is underneath my breasts, now, snug against my ribs. He's still kneeling in front of me, and I feel my legs parting just a little bit, trying to open themselves to give him access, because maybe it isn't as sinful if I don't ask and he just—

The door opens, and Mrs. Medlock steps through it. "Martha! Mary is our *guest!*"

Now it's Martha's turn to gasp and jump back. I'm filled with the scorch of shame, but Mrs. Medlock doesn't so much as look at me. All of her ire is reserved for Martha.

Dickon seems unconcerned. "Suppose I'll have to make different clothes then, won't I?"

Mrs. Medlock isn't amused. "I'm certain you will. For pity's sake. What do you think Mr. Craven would say?"

Dickon looks at me again, a brief, hot gaze, before he turns back to Mrs. Medlock. "To you, or behind closed doors?"

Mrs. Medlock shakes her head. "Well, I suppose

you'll see for yourself soon enough. Shoo, now." Then, to me, "He's expecting you in his office."

"Does that mean—?" Hopeful relief neatly replaces the hunger in my belly.

"Yes," Mrs. Medlock says, thankfully. "The Master came home for you."

4

MARTHA AND DICKON leave me to get dressed by myself, and I'm grateful for the time to clear my head. I pull on my rough commune garments and let the scratch of wool on skin remind me who I am, and where I belong. I am a child of the Kingdom. I will act like one.

But then no one comes to fetch me, and between boredom and anxiety, I find myself itching again, now with naughty possibilities. When I've touched myself before, I imagined vague things; now I want to do it again with the memory of Dickon and Martha's hands, their attention and their praise, fresh in mind.

I have to leave this house soon. Before I do something I can't take back.

I go over to the window and look out over the grounds, trying to calm my racing mind, to distract it with something soothing. The yards seem overgrown, still winter quiet even though it's the beginning of spring. I trace a maze of paths and walkways, brambles and hedges, until I see something red flash in the corner of my eye.

It's her. The woman from last night, my first taste of how this place would change me.

The glimpse is fleeting. The woman seems to disappear just as quickly as she appeared, somewhere between a wall and the house. I don't make a decision so much as I let impulse carry me out of my room and down all the flights of stairs to the ground floor, where I find a door that lets out into the gardens.

Outside the air is bracing, especially with my hair still damp, but it's not too cold as long as I keep moving. I follow a path that leads me deeper onto the grounds and it's even more overgrown down here than it looked from above: the gardens are choked with weeds, and the plants that have managed to thrive are wild and overgrown. Still, I can tell that the soil here is far richer than what we had on the commune, where if we stopped working, the plants would die almost instantly. I could do so much with a place like this.

Some brave daffodils are starting to bloom again, shoving against the disorganized riot to put out their blossoms, and I'm captivated by these slivers of beauty amidst so much decay. I can't figure out which way the woman in red was going, or where I last saw her, so I let the flowers lead me, moving from a stand of stunted peonies to the first buds of a rosebush to a lavender bush just sprouting purple. I'm crushing a piece of it between my hands, inhaling the scent, when I hear singing. This time, I follow the sound, as captivated by the tune that is so unlike the hymns I know as I am by the idea of seeing her again.

The song gets louder as I round corners and cut across paths. Finally, a turn brings me to a high stone wall with a metal door sitting ajar in its center. Mrs. Medlock said some of the house was off-limits, but the door is open, I reason, as I peek my head around to see what's inside.

She's led me to the strangest and most beautiful garden I've ever seen. This place, at least, is well-tended to. Rosebushes are already blooming, and so are patches of lilies and climbing vines of star jasmine. The space is dotted with oddly-shaped stone benches and oversized birdcages; they must bring livestock through here sometimes, because hooks to hold their leads are bolted into the stone walls. The longer I look, the stranger it gets: I see a wooden cabinet open to display whips and bridles, but why would you ever let a horse in where it could trample so many delicate flowers? There's also a picnic table with a padded leather top no one could think of eating on.

And then, finally, my eyes light on the songbird in crimson. The woman I saw stands on a bench with one leg thrown over the shoulder of a man in a plaid shirt whose face is buried in her secret nest. He's thick in the shoulders, with rough hands that grab her skin. She doesn't miss a note even as her entire body tenses and a shudder runs through her along with the final note. Our eyes meet, and she smiles brightly at me as the man pulls back to wipe his mouth.

"Not bad, little slut," the man tells the woman whose body I can't stop staring at, breasts so much fuller than my own beneath the silk, and from the glimpse I saw, no hair at all between her legs.

"Now, now, Ben Weatherstaff, you know perfectly well I didn't miss a note. Am I your favorite little slut?" She laughs, and I'm startled to hear that word used here like a prize and not a shame, as I'm used to hearing it at home. Intrigued, I start to walk into the garden, my feet carrying me forward without conscious thought.

Suddenly, my way is blocked by the enormous man she called Ben, and he looks angry. "You don't belong here!" he growls.

His words break the spell I was under, and all of the fear I didn't feel before rushes through me like a flash flood. What am I doing? I turn and bolt, running back to the Manor as quickly as I can find it, finally bursting through the doors with a sheen of sweat on my skin and my skirts knotted around my ankles. I try to find the staircase that will lead me back to my rooms, but the hallways twist and turn on me, and I can't seem to locate any landmark I remember.

As I pause to catch my breath, I hear a voice

through one of the doors. The low, masculine tone is commanding—and clearly deeply frustrated. "She's been here less than 12 hours and you've already lost her?"

Are they talking about me? I draw close to the door the noise seems to be coming from, and press my ear against it so that I can hear better.

"I'm sorry sir, but we—" That's Mrs. Medlock.

"Find her," the man rumbles, "and don't let me see you until you do."

There are footsteps, and I realize too late that I should have moved when the door opens and, without it to support my weight, I tumble into the room.

This is the warmest place I've been in this house yet. A fire crackles in the grate, and the floor is mostly covered with a thick fur rug. The furnishings are sparse aside from an imposing desk, behind which sits an even more imposing man.

So *this* must be Uncle Arch. He's wearing traveling clothes, but even dusty and creased I can tell that they've been well tailored, perhaps by Dickon. I can also tell he's tall even when he's sitting, and his gaze is razor sharp. He's beautiful like the man in a painting I saw last night, same high cheekbones. Sad, dark eyes. But no, the artist got too much wrong. This man has a sharpness to his features. A danger.

As I look him over, he does the same to me. I can almost feel the power of his assessment, and it feels... heavy. Shyness forces my gaze to the floor, and when

I look up again, he looks hungry, I think, in a way I can't imagine an uncle should look.

"That will be all, Mrs. Medlock," he says. She walks out of the room and shuts the door behind her, leaving us alone together.

He doesn't speak, so I do. "I appreciate you returning to meet me, and I don't wish to bother you any further. My mother said…" I try to add more strength to my voice before I continue. "I'm here for my painting."

He doesn't respond, just keeps *looking* at me, his gaze unnerving in its singular intensity.

"I believe…it's a portrait of your late wife? I understand Aunt Lily was a great beauty. And the portrait was…people said it was one of my mother's greatest." His silence makes me anxious and my words come out too fast, tripping over each other. "The last of her works before she retired to the Kingdom of Love. She left it in your care, in case I needed it. And now I do."

As I'm talking, his face remains inscrutable, save for that sharp-edged hunger. It makes me self-aware in a way that feels wrong. Even without my mother's warning, I'd have been on edge. Knowing that my nipples have pebbled beneath his stare, the faint disappointment that I'd worn something so homely to meet him…every good part of me that's left is screaming that I should run as fast and far from him as possible. I could be back at the commune before nightfall if he's willing to call me another cab.

"Do you know how many paintings are on this property?" Uncle Arch finally asks, his voice cracking like a whip through the still air in the room.

Of course I don't. I can't imagine anyone does, given the size of this place. "But this one belongs to me," I remind him.

"I hardly have the time to deal with this. If you are certain that what you want is to take that painting and leave?" He waits for my nod. "Then it will be on my time, and not yours. I can't say how long it might take me to get around to it. Of course, in the meantime, you'd be my honored guest."

Despite the sinking of my stomach and still-protesting conscience, I thank him.

"But if you're going to stay here, there are rules," he says, his tone lower now, reverberating through my body.

"I can follow rules," I tell him, swallowing down the bitter taste of untruth. If I had followed the rules, I wouldn't be here, but the thought of this man knowing what I've done is humiliating enough for me to compound my sin with a lie.

"One." He leans back in his chair, flicking his gaze over me again, ruthless, casual. "You are to obey every member of this household, no matter how lowly. Whatever they say, you do. I do not want any trouble from you."

He rises to his feet and walks over to me. He's even taller than I imagined, with broad, strong shoulders and a narrow waist. His body feels powerful but contained—very different from the righteous, wiry men I've always known. He pauses to see if I'll protest, then continues, circling me now as he speaks.

"Two. Parts of the grounds are forbidden. The garden you so blithely strolled into just now is off-limits. As are my quarters."

He's close to me now, close enough that I can see the full power of his body, even as his clothes try to hide it: his muscular thighs, broad shoulders, corded forearms. I can feel the heat radiating off of him, and something else, too: pure power, intoxicating enough to make my knees feel wobbly. He's more potent than the liquid the Petersen boy let me sip, and I nearly step toward him.

You can never, ever trust Archibald Craven.

"Three," he continues, apparently indifferent to the effect he's having on me. "Some nights, you may find that I am entertaining guests. Sometimes you'll be warned in advance, and you are to stay in your room from the time the sun sets to the time it rises. If you haven't had warning and you see guests in this house or its grounds, you are to immediately go to your room and stay there. Do not engage with them, not so much as a word. You are not invited to attend the entertainments. Do you understand?"

"Yes," I murmur, my voice as small and helpless as I feel. Is the lady in red a guest? Why didn't Mrs. Medlock just say so when I asked yesterday?

He's behind me now, and I feel the suck of air when he inhales against the back of my neck.

"Have you bathed?" he asks.

"Yes."

He steps away from me, and then comes around so that he's facing me, leaning against his desk. "Take these grotesque clothes off," he commands.

The shame of this morning—how easily I forgot myself—comes over me again. I already feel naked in front of this man. Is he really going to make me—

"Obedience, Mary," he intones. "Don't disobey me the first time I ask you to do something. You are here on my charity."

So I do as I am asked. I strip off every layer, feeling his eyes on me the whole time. When I am finally done, I face him, and I can see that he is unashamed of how he's looking at me. His cock is hard in his pants, a thick rod much bigger and more imposing than the boy's was.

"Hands on your head. Lace your fingers."

This time, I obey instantly. Uncle Arch prowls up next to me again, dipping his head to inhale at the skin of my collarbones, his warmth tantalizing close to my bare breasts.

"Mmmm," he murmurs, and I'm molten between my legs, slick and ready for—I don't even know what. *Something.* I suck in my breath to keep from making a sound.

Then he moves away again, all business. He rings

a bell on his desk, and stands staring at me, arms crossed over his chest, until Mrs. Medlock rushes in.

"Sir?" she asks.

"Her clothes smell like a tragic childhood. Burn them."

But what will I wear? I don't have time to wonder.

"Put your arms down," he commands me. "And stop blushing. Your body's as perfect as I've ever seen. Shame doesn't fit it well."

Then he stalks off through the open door, leaving me alone with Mrs. Medlock. She doesn't seem shocked, like she was this morning with Dickon and Martha. Instead, she dutifully gathers up the pile of my clothes and leads me back to my room. It feels like it takes forever this time.

I shiver as I march through the cold of the hallways, bare for anyone to look upon, trying not to disobey again by wearing my shame.

5

I WAKE IN DARKNESS, some deep part of the night, to the sound of a man's voice. It's a low rumble, almost a purr, the sound faint and echoing. He's not in my room, I think. I hope. Perhaps in the hall outside?

I lie there for a few minutes, waiting, straining to hear what he's saying. I think I catch the edge of my name—*Mary*—but it could just be the sound of this old house shifting itself. A pipe clanging in the walls. Floorboards settling in the cold. *Go back to sleep*, I urge myself.

But then I hear it again. If not my whole name, then a sound like *mmm*, like satisfaction, that tugs low in my gut. This isn't an entertainment, surely, and if I can learn anything that will help me survive my time here... I throw off my covers and get up to see if I can locate the source of these noises. If anyone asks, I can say I was sleepwalking.

How comfortable I am already getting with lies.

Mrs. Medlock brought me a robe to wear while my clothes are being made, and I'm grateful for its warmth as I slip it around my shoulders. I pad through the halls of Misselthwaite Manor silent as a ghost, my bare feet gliding along the worn wooden floors. In the dark it feels even bigger than it did in the daylight, like the house has expanded, somehow, and the night itself has come inside.

I go down one flight of stairs, but everything's locked on that floor, so I descend again. Here I find a long-disused parlor, its furniture covered in dust cloths and cobwebs forming lace in the corners of the windows. I'm wiping them away with one careful finger when I hear it again. That voice.

I'm closer to it here than I was before. I still can't quite make out what it's saying, but I can tell it's a man's voice. It sounds almost like Uncle Arch, I think, but without the commanding edge that threatened to scrape me raw in his study. Whoever this is sounds…sleepy. Relaxed.

The thought of Uncle Arch compels me. He holds the key to my future, so perhaps it's not surprising that when I think of him, I think again of power: raw force radiating from the man who stripped me naked and then flayed me with the whip of his gaze. No one has ever made me feel anything like that before.

I want to see him again.

No. I need to.

If I can study him, I can understand him. If I can understand him, I can break this spell he has over me.

No earthly man can possibly have the sort of power I've assigned to him. The only way to make it through my time here as unscathed as I can is to find a way to make him human. Just a man. Well-built and clever, more than any men I've known at home, but a man nonetheless.

Of course, I have no idea where to find him in this haunted pile.

I try room after room, but they're either locked or abandoned. But every time I think about giving up— going back to my room and trying again in the morning—I hear that low whisper and it urges me onward. I want to find it.

Eventually I decide to risk going down to the first floor. From my limited exploration so far, it seems to be the most inhabited, so it's where I'm most likely to be discovered. But maybe it will at least give me a clue about where I can find Uncle Arch, or whoever's making these noises. Maybe even both.

Instead, I find myself in a library. It's a long, narrow room, its shelves stacked with books from floor to ceiling. Moonlight filters in through the windows, washing the room in a pale, ghostly light that almost makes me wonder if these rooms really are haunted.

"Aunt Lily?" I whisper, but no spirit answers.

There are no paintings on the walls here, because there's no room for them, but the place does seem to be filled with sculptures I don't understand. A collection of silver shapes—some long and narrow, some shorter and rounder, almost like bullets but not quite —sit on the mantelpiece over the fireplace. All of their bottoms are flared and flat. A collection of finely made riding crops is hung near one of the windows. And everywhere there are keys—ornate brass and simple silver, like the collection that hangs at Mrs. Medlock's waist has been hung around the room for anyone to find.

I'm not interested in the keys, though. Instead, I find myself drawn to the books. We didn't have any on the commune, except the Bible, of course. How many stories are crammed into this room? What worlds are contained within these pages?

I slide a slim volume off the shelf and admire the oxblood leather binding. It feels surprisingly light in my hand, almost weightless.

When I open it, though, I find that it's been illustrated with the filthiest images imaginable. Each drawing is richly, almost painfully detailed: the hot pink flower between the thighs of a woman being held open for inspection by a group of men. The veins in a man's cock as he pushes it into the anus of a woman who looks...who looks like she's *enjoying* being stretched so wide.

As I flip through the pages, my fingers furtive and guilty, I see bodies intertwining in ways I never dreamed possible, each one introducing me to another degrading, beguiling act. I barely know what I'm looking at, but the place between my legs begins to throb with want, like it always does lately.

I slam the book shut, flinching as the sound echoes in the empty room. I put it back on the shelf hastily, so that if anyone comes, they'll find me empty-handed. But I don't hear anyone stirring.

I reach out and take another.

This one has the same subject matter, though its illustrations are less detailed, and done in black and white instead of color. Somehow, though, they're just as erotic. The bodies almost feel like they're in motion, and I imagine that I can hear them: the women's sweet sighs and the men's lusty groans. The cry she might utter when he spanks her exposed buttocks. The wet sound of his fingers in her mouth and between her legs.

The pulse of my need has gotten too strong to ignore; I'm not wearing underwear, and I can feel my own slickness dripping down the inside of my thigh. I put this book back on the shelf, too, and seek out a third: something small enough that I can take it back to my room and page through it while I touch myself.

I slip it into the pocket of my robe, and just as I do, I hear footsteps outside the room. I glance around to make sure I haven't disturbed anything, and my gaze falls on the silver bullet-shaped things on the mantelpiece. There are so many of them here, and this one is small enough to be easily missed.

Impulsively, I grab one and slip it into my other pocket before hurrying out of the library and into the cold, dark halls.

I try to be soundless, just a shadow moving along

the walls and floors, but I've only gone a few steps when I hear Mrs. Medlock say, "Mary."

Too flustered to try the sleepwalking lie, I turn around, hot-cheeked and shame-faced.

"Were you in the library?"

"No. I wasn't. I was just—"

"That room," she says. "Is not for you. Nor is any room in this house but your bedroom, the kitchen, and the hallways between. Do you understand me?"

"I heard—" I try, but she doesn't want to hear this either. Instead, she marches me up all of the stairs and locks me in my room, telling me Martha will come and let me out in the morning.

I hold my breath until I hear her footsteps disappear down the hall again. Then I pull my treasures from my robe pockets: the book, and the bullet. I hide the bullet under the bed, and then tuck myself under the covers to peruse the book.

It's every forbidden thought I've ever had, rendered in ink and paint. Men and women, men and men, women and women, groups of three, four, five, and their bodies are engaged in every possible sin. My heart sticks in my throat, and I half expect God to appear to strike me down. Surely I've sinned too much already. But He doesn't. Instead, I get wetter and needier between my legs, wanting so much it *hurts*.

Finally, when I can't bear it any longer, I let my fingers find my softness, stroking myself open, imagining what it would be like if these illustrations came to life around me. A cock, hard and rough and ready, being pressed against my closed mouth. Someone's lips and tongue on the tender peaks of my nipples, his fingers where mine are, so close to pushing inside. In some of the pictures the men are kissing the women's clits, licking them greedily, and I can barely consider it before that familiar sensation shudders through me, a quaking. I feel like one of the electric lamps I haven't quite gotten used to yet, lit up and sparkling.

It's not enough, though. Fear and adrenaline and desire have me wide awake, and I keep turning the pages, touching myself, shivering with pleasure at each new vista as it's unveiled. Women with their legs behind their heads, their rears in the air, taking two cocks at once, and sometimes even three. I don't hear the voice again, but I think of Uncle Arch's hardness in his pants anyway, straining for me, and the world goes white. When I fall asleep at last, I'm damp with sweat and wrung out with pleasure, my hand still tucked shamefully between my legs.

6

MARTHA LETS me bathe by myself the next morning, and I'm grateful that I'm not being led into another temptation. Though is it already too late for me?

The commune led me to believe I'd be degraded beyond recognition, living out here among opulent sinners, but as I look in the mirror, last night didn't mark me. My skin looks like it's still lit from within. And I feel as much like myself as I ever have, actually, not different, or worse. Maybe even...better.

That is a dangerous thought to have.

When I'm clean, Martha walks me back to my room, and Dickon brings me clothing. It's nothing like what the woman in red wore—much more akin to Mrs. Medlock or Martha's simple, modest dresses, though they're made of materials I could never have dreamed of, before, plush cashmere and soft brushed cotton. They also fit me differently, outlining the shape of my body instead of concealing it indifferently.

There are undergarments too, but for now I simply want to enjoy the feels of this fabric on my skin.

The first outfit is a blouse and skirt, and I slip into them easily. "Much better," Dickon pronounces when he sees the effect.

"Not that I have anywhere to wear it," I remind him, trying not to sulk too obviously. "Why won't Uncle Arch let me look around? I'm trapped up here with nothing to do while he runs his business. I have no idea if he'll find the time to look into my painting next week or next year."

"What, you can't amuse yourself?" Dickon asks, and for a moment I wonder what he knows about how I spent last night.

"I'm a farm girl," I tell him, trying to sound simple and innocent. The me of only a few days ago who already feels distant. "I'm used to having chores to do. Being inside all day, just sitting around...it doesn't feel right."

Dickon is unmoved, but Martha takes pity on me. "You can probably wander around a *little* bit," she says, indicating that I should take the clothing off again. "Really the most important thing is to stay away from the Garden."

Something about the way she says it tells me she's talking about one space in particular. I remember what I saw yesterday, before that big burly man pushed me out. The place the lady in red led me to. "The one behind the stone wall? With the metal door?" I ask.

Dickon smirks. "Nice work, Martha," he says under his breath.

Am I not even supposed to know that the garden exists? Arch did mention it in his list of forbidden places yesterday.

Martha shrugs. "She probably knows a lot of this already from her mom. Right, Mary?" She takes the clothes I've stripped off and hands me a dress to try on. I'm still not used to being naked in front of her, let alone a man like Dickon, and my hands fumble as I try to figure out how to put it on—do the laces go in the front, or the back?

Martha solves the problem by taking the dress out of my hands and indicating that I should hold my arms up. She slips it over my head, and the rush of soft fabric on my bare skin is a sweet little whisper. I glance over my shoulder and see her smiling conspiratorially at me.

"Anyway, who doesn't know how famous Grace Lennox was?" She adjusts the dress to my frame. "Or what she and the wicked Mistress Craven got up to in the Garden."

I don't, but I'm not about to tell her that. My mother rarely spoke of her life before the commune, and she certainly never gave details. Now I'm curious not just about the gossip, but about the woman she was before me. Sister Grace, the stern and devout mother I knew, seems to have nothing in common with Grace Lennox, the artist these people mention so casually.

The dress laces up the back, it turns out, and Martha pulls the ribbons back there tight and then tighter while she talks. Every tug forces a little breath out of my lungs. "It was a sight to see, they say, in those days. Mistress Craven had a rose-covered bower at the top of the tree in the center of everything, and from her throne, she inflicted the most exquisite torments on men and women alike."

Dickon takes over to pull the last ribbons tight before tying them off. His fingers linger at the back of my neck for a moment. He tugs the back of the dress down, his hands sweeping along the curve of my rear, and he checks the fit of the waistline, every touch brusque and professional. It still makes me feel a shameful, burning need, a desire to drop to my knees in front of him and find out if people really do the things I saw in those illustrations. All the vague things I used to want, my imaginings a blur of skin and sweat, have been turned into vivid, specific images that make my stomach tighten and twist. I can't tell if it's because of fear or need or both.

Maybe they're the same thing.

"Your mother was one of the lucky ones—rich enough to pay the membership fee, loved enough not to have to. She didn't come to be admired, but of course she was adored regardless." Martha shakes her head. "Master Craven was desperately in love with his wife. Not many men would have let a woman run wild like that, but he loved it, they say. And Lily loved Grace like a sister."

Dickon's come around to the front of me now, and I can feel the way his design, with its tight stays and low neck, has pushed my breasts up and revealed the roundness of their tops. He stares at my curves as Martha chats away. "Grace loved what Lily had done with the place. Called it a fortress of beauty. The work she did in the Garden was her most coveted, and usually snapped up on the spot. The art world was furious to be cut out. She'd laugh with Lily about it, so Ben says."

Ben is the same enormous man kissing between the legs of the woman in red. I'm getting to know everyone here and I'm not sure I'm comfortable with that.

Martha continues. "She said art was only worth what the buyer was willing to pay, and it was hardly her fault that these buyers were trying to impress each other. Apparently her affectation not to care about the money wasn't much of an affectation at all, though."

Dickon bursts into the conversation with a question.

"Did you really bathe with buckets in your cult?"

Martha smacks him before I have to answer.

"Sorry, in your *commune*."

"Hush, you savage." Martha turns back to me. "Anyway, Arch really does care about money, so he was happy as could be to pocket the commissions. Lily was a shrewder businesswoman than anyone but him seemed to realize."

Dickon's gaze wanders over the little show my breasts are putting on and I notice that his cock is as hard as Uncle Arch's was yesterday. He's not trying to hide it, either. He gives me a little grin as he touches himself roughly, adjusting his length in his pants.

Martha isn't paying attention to him. She's still telling me the story of Uncle Arch and Aunt Lily. "He gave her free rein to reign…until, of course, she fell to her death," she says. She's caught up in the story too, color flushing her cheeks and her eyes bright with enthusiasm. "After that, he never set foot in the Garden again, and left the running of it to Ben Weatherstaff. Now *he's* got a cock like a—"

"Should this be tighter?" Dickon's question cuts her off mid-sentence and is accompanied by hands cupping my pushed-up breasts. His tone is as sharp as his dick is hard. Whatever she was about to say is off-limits to me, even more so than the Garden, apparently.

Martha takes his cue this time. She bustles over to the other side of the room, pretending to be distracted by sorting a pile of my belongings from the commune. "That's the legend, anyway. Now it's some sad, dead courtyard. He just hates to be reminded of it is all, so he wouldn't want you asking questions about it." She looks at me again, making sure I meet her gaze. "Do you understand, Mary?"

I nod that I do.

The door swings open, and another man walks in, one I haven't seen before. "Master Neville," Martha says, dipping into a little curtsey.

I recognize the name: Neville Craven. Arch's brother. I can see the resemblance between them, but where Arch's features are classically handsome, Neville's seem cruder, somehow, the generous curve of his mouth brushed with something cruelly dangerous. If the Manor belongs in a fairy tale, he is the beast, I think: his eyes devour me, and every place they land turns numb. It's nothing like the heat I felt moments ago, when Dickon's admiring gaze stroked me up and down.

Neville comes to me without a word, and Martha and Dickon back away from me, giving him space. "Mary Lennox," he says. "I'm Master Neville Craven."

He pauses, and I hold my breath.

"Welcome to Misselthwaite." The cold rush of his breath brushes against my neck when he speaks. He kisses each of my cheeks, one and then the other. His touch is soft, nearly featherlight.

But somehow, it feels like both a promise and a warning.

AFTER MY FITTING FINISHES, I'm left alone in my room for most of the morning. The sun is high overhead, hidden by a thin layer of clouds, when Martha finally comes with lunch and tells me that as soon as I'm finished eating, I'm to return to the Master's study.

I barely taste the food as I swallow it—a cold chicken sandwich, accompanied by a samovar of hot tea that comes with sugar and cream. A week ago I might have cried at the luxury of this kind of meal, and of a morning without chores on top of it. Now all I can think about is what will happen when I see Uncle Arch again. After meeting Neville, I'd changed back into the simple blouse and skirt, but I wonder now if that was a mistake. If I'll look too plain.

Martha accompanies me downstairs, following me as tightly as a shadow while we make our way through the maze of hallways and rooms. I wish she'd leave me alone to my thoughts, but at the same time I'm grateful for her companionship: I'd get lost if she'd sent me by myself.

When we get to the study door, it's closed, and I hear voices coming through it. They don't quite sound like they're arguing, but they're working up to it. I pause on the threshold, not wanting to interrupt. "You aren't looking at the bigger picture, Archie," someone is saying. It sounds like Neville. "You've always lived inside your little fantasies, but it's time you understand reality. If you persist in this, you'll only be hurting yourself. Don't look at me like that, I don't take pleasure in teaching you these lessons."

At that, Martha sweeps by me and pushes the door open. The men inside fall silent.

Neville is there, Dickon, along with Uncle Arch and Ben. I glance between his legs but I can't see his cock, or what it might be the size of.

There's also a man in a red coat, younger than the rest. My age, maybe a few years older. I recognize him immediately as the sad young man from the portrait, the one I'd thought might be Uncle Arch. I can see the differences now. His eyes are a bright green where his father's are a brown so deep they're almost black. His hair waves softly, unlike his father's disciplined straightness.

No one greets me as I catalog their contrasts. Instead, Neville looks between Arch and the man in the red coat. "Your son agrees with me," he says to Arch. "Don't you, Colin?"

So he's my cousin, then. Uncle Arch's son. Only not quite, because none of us are actually related. The look on his face is wary, like he doesn't trust or like anyone in the room. Even his own father. Perhaps he heard the warning, too.

Colin shrugs. "I don't want anything to do with it," he says. "Do what you please. You will anyway."

"It's not up to you," Uncle Arch intones. He doesn't look at Colin when he says it. His gaze seems content to fall anywhere but on his son's familiar features.

Neville turns to me at last. "Look how perfect she is," he says, gesturing at my body. I'm at once proud and ashamed of how it looks in my new clothes, plumped and on display. Though if they know people like the woman in red, perhaps they're still unimpressed. My breasts are smaller than hers, and you can't even see my knees.

"Innocent as a child," Neville continues, "but, in fact, a full woman. Such a rare prize."

I have no idea what he means by this, but he seems convinced, and so does Ben. I can't read the look on Colin's face, let alone Uncle Arch's. I've never thought of myself as a prize. Until recently, I wasn't supposed to think of myself at all.

"I said no," Arch says. "Leave the idea alone, brother."

Neville sits down in one of the overstuffed armchairs, shrugging like it's all the same to him. "Well, we can table it for now. I'm certain you'll come around once I start gauging preliminary interest."

Arch looks furious, like a storm cloud boiling over. "I haven't given permission for any interest to be gauged."

"You don't have to," Neville tells him. He sounds positively cheerful. "Ben, can you work with her?"

Ben looks me up and down, frank and unsparing. "If we can advertise truthfully," he says. "But wasn't she kicked out for whoring herself?"

That one kicks me in the stomach. They keep talking about me, but no one has said a word to me since I entered the room. My greatest shame, my biggest mistake, is being discussed openly yet I have no idea what the discussion is, or how they would even know about my expulsion from the Kingdom. Frustration and humiliation prickle under my skin, a mix of emotions I can barely contain.

"I am not a whore," I interject, hating the shrill edge to my voice. "And if I can just have my mother's painting, I will leave here and you'll never see me again. Please. Give it to me, so I can go home."

Arch turns on me, and the look in his eyes is like a brand, it burns so hot. "This *is* your home!" he roars. His voice almost makes the room shake. "You have nothing and no one but me. And I do not like your attitude. If you want to walk out of here with anything at all, you will do as you're told, and right now, that means you will strip below the waist."

I want to run, but Ben's moved between me and the door, where he's standing with his arms crossed, his body a formidable mass. Neville is straightening the cuffs of his shirtsleeves. Colin shakes his head and lets a heavy sigh escape. "Can I go," he asks, "so at least one of us doesn't have any more sins to bear?"

My eyes lock on Colin. Uncle Arch's son seems nothing like him, despite the similarities in their features. He's the first person since I arrived who has named what this place seems to specialize in. And he's certainly the only one who seems to understand the shame a sinner should rightly feel. As he stalks out past Ben, I feel the full force of my own mortification, but no judgment from him. It buoys me. If doing what I'm told gets me what I need to leave this place forever, I can spend the rest of my life atoning for the sins committed outside the walls of the Kingdom of Love.

Right now I'd do anything to be back among people who didn't confuse me. People whose simple desires were righteous, like harvesting enough apples for us all to eat pie. Pleasures I could take part in without fear. If I can't remove myself from Misselthwaite, my grace will keep eroding until there's nothing left.

So yes, I will strip for these men, if that's what it takes. It certainly won't be the first time I've debased myself in this house.

I undo the button at the top of my new skirt and

let it fall around my feet, exposing myself to the men in the room. I feel their eyes everywhere, stroking and assessing my bare legs and seeking the tiny slit between them, which is already starting to swell at all of this attention.

Dickon moves behind me, and he takes my arm and guides me. His touch is gentle. He leads me to a chair in one corner I hadn't noticed before, older than the rest, with leather straps hanging from its arms and legs and a pair of stirrups for my feet.

I sit down in a daze and watch as he buckles me in: one wrist, and then another, his fingers making fast work of leather and metal as he binds my ankles in places. A pause, too brief for anyone else to notice, for him to flash me the smallest smile of encouragement. Then he moves something at the side of the chair, and the stirrups part my legs for me as Ben steps forward.

Neville has turned on a lamp and bent it to shine right between my open legs, so that there's nowhere to hide: they can see my pink wet center, the hot empty core of me, on full display. I make a little noise —of pleasure, of shame, of anguish—and Ben shushes me. Then he pulls up my shirt so that my breasts are exposed too, my nipples tightly pebbled and my skin turning to gooseflesh all over.

"Lovely, responsive nipples," he observes, reaching down to give one a tweak. His fingers are calloused, rough where I'm soft. "They're supple, even when hard. I know many a man who'd pay for a suck or a pinch." He flicks me then, and I want to squeeze my legs together, to cover myself up and give myself some pressure on my cunt, but I can't. The men watch me squirm against my bindings with mild interest.

"Has a man ever touched those before?" Arch asks. His stare is somehow more intense now than ever.

"No."

"What about your pussy?" Neville asks. "Have you spread for anyone like you're spreading for us?"

"No. No. I—" *Pussy.* It's a word like *clit*, defining in an instant both a place and a feel.

"Religious girls often take it in the ass," Dickon says, sounding sympathetic. "Doesn't break anything or plant a seed. Has a man ever fingered your asshole for you? You can tell us, Mary. Be honest."

"No!" I'm shocked at the thought, but too embarrassed to tell him. Instead, I stare into his eyes so he sees the truth in mine. "No one's touched me anywhere. Ever."

"No one is *this* innocent. Surely you've seen a man's penis before?" Uncle Arch asks.

I don't know what to say to this. Will I get in trouble if I tell the truth? Will I get in more trouble if I lie?

They take my silence as a yes, and though Arch frowns, Neville lets out a low, filthy chuckle. "Dirty men on that freak farm," he says. "But all of them married to the idea of virginal brides, eh? Never quite understood that, myself. I'd rather a woman be skilled than pure. But if that were the case, none of us would have a paycheck, eh, boys?"

Dickon isn't sidetracked. "She might use her mouth instead," he observes. "Is that it? Do they ever tell you that being on your knees will get you closer to God?" I begin to nod before he continues. "Have the men ever put cocks in your mouth, told you their cum was a sacrament?"

"No!" And God help me, another piece of my soul erodes as I get wetter at the thought.

Ben confers with the other men silently. "She's very insistent. I'm inclined to believe her," he says after a while. Then he kneels between my legs and uses his hands to spread the lips of my—*pussy* apart. "Cunt's gorgeous," he continues. *Cunt.* A word even more descriptive. Tight in my mouth just like the channel inside me that he slides one thick, work-roughened finger far inside.

"Soft and warm and wet, just like you want 'em. Let's just see..."

I can't help myself. No one's ever touched me there before, and I'm so, so needy. I want more, so I buck my hips forward, gaining a fraction more of him. My inner muscles spasm around the intrusion, pulsing, and the white hot that came over me so many times last night comes again. I hear myself gasping, feel myself pulling against my restraints. Ben waits until I'm done before he pulls his finger out again, and I feel the loss keenly.

"Intact," he says, rising to his feet and facing the other three men. "And what an orgasm. Neville is right about one thing: she's exactly the whore we've been waiting for."

8

As soon as the last strap is unbuckled, I go running. My shirt is still rucked up under my arms, tangled on itself, and it's all I can manage to pull my skirt on as I skid out the door. I barely remember the afternoon they kicked me off the commune, but I can recall the word *whore* in everyone's mouths clear as day. Now I know they were right about me. Sister Rachel and the council, they saw it long before I was ready to admit the truth.

I'm a whore. A shameful, dirty, irredeemable whore. Headed straight to hell, just like my mother used to warn me would happen if I allowed my self-ishness sway. I wanted it, what Ben did, and I wanted more.

Worst of all, I still do.

My feet churn up dirt and mud, and tears track down my face as I run. I don't know where I'm going.

Of course I can't outrun what's taken root inside of me, but I don't know what else to do.

I almost run headlong into the door of the Garden, which is locked and sealed up tight. I know no one's there, but I beat against it anyway with one ineffectual fist. I want to be allowed inside there; I want to tend its beautiful flowers, to be among growing things again. I have spent my whole life learning how to plant and sow, to nurture heaven's beauty in a hellish land. I could almost laugh at how I once thought rocky soil was the devil's trial for me.

What kind of devil is Uncle Arch, who looks at me like a starving man would manna? Why won't he simply let me leave and give us both salvation? And if I must stay, why won't he let me be *useful*?

I sink to my knees, ruining Dickon's careful work in an instant. My skirts are wrecked with mud. I let my head rest against the door's cold, unforgiving metal. The touch that comes against my shoulder is gentle, but it startles me anyway. I jump to standing and whirl around to see Colin standing there with his hands in his pockets, looking slightly ashamed of himself. "I'm sorry," he says. "I didn't mean to startle you."

"It's okay." I remember how proud of my looks I was just a few minutes ago. Now I understand why the elders were always going on about pride coming before a fall. My hair is disheveled, my face wet from crying, and my brand-new clothes—my first ever brand-new anything—are muddy and wrinkled. I tug my shirt down so that it covers my breasts, at least.

"I don't want…you don't have…" He seems unable to articulate whatever thought is wrinkling his aristocratic forehead.

"It's okay," I tell him. "I understand." And I do. Any man who willingly bears his burden of sin is a brother, I was taught. Colin's burden looks heavy enough without trying to explain himself to me. "I know what I want. And I know the cost I'll have to pay for it."

"I don't think you have the slightest idea what you're paying," Colin says. His hand reaches for me, seemingly involuntarily, but we hear it at the same time.

"Mary, dear," calls Neville. I leave Colin's hand hanging in midair and turn down a laneway, hurrying so Neville won't be able to catch up to me. My eyes are scanning the ground, watching for rocks or broken paving stones, so I run right into something warm and solid.

This time, it's Archibald Craven.

I step back from him instantly, almost cowering in fear. He must have come to discipline me for running out of that room. But what did he expect? He thinks I'm a whore.

"Mary," my uncle says. "Are you all right?"

I'm not, and I know he can see that. Is this a test? What does he want me to say? My mother's voice in my head is fainter than it was when I arrived, but no less urgent.

Remember one thing.

"I was going to take a walk around the gardens," he continues. "Would you consider joining me?"

You must promise me.

I want to say no, to spit in his face and run again, but I'm frozen in place. Neville might feel dangerous but Arch's power holds a pull too strong to even think about resisting. I wonder if my mother felt it too. If she knew that no promise I made would keep me truly safe.

"It's nice to have a new face here," he says, and his voice is gentle, like he's talking to a small, scared animal. As though what happened in his office was all a bad dream. "I don't spend much time at the Manor these days, and when I am home, I tend to take it for granted. Seeing you here has reminded me to try to enjoy the grounds a bit." His gaze on me doesn't waver. "I would appreciate your company."

Maybe it's the fact that he's asking, not telling. Maybe it's the way he makes me feel when I'm near him, something magnetic and primal that I don't understand. Or maybe it's the fact that I think I catch an echo of Colin's sadness in his eyes.

I can't explain it. I only know that instead of saying no, I drop my head and tell him, "Yes."

We fall into step together, my shorter legs having to go double time to keep up with his long ones. The clouds have thickened overhead, and the day is gray and soft all around us. For the first time, I let myself look at him not as my uncle, a man whose power over me is iron-fisted and absolute, but instead as just…a man.

He's handsome, I realize—gorgeous, actually. He's tall and lean but with those same broad shoulders under his coat. I watch his throat work as he swallows, noticing where his shirt is unbuttoned and the patch of skin it reveals. The strength in his hands and arms. Something inside of me trembles in my stomach or my lungs.

He's older than I am, I remind myself, *at least in his forties*. But his brown hair is only lightly threaded with silver, and girls my age marry elders on the commune all the time.

Not that Arch would—not that I would—it's impossible.

We walk in silence, and as we move, I see the gardens coming to life around me. The plants are still wild and overgrown, rambling into the path or twining up around each other into a mess of flowers, but I see hints of civilization: staff arranging tea lights along the path that runs against the side of the house, strewing flower petals on the paving stones. We pass by the kitchens and I see lights on, hear clanking and laughter, smell something so delicious I want to pause and savor it.

Arch keeps walking, though, so I stay at his side.

"You know," he says at last. "There's nothing shameful about being called a whore."

I keep my gaze carefully away from him. I appreciate him trying to be nice, but I know he's wrong. It's one of the worst things a woman can be. I listened to my elders. I've read my Bible.

"Yes," he continues. "Some people attribute negative connotations to it—especially in that cult you—"

"It's not a cult." I can't stand listening to these people talk about my home like this. "How can you say that? I had a happy life until I was thrown out."

Arch scoffs. "For looking at a man's penis? Mary. You're a grown woman. You should be enjoying your body." I expect to find him looking at me, his gaze emphasizing my breasts or my waist, maybe his cock hard in his pants again. But instead, he's looking at the ivy growing along one of the garden walls when he says, "All I want to tell you is that here...in this manor, with these people...a whore is a woman who knows how to enjoy her body. It's a compliment."

I steel my resolve. I will not let this man confuse my mind. "Well, I'm not interested in enjoying my body or being a complimented whore," I tell him. "All I want is to return to the Kingdom."

"You can go."

Colin made that clear just a few minutes ago, but it's not that easy.

"I can't leave empty-handed."

Arch nods. "Ah. The painting. I've been looking into it."

My heart quickens. "And? Will you give it to me?"

"I'm afraid it's been misplaced. You must understand that I own a lot of art, in a lot of locations. These things take time. Patience is a virtue, or so I'm told."

My heart sinks, even as I recognize this is the closest to a joke he's likely ever come. He's trying to soften the blow. It doesn't work.

"I won't have any virtue left soon." I pause, waiting for him to correct or ridicule me, but he doesn't. "I have to sell the painting, and fast. It's the only hope I have of going—" I almost say *home* again, but I recall his reaction earlier. "Back to what I know. If I had money…the elders might look the other way regarding my sins. And I could return to my life, as if all of this never happened. I could even marry, maybe."

I try to imagine returning home: the gates opening for me. Being welcomed back by the other girls. Sitting in the dining hall, working the fields. A strange feeling rises in me. The images have no shine to them, no shimmer that tempts me the way they ought.

"Is that what you want?" he asks.

"I might not be allowed, but a good dowry would help. If I were an elder's wife, then no one would tempt me. I'd be safe again, there."

I wait for him to condescend to me, or put his foot down. Instead, his voice grows softer still. "Oh, Mary. Do you truly believe that temptation is only possible outside, when it's given permission? You have already proved that wrong."

I hang my head. It's true. I didn't ask to be tempted inside the walls of the Kingdom of Love when the Petersen boy found me. I had all but asked *him*, given how he found me.

"How do you know what happened?" I ask, something that's been shadowing the back of my mind.

"I make it a point to know things." He's quiet for a moment. Though I'm bursting with questions, I know he will not be rushed. "You remind me of Lily," he finally says.

I'm shocked to hear him speak his dead wife's name—the way Mrs. Medlock and Martha talk about her, I thought that word might be forbidden on this property. "She never fit anywhere but here," Arch continues. "Just like you."

He glances at me sideways, and for the first time, his gaze doesn't feel like a hammer swinging down on me, brutal and final. His words are another story. If he thinks I fit here, if I *am* the whore they say...but no.

No. I can't accept that. *Maybe I can charm him into giving me the painting,* I think. *Maybe the secret is just to be nice to him.*

"I don't think that's right," I say, picking carefully through a piece of path that's sharp with fallen sticks and wayward brambles. If only I had some boots and some tools, I could clear this before lunch. "You haven't seen how I fit there."

He steers us away from the path we were on and onto one that's lined in soft moss. It's still cold, but the soles of my bare feet are nearly numb by now, and either way, I appreciate it. The path dead ends into a quiet little corner of the gardens, where Arch indicates the bench of a picnic table that sits under an ivy-covered wall.

"Sit," he says. "I'll show you."

I hesitate for just a moment before I follow his instructions. I wonder if he'll join me, but he doesn't. Instead, he stands in front of me, legs apart, hands clasped behind his back. I feel as exposed as I did when I was naked in front of him.

"You took something," he says. "From the library."

Fear grips me by the throat, as sudden as his words. The shadows in this lonely part of the garden seem to turn darker, more menacing.

"I took a book from the library," I admit, eyes cast into my lap. "I thought it would be okay as long as I returned it. Isn't that how libraries work?"

He shakes his head once, dismissive. "Not a book."

I drop my eyes to his feet, face heating with shame. "I'll bring it back."

"Look at me."

I do, and his eyes are blazing, now, cold power radiating off of him like electricity.

"What did you think you were going to do with it?" he asks.

I know better than to try to be clever. I haven't learned to lie, yet, something I'd considered positive until now. "Nothing. It was a souvenir. Before I went back, I'd try to sell it. It looks like silver. I couldn't keep it, and it might be valuable."

"Do you know what it's for?" he asks.

It's for something?

"It's a sculpture, and like you said, you own so much art in so many locations..."

His eyes narrow as I repeat his words back, but his tone doesn't change when he says, "It goes in your ass."

"What? Why?" He steps closer, towering over me. I keep my eyes on his, tilting my neck back, baring my throat.

"If I tell you," he says, and his voice is like a knife bladed in silk, stinging and soothing at the same time, "you have to do it. And if I don't tell you, you're going to be punished. Which will it be?"

I recall my punishments at the commune in quick succession: the nights I spent sleeping in the chicken coop when I failed to clean it out properly, or the time I took too long at bathing and wasn't allowed to clean myself for a month. I don't dare think what a man like Uncle Arch might do to me if I provoked him. It might be ugly. It might be permanent.

But he makes it sound like the other thing could be a punishment, too.

"I don't know," I tell him, trying to buy time. "I don't want to be punished, but..."

He decides I don't have a choice. "Go upstairs to your rooms," he says. "Take that sculpture, as you call it, and put the narrow end in your mouth. Keep it in there while you strip off all your clothes. Then you bathe. Suck on it while you do, like it's the most delicious cock you've ever fantasized about. When you're clean, get on the bench in the bathroom. The one facing the mirror."

He shoves my legs open and steps between them, and I'm helplessly aware of how naked my pussy is under my skirts. My cunt.

"You spread your legs," he continues. At first, he seemed angry, but there's something else animating his instructions now, a hunger that reminds me of the way he looked at me during our first meeting. "High. You watch yourself finger your clit until you're so wet you can lubricate your tight little asshole with it. Finger yourself slowly. There's a tube of oil in the cabinet if you need it, but I think you'll find you won't. I think you'll hate every second of loving it."

It makes my skin feel too tight, hearing him say all of these filthy things and looking at me like this. Can he see my cunt quivering as he talks?

"Then, and only then, do you take the silver plug out of your mouth and push it into your asshole. You'll stretch. It may hurt. Go slow. Feel how it stretches you. How it invades your most private place and impales you like a beautiful whore."

I'm hot all over, now, my nipples stiff peaks under my shirt and my pussy pulsing its needy rhythm between my legs. My breath comes in short wet gasps. It feels like I do when I touch myself, how it did when Ben touched me, but no one is touching me at all. What is he doing to me?

"You have a choice now," Arch says, his voice ruthless, savage. "I can punish you for what you stole, or you can use the silver plug exactly the way I just described. My punishments are not trifling. You will be sore. You may bleed. But you will pay back what you owe me, and you will never steal from me again. Anything I choose to give you will be earned."

The Council has spanked me raw more times than I can count: I've been turned over an elder's knee and smacked with a paddle since I was a girl. The pain of those encounters come roaring back to me, but it's a pain I know well. It's something I understand.

"Punish me," I tell him.

"As you wish."

He doesn't tell me what to do, instead showing me with his hands: he tugs me up from under my arms and turns me around so I'm facing the bench. That's when I realize this isn't a picnic table at all: it was built for someone like me to lie on top of, on my stomach, with my knees falling open onto either side. Arch hikes my skirt up around my waist, and I flinch with shame at the way I'm exposed.

I hear the snick of his belt being undone, the sound of it being pulled from its place around his waist. When the elders spanked me, it was almost always one of the women, someone sour-faced and ancient with wrinkles. They usually did it with my underwear on.

It never felt like this.

"You have a perfect ass," Arch growls. My hips tilt up involuntarily when he says it, like some deep-down shameless part of me wants him to keep look-ing. "Firm and plump and begging to be spanked, and fucked, and spanked again. It should be red and tender and always leaking with cum. I don't know how a slut as perfect as you could think you belong anywhere but here."

I want to tell him to stop saying that, that despite what he and the woman in red believe, that a slut and a whore is not what I want to be—but before I can, his belt across the backs of my thighs cracks the words right out of my mouth. The blow stings, but as soon as the sensation dissipates, I realize I'm left with nothing but a rising, wicked heat.

"Are you sure about this, Mary?" Arch asks, his voice languid and caressing as he smacks me again, and again. "You should take the plug. I'll give you time. We'll meet back here in an hour, and you can take this same position on this bench and you can show it to me."

I force my focus away from the pleasurable ache that's blooming everywhere below my navel. I think about the bench. I feel the way it's solid underneath me, the bite of its cold stone against my bare knees.

And I realize something. "I've seen another bench

like this," I say. One that looks more comfortable. "There's a wooden one, with cushions—"

Arch reaches down easily and grabs me by the hair, forcing my head up and making my scalp burn. "Where?" he growls.

"Behind that wall," I tell him, relishing the feeling of his body like this, so close to mine. "Where Ben and the crimson woman were."

He lets my head drop just as quickly as he grabbed it.

"As I told you," he says, voice icy now, "that garden is forbidden. Ben and Robin have earned their places here, along with my trust. But you, with all your talk of godliness, you steal and sneak and demand. I'm out of patience."

"I didn't know it was forbidden when I—"

He isn't interested. "Get up," he commands, so I do. I'm barely sitting before he flips my skirt down again, and I don't know what to do with the fact that I'm also disappointed to be covered up.

Then he pins my elbows together, one firm hand holding me in place, and all but drags me back to the house.

The tea lights are all lit now, and the paths strewn with fragrant rose petals, so there's plenty of light for the staff to see their Master treating me like a child throwing a tantrum. They aren't brave enough to make eye contact with me in front of him, but I seethe with humiliation all the same. I'm furious and muddy, wet and tear-streaked and still, somehow, hot between my legs when Arch tosses me into my room like a rag doll and shuts and locks the door behind me, trapping me alone in here once again.

"It was a mistake to give such a contrary girl a choice," he tells me through the door. "You'll report back to me at dawn with your ass plugged with what you stole, or you'll leave this manor with what you brought—nothing."

9

It's LATE when Mrs. Medlock brings me my dinner on a tray. She doesn't linger, and locks the door behind her.

I tried to look at my borrowed book again to pass the time, but the images just reminded me of all the disgusting things Arch told me to do with the little sculpture, and the excitement I felt unnerved me. I slammed it shut. Now it seems to taunt me, sitting on my bed while I eat cold chicken. I'm glad I didn't take one of the bigger ones, I think—at the time I just wanted something that was easy to conceal, and I'm glad of it now.

When I finish my food, I take the silver object and rest it in the palm of my hand. His instructions ring through my head as I weigh it. It's heavy, cold, and smooth. What would it feel like...inside of me? The idea half repels me, but I have to admit I've imagined something similar when I touch myself—something bigger and firmer than Ben Weatherstaff's finger to clench around. Something to get inside of me and take me apart.

Here, in this manor, with these people...there's nothing shameful about being called a whore.

Uncle Arch wasn't lying. He meant what he said, truly believing that the sinful nature I've worked so hard to deny is no sin at all. I put the plug down and open the book again. Flipping through the illustrations, I try to find someone with an object like this. Before I've gotten halfway through, I hear sounds from the grounds underneath my window.

I know that up close it's all overgrown and wild, but from up here the gardens look like a fairyland: the paths are candlelit, and people are coming up and down them, light on their feet. I can't make out anything distinct, but the snatches of chatter and laughter that float up to me sound joyful and easy. I peer through the darkness between us to try to make out what they're wearing, but all I really catch is colors: peacock blues and greens and lemon yellows on the women. Formal black and white on the men.

The house is alive. It's a party. The entertainment I was warned about.

It feels like providence. Surely it can't be a coincidence that a distraction comes just at the moment I'm allowing the temptations of Misselthwaite to take root.

This is the moment I didn't realize I was waiting for.

Arch instructed me specifically to stay in my room when there were guests, but a party means the staff will be too distracted to notice one more girl in the crowd. If I can just make it out of my room, surely I can find another painting as valuable as mine is supposed to be. It's a trade he still comes out ahead on. After all, seeing my mother's greatest work would have meant something to me. I hope that selling a piece that means nothing to me will still be enough of a sacrifice for my prayers to be answered.

If I can find something small enough to conceal, I could leave on foot for the nearest town. I still have the number of the man with the taxi; I'll call him from there. I could be home by dawn, just as Uncle Arch is coming to look for me, to see if I followed his instructions.

I can leave this confusing, tempting, terrible place behind for good.

When Mrs. Medlock comes back to collect the tray, I'm ready. "What's happening downstairs?" I ask, trying to sound casual.

She clicks her tongue at me and seems to fight her desire to respond with her clear orders not to.

"Don't bother yourself about all that," she finally says. "You'll be staying up here anyway. They'll all be gone by morning."

"Of course." I don't want to arouse her suspicions. "It's just that I'd like to have a long, hot shower before bed. And perhaps drink some tea? It won't be easy to fall asleep with a party going on. Uncle Arch asked me to meet him at dawn; I don't want to disappoint him by oversleeping."

I can hear a small quaver in my voice. It's my lack of confidence in lying, but it seems to strike her as fear of the Master of the house. Mrs. Medlock gives me a look of pity I very nearly feel guilty for, but then she nods and begins to gather me fresh towels and a robe. I smile at her and accept the armful of bathing things. My heart races though I've not yet taken a single step out of bounds.

"I'll make you some chamomile from the gardens and leave it on your bedside table," she says. She has been kind. Hopefully she won't get into any trouble for my deceit.

We step out of the room together before parting —her to the back staircase, me down the hall to the bathroom.

I set down my towels and turn on the water, wincing a bit at the waste. Then I sprint out into the hallway and scamper down the stairs as fast as I can, my heart pounding now as much from exertion as fear. The tea tray is rattling in the kitchen as Mrs. Medlock assembles it, but the kettle isn't whistling, so I tiptoe on.

Where can I find a painting that won't be missed immediately? Not one of the front rooms or formal staircases. There was a music room I vaguely remember from my wanderings, as expensively decorated as all the others, but the dust covers tell me it's out of use.

I try to orient myself. Was it next to the hearth room or the blue guest suite? I try a few locked doors before realizing I'm in the wrong wing.

Confident, heavy steps sound from my right in a stride I recognize. Uncle Arch. Of course.

He won't step foot in the Garden.

I leap through the closest open door and press myself against a wall, my shaking hands over my mouth as I wait to be found out. What punishments would he add to my sentence?

His tread slows as he passes the door, as though he senses me.

I hold my breath.

One second, two.

Finally, with a long sigh, he carries on down the corridor. The faintest scent of him remains as his steps fade. It's my turn to sigh as I spot my safest course of action—a pair of French doors leading outside. I try to regain control of myself as I push open the heavy door and step into the cold night air.

My plan, insofar as I have one, is to hide outside in the crowd until the party seems underway. Once I find a vantage point, I should be able to see who is coming and going through the palladium windows that line the hall. Then I can sneak back in and find something—anything. Even if it won't fetch as good a price, even if it won't provide a dowry.

As soon as I have a painting in hand, I'll be out the

door, and I'll never see the Craven men or this strange place again.

And if I dream of it, or of *him*, surely the memories of lust are less a transgression than acting on them.

I cling to the side of the house, skulking in its shadows as I watch the procession of guests making their way along the candlelit paths. It might be harder to hide among them than I'd hoped—they're all so brilliantly dressed, and what I hadn't seen from above, masked so they appear like a parade of brilliant specters. I changed out of my muddy, garden-ruined clothes earlier, but my face is still dusty with tears and dirt, and even if I was clean, even if I had a gown of my own to wear, I'm not sure I could ever look as confident as these people do.

Not everyone walks. Some crawl; some crawl at the end of gilded leashes. I see whips like the ones that were in the library, but these are larger and stranger, made of thick black leather and edged in glinting chrome. A man walks by wearing a version of a horse's harness. Another follows, naked except for his cock, which is locked in a golden cage.

It feels like a lifetime ago that I was shocked by Robin, the woman in red, in her skimpy dress.

As I follow their snaking path, watching them accept glasses of champagne from waiters in crisp tuxedos, I wonder if that easy assurance is a result of money or their beliefs, so different from my own.

The path turns, and I have to step away from the

wall of the house, so I find a hedge to duck behind. I'm just in time as Dickon appears around a corner, laughing. Piano music is lilting through the air and his long fingers twitch as though longing to play along. In the candlelight, in the moment, he looks handsome and charming, hair tousled and eyes sparkling. A boutonniere of snake's-head fritillary adds a touch of personality to the white tux he wears. If anyone has the answers to how I could own my power like they all do, it must be Dickon.

Then he spots something in the crowd, and his devilish grin disappears. He grabs one of the attendees by the arm—a man in a tux that looks suspiciously like those the servers wear. Unlike their plain black silk masks, however, his is a shimmering silver. Dickon pulls it off his face, and the man looks startled, and then afraid.

"Playing guest tonight, are we?" Dickson asks. This time, the twitch of his fingers summons Ben Weatherstaff. I take a step further back into the shadows.

"I—" the waiter stammers. "Someone gave it to me? I didn't think—I was just—"

"You *work here*," Dickon reminds him. He tosses the mask into the grass, and it tumbles into my shadow, a sliver of temptation in the moonlight. "You wear the black silk unless you can afford the price of membership. We pay well, but not nearly that well. Ben, perhaps you could find a few bathrooms in the staff quarters that need to be cleaned so that no one else accidentally 'gives him' anything to distract from his duties?"

Ben hauls the man away by the lapels.

"Ah, my dear, that shade is perfection on you," he tells an older woman, with a cheeky once-over her husband seems to appreciate. "I've set aside a bottle of the Plénitude Rosé that you like. Shall we?" As he leads them off, I see my chance.

Not for stealing art, but for stealing a moment of pretense.

I dart forward and grab the mask, sliding it into place. The dress I put on earlier is made of cream-colored cotton, and though it isn't as beautiful as some of the others here, the mask and the dress look well matched together. If anyone on staff sees me, I can tell them that I'm a party guest who got lost.

"Playing little servant girl, are we?" a man asks, reminiscent of Dickon's words, but so much more lecherous in their delivery. He's fat, thick-fingered, and leering. "Want to serve me?"

"No, thank you," I tell him. Now that I have a disguise, I find it slightly easier to speak up. Yet it doesn't change how I feel on the inside. I'm still Mary Lennox, fallen from grace and far from home. I'm still drawn to the desires that led me here to begin with.

This was a foolish idea. I need to get back into the house. Mrs. Medlock will eventually notice my shower running for too long. I have to find a painting, and then flee.

"Harry, leave her alone," someone else says. A woman in a jade-green dress—if you can call it that, it's so wispy and insubstantial—takes hold of my elbow. "You'll have your pick of pretty young things once we're in the Garden," she tells him. "Consenting ones, mind you."

"Oh, thank you, but I—" I start, but she cuts me off.

"No need to be nervous," she says confidingly. "Just head right through there, and we'll take excellent care of you tonight. First time, darling?"

"Yes," I say. She's still leading me along the path, and my mind is blank: I can't think how to explain that I need to leave without making her suspicious. She also smells intoxicating, perfumed by the same fresh white flower scent I remember from the woman in red whom I met on my first day here. The smell makes me dizzy, and the next thing I know, I'm at the gates to the forbidden Garden.

Strings have joined the piano, the clinking of glasses, and the occasional low moan. Pain or pleasure? It's impossible to say. Another world is in front of me. The woman sees someone else she knows, and as she goes to greet him, I take a few steps back into the crowd.

I could turn here, I think. *I could run back to the house.*

I want my painting. I want my life back. I want to leave this place, where I'm held powerless, inspected like livestock, tempted by things I barely understand.

I want to stop worrying about what I want and simply be told what I need.

And yet, even more than all of that, I want to know what's happening on the other side of that wall.

10

JUST ONE TINY bite of the apple can't hurt, Eve must have told herself.

Of course that wasn't true, a lesson I ought to have learned by now. Nothing makes the taste sweeter than forbidding the fruit, and the pain of the punishment never seems to quell the desire for it.

Inside, the Garden is still bordered by four high stone walls, the way it was when I first got a glimpse, but that's all that hasn't changed. Around me everything is a blur of sound and motion. I hardly know where to look first.

There are riotous sprays of flowers everywhere. The only thing to rival their color are the guests: the silks of the women's dresses and the flowers and feathers they've woven in their hair are even more brilliant against the stark blacks of the men's suits. There's more champagne in here, each glass sparkling golden or pink, but also trays of chocolates being passed around and fed into willing mouths.

Mine is watering.

Robin, clad in nothing but a ruby choker, steps in front of the musicians and begins to sing the melody I'd heard her practice with Ben. Looking away, I'm shocked to find the livestock hooks on the walls have people chained to them. Above us, dancers sit in hoops suspended from the trees, twisting and turning their bodies into artful, impossible shapes.

Every nook, bower, and grotto is filled by bodies moving like the illustrations in my library book come to life. It takes several long moments before the scene separates itself into distinct images: a man wearing nothing but a pair of thin white briefs and a gold collar around his neck drops to his knees in front of a woman and ducks his head under her skirts. I can't make out what he's doing, but I think I can imagine it, and I'm glad no one can see my cheeks go scarlet under my mask.

I turn away from them and watch a woman leaning over that wicked bench as a couple of men spread her ass and slide their fingers into her hole, chuckling filthily to each other as she squirms. Is that how Arch saw me, I wonder? Was I that exposed? Could he tell that, as much as I hated the idea of what he described...I was curious about it, too?

On a small stage, a man applies clamps to a woman's nipples before spanking her with a many-tailed whip. She cries out, and the sound is equal parts agony and ecstasy.

This place is all sin and decadence. It's the worst of the world outside. It should scare me, and in truth, some of it does.

But it also feels like I belong here, amid all of this strangeness and indulgence, the way I've never belonged anywhere else. Uncle Arch was right about me. I *am* a whore, albeit an inexperienced one. That yearning I've felt for power is braided with desire and rooted in my selfishness.

I know this is wrong, but I want to try it anyway.

I spot Ben Weatherstaff, his cock hard in his pants and, indeed, thick as a rocket. He's strapping a blonde woman into a chair like the one he put me in earlier, except she isn't resisting, and she doesn't seem ashamed or frightened. She laughs as he pulls the strap on her wrist, urging him to make it tighter, and she sighs with relief and satisfaction as he spreads her legs to reveal the cleft of her pussy. I watch as he strokes her there, easy as anything, until a shiver goes through her, a spasm like a quake. Then he feeds those same fingers into her mouth, letting her taste herself, and she suckles at him as greedily as a newborn at the teat.

I watch them too long, because as I turn away, I realize someone has caught sight of me. Even in a mask, I recognize Neville: his black hair is loose, tonight, brushing the tops of his shoulders. He looks dashing and dangerous, and I know I can't let him catch me.

I dart through the crowd, trying to put space between us, but the calm smile on his face tells me he isn't worried. He knows he'll have me.

It's just a question of when.

I'm slipping around a trio of people, all of them kissing and caressing each other, wondering if I've lost him at last, when I feel a grip on my arm.

It's not Neville.

It's Colin.

"I have her," he says to Neville, who's just caught up to us in the crowd.

"Do you? Because if she's ruined, she's worthless."

Colin's sad eyes flash with fury. "She is not yours to value, Uncle Neville. She doesn't belong here."

Neville laughs. He seems dangerously at ease, not in the least chastened by Colin or his words. I am, though. Arch says I belong, the wettened pulse between my thighs agrees, but Colin looks at me as though I am still a godly farm girl and makes me wonder.

Do I *truly* belong, or do I simply wish to shed the burden of my fears?

"We'll talk later," Colin says, dismissing Neville. Then he leans and murmurs in my ear, "Come quietly if you don't want my father to find out you were here." His breath brushes against my neck and after all I've seen, I'm highly sensitized, feeling ticklish and hot. But Colin's next words send me crashing back to earth.

"Consider yourself lucky I got to you first," he says. "Because Neville Craven wouldn't be gentle."

He leads me out of the Garden, heedless of my reluctant feet, and to a shed at the edge of the property. There are no tea lights out here, just the half-full moon in the black sky, and when he closes the door, there's not even that. I inhale the stink of motor oil and sawdust as he lights a lamp, and then bends me over the tool counter before picking up the skirt of my dress.

He leans over me again, and this time, I can tell that the brush of his breath on my neck is deliberate. "Do you know what you nearly got yourself into?" he asks.

"I just wanted to see the Garden. I wasn't trying to get myself into..." And I wasn't—not at first—but I know that if Neville hadn't seen me, if I hadn't run headlong into Colin, that I could have gotten myself into nearly anything at all. I feel myself shudder deliciously at the thought as he runs a hand over the exposed curve of my ass.

"Do you want me to punish you?" he asks. "Is that what you want? Because I don't, but I've been told that's the way you are used to learning in the commune."

Here he pauses to smack me, the sting startling a helpless cry out of my mouth. After that the slaps come down in a continuous rain, my skin pinking all over as he tells me, "You simply do not understand the world of my family. We are not good men, Mary. And we will not be good for you."

I'm already bruised from Arch's belt this morning. Tears are streaming out of my eyes; I can't remember when they started falling. The confusion I've felt since I reached the Manor seems to have boiled over inside of me: what he's doing hurts so much and it feels so good.

"I'm sorry," I say. "I'm sorry, I'm sorry," and I'm not sure if I'm apologizing to him or myself or God, because I know that if he did take his cock out right now, if he pressed it against my entrance and asked me what I wanted, I would beg him to fuck me with it.

He doesn't, though. Instead, he stops spanking me and starts stroking the marked-up skin instead, tender and careful. I push into the touch like an animal wanting to be petted.

"Why are you not good?" I ask. The remorse with which he touches me now speaks to a gentle nature at odds with the spanking I just received. "What torments you? Why do you torment me?"

His hands still. "You," he says. "You do not deserve to be molded and trained into a creature for men like us to break. You deserve to choose happiness. And so you cannot continue on with this curiosity. Forget about the Garden. Forget about everything you saw."

There's nothing to do but agree. "Yes," I lie. It's so easy when he can't see my face.

"Neville has never known happiness, so he delights in taking it from others. He would sell you to the highest bidder and never lose a wink of sleep."

"What?"

But his hands are back on my ass, running down the backs of my thighs, pulling my legs apart. I can barely focus. "You need to keep away from him," Colin says. "Stay in your room. I'll take care of him. But first, I'll take care of this."

His hand slips into the warmth between, until his fingers are ghosting against my pussy. What they called my *cunt*, his palm sliding against the wetness that's accumulated there. He flicks his fingers against my clit.

"Oh!"

"A little release," he says, doing it again. Then he flattens his fingers, rubbing against me hard and fast, and I hear myself whining in the back of my throat. "It feels better when someone else does it, doesn't it? An orgasm will help you sleep. Then tomorrow you can start fresh."

"But I don't—" I stop myself before blurting out another lie, this one senseless. Back at home, I would have protested all the way to hell that I had never touched myself like this. Colin knows, though. He knows and he doesn't judge me.

He slaps my pussy, and it feels even better than when he spanked my ass. "Shush," he tells me. "I'm going to get you out of the trap you don't even know you're in."

His fingers are driving me crazy, stroking and flicking me, spreading my wetness all around, exactly where I need them and still not enough. "I can't, I can't," I pant.

"You can. You will."

He makes good on his promise: he pinches my clit one more time, firm and commanding, and I come with a helpless cry. Then, before I can even recover, he flips me around and presses me back against the tool bench. I'm almost glad he's holding me in place —my legs are shaky as he tugs his length out of his pants and starts to stroke it firmly. His face is more relaxed than I've ever seen it as I follow his gaze down to his cock.

It's hard and huge like his father's, but I've never seen a Craven man bare before like this. It jumps, like I remember means it likes this, and grows slick with my juices as he pushes into the circle of his fist. With his free hand, he tugs my dress up over my breasts and pinches a nipple. I cry out again. He shudders and comes, hot spurts landing on my sternum, my breasts, my belly.

It's shocking and filthy and I feel degraded. I feel like I want his hand between my legs again, with his cum there this time, too. I'm in hell. I'm in heaven. But his face has shuttered again. Whatever secrets haunt him, they've returned to their posts.

"Go back to your room," he growls like an animal

who regrets catching his prey. I'm too stunned by what's happened to do anything but obey.

Obey, and send up a desperate prayer that no one in the Manor sees me sneak back in, covered in cum and desperation.

11

I MUST NOT BE DAMNED yet, because my prayer was answered. The water still running in the shower was cold, but soothed my aching bottom and rinsed away all evidence of debauchery.

I drink lukewarm tea and watch the sun rise through the windows across from my bed. At first, I think I'm hallucinating the lightness that suffuses the sky, black shading to purple, but the stars start to disappear, and I know the dawn is on its way. I haven't slept a wink. How could I?

I keep turning what happened in the Garden over and over in my head. The array of clothes and of bodies. The sounds I heard: moans and whispers, the smack of skin against skin and the crack of those leather whips whistling through the air. The scents of champagne and sex, thick mineral sweetness. The wetness between my legs, the hardness of my nipples, and the want that made my whole body sing like a plucked wire.

This is the world of the Cravens. This was the world of my mother.

This was the last place on earth she wanted me to end up, and yet here I am, dreaming of returning through the wrong set of gates.

My ass gives a throb. I turn over onto my stomach seeking relief. I can't help remembering what happened after Colin's spanking. Remembering the other sort of relief he gave me. How his fingers felt, working between my legs, and how the pleasure moved in counterpoint to the pain. The look on his face as he touched himself, dark and hungry. My fingers don't bring the same feeling.

He was right. It is much better when someone else does it.

I won't be able to fall back asleep with the light starting to brighten, so I get out of bed and drift over to the window. Below me, the staff is cleaning up last night's revelry in the breaking dawn light, gossiping and laughing as they collect the burnt-out tea lights and make piles of discarded coats and forgotten hats, even a lost shoe or two. *They know more about what happens during the Misselthwaite parties than I do*, I think jealously.

"Careful. Someone broke a glass over there," a male voice says, and I look down to see Uncle Arch among the servants, already carefully dressed like he's on his way into town. He looks so sharp-edged, nothing like the debauched revelers who crowded the grounds last night. It's hard to believe he ever walked among them, happy and in love with Aunt Lily.

I imagine what he'd say if he knew I was there. A shiver passes through me, rippling outwards from my clit. I want to see him again—to try to figure out why he hosts these parties, but doesn't attend them, and if it has anything to do with Colin's haunted grief. So many mysteries in this house.

Then I remember that he and I are supposed to have an appointment this morning. I glance at the sculpted silver, which is sitting on top of the dresser, its shimmer just visible in the dim room. After Colin's punishment last night, I'm not sure I'm afraid of Uncle Arch anymore—they did worse all the time on the commune, and I never liked it half as much as that spanking.

Instead, I find that I...want to please him. I like the idea of showing him obedience and seeing how he reacts to that instead of my willfulness. He spanked me yesterday, but he spoke kindly to me, too. I watch as he walks through the crowd of staff. So unlike them, so unlike his brother and his son. From a distance, his proud figure could almost look lonely.

The sun is just barely peeking its head over the horizon, but still, I don't have much time. I select a dress for the day, grab the plug, and drop it into my robe pocket before opening the bedroom door. The fact that Mrs. Medlock never returned to lock it means that my ruse was successful. She trusted that I did exactly as I said I would.

And Uncle Arch must have stayed far away from my attic.

I lock the bathroom door behind myself and then regard my reflection in the mirror. It's not something I've ever had the luxury of doing much of. I wonder if I truly look different, or if my own face just isn't as familiar to me as it is to others. I wonder if it's as pleasing as Martha's, and Robin's. But there isn't time to linger over the question. What did Arch tell me to do to prepare myself?

I remember the slow drawl of his words like a finger stroking up my spine, a delicious tease.

Put the narrow end in your mouth.

The object isn't over-large, but it is heavy on my tongue, and I find I have some trouble swallowing with it in there. The discomfort fades, though, as I remember his next instruction.

Strip off all your clothes.

Arch's voice rumbles in my head, and I imagine his stark, impassive gaze on me as I pull my night-gown over my head and step out of my underwear. He praised my body once. Would he do it again?

Suck on it while you do, like it's the most delicious cock you've ever fantasized about.

I'm more determined than ever, now, to do exactly as Arch instructed. More than that, though, and I know it's foolish to think, because I'm still a girl, mostly, barely a woman yet, but—I do want to please him. Any way I can. Would he enjoy how this looks, my mouth stretched open, drool gathering at the corners, as I strain myself to please him? Is it his cock he hoped I'd imagine?

Because I am. It must be like Colin's but not exactly. Larger, perhaps. I imagine licking it, making it jump. Making him groan. It would slide so easily into my waiting mouth.

This time when I put the object in, it's warm and wet, and it slides in easily. I run myself a bath with hot water, using the taps the way Martha taught me.

When I sink into the tub, it's a revelation: it feels almost as good as Colin's fingers on my clit did last night. My body is immersed in warmth, floating suspended. The thing on my tongue is the only thing that keeps me tethered to the task at hand. Once I'm clean and cozy, I get out and prepare myself to carry out the next piece of Arch's instructions.

These are rather more...intimate than what came before. I sit on the low bench, facing a full-length mirror, and, his voice in my ear as I do it, I spread my legs open wide.

I can see myself like I never could have imagined,

perfectly clear in the glass in front of me. Colin's punishment has disappeared already, leaving my bottom unmarked. I'm flushed from my bath, pink and white everywhere.

My thighs are strong from the hours spent doing farm chores, my stomach tight and flat. My breasts sit high on my chest, my nipples stiff red peaks, and I reach down and tweak one experimentally, like Colin did to my clit last night. The sensation zings straight between my legs.

I look obscene: my mouth closed around a silver pacifier, my wet cunt on display for anyone to see, like the woman at last night's entertainment. *But there isn't anyone here*, I remind myself. The door is locked, and Arch *said* to touch myself, so I do, my hand tracing a path down between my breasts to the warm hollow of my cunt. I stroke myself there, pressing the heel of my hand to my aching clit, swallowing moans that want to escape my stuffed-full mouth. I teeter on the edge of an orgasm and pull myself back just in time. Arch didn't say anything about coming.

Instead, he told me to finger myself...there. Lower.

Your tight little asshole.

My fingers are dripping and slick by the time I brush them against my hole, pressing one in slowly. What did Arch say I would feel? *Invaded*. And it is like that. But it's not...bad. I imagine his hands where mine are, fine and strong and competent, splitting me open while my pussy twitches and my throat swallows helplessly.

The sun is starting to shine through the windows, the world outside turning from pink to yellow, and I know I need to hurry. I'm not fully ready, though, and when the plug presses against my entrance, it hurts a little bit. The pain takes me out of the moment, and I wonder if I can do this after all. Maybe I should stop. Give up.

But he would be disappointed, so I keep pushing, and there's the slightest amount of give. An inch of the thing slides inside of me. It feels like a victory.

I keep going.

I touch myself while I push it in, the thrum of my clit making everything below my legs feel swollen with want. There's so much pressure inside of me but not where I need it most. I remember Ben's finger piercing me in Arch's study, and it takes everything I have not to come again. But the memory unlocks something, and my body opens. Now the object is seated inside of me, as deep as it will go.

I don't have time to admire what I look like now, with the tantalizing hint of silver belying what's happening inside me. I pull my fresh dress and a pair of shoes on. Then I rush down to the gardens, the strange stretch of the thing inside of me accompanying every step.

I sit down gingerly on the bench, shivering in the cool morning air. The sun is up, but only just, and the morning dew is crystalline on each blade of grass. I can almost smell the scent of last night's party on the air still: the pop of champagne. The sweetness of the strawberries. The heat of all those bodies.

I wait and watch as the sun slips all the way over the horizon, and then rises above it. I'm trembling with the chill, now, my asshole clenching around the weight inside of it. My stomach rumbles for breakfast.

I don't move.

The sun comes up high enough to touch my face, a gentle caress that doesn't make up for the fact that I am still alone. Full, sore, anxious to please, to show off my bravery. But apparently that's not enough for him.

Because Arch doesn't come for me.

12

EVENTUALLY, the day's warmth starts to feel like an accusation. Who did I think I was, that I might matter to a man like Archibald Craven? It wasn't intended to be a *date*. It was a punishment. And being deemed beneath his notice stings more than my spanked bottom. I stand up and make my way back to the house, the object in my ass an unwelcome reminder that follows me with every step.

As I step in through one of the side doors, I hear raised voices, and I can't help following them down the hallway. Did something happen? Maybe Uncle Arch got caught up in some sort of household business and couldn't get away.

Wishful thinking.

Instead, I find Colin, Dickon, and Mrs. Medlock in the library. In the daylight, the walls of books look even more impressive—and the absence of the thing I took is much more obvious. Mrs. Medlock is wringing her hands. Worry twists her features into a version of her I haven't seen before.

"I haven't been dusting in here as regularly," she's telling them. "So I'm sorry, but I can't tell you when it went missing."

I know that she knows *exactly* when it went missing. After all, there's only been one person in this house, and in that room, who isn't on staff. And from the look on her face when she sights me before the men do, she isn't very happy with me for it.

"My mother collected all of these personally," Colin is saying. Oh, no. Arch didn't mention that part, but it does explain why he was so cold to me. "And they're about the only things left in this house that belonged to her, so I don't need to explain to you how important it is that we find it. You know how my father—"

I step in, and he breaks off at once, eyes shuttering.

"We can look into it," Mrs. Medlock says. "But that door was locked last night. There's simply nothing to be gained from pulling the membership list."

"She's right," Dickon adds. "No one who can afford the Garden is sneaking around stealing party favors. I vet each member as thoroughly as Ben vets the girls, and we've never had a problem before."

"I have it," I say, before they can reach the conclusion on their own. All three of their heads turn toward me in unison. "I can go get it right now, if you like."

I get a ghost of a nod from Mrs. Medlock that can't cover the pang I feel at Colin's visible disappointment. Arch already knows I have it, so I can't get in more trouble, but if I'd known it was Lily's...

Well, I can't say if things would have gone differently, but I didn't know.

No one says anything, so I turn to go. My plan is to go upstairs, remove Lily's plaything, and then wash and return it. It can be like the whole thing never happened. But before I can make it two steps, I feel Dickon's hand on my arm. "Not so fast," he says. "Bend over that table, there's a good girl."

He moves with me, never letting go of my arm, and before I know what's happening, my hips are pressed against a small backgammon table, my ass on display. Dickon lifts the skirt of my dress to reveal me to the room. I stare at the pattern in front of me, willing the black and white to absorb my shame, somehow. He strokes one of those thick, observant fingers along the backs of my thighs.

"You naughty girl. Where were you last night?"

I look over my shoulder at Colin. His disappointment remains.

"In the Garden where she didn't belong," he says. "She got a punishment, for all the good it did. She's lucky no one else got to her first. She would have been split in two."

"Jealous?" There's a grin in Dickon's voice. "Here,

now, little one. I didn't expect it out of you. Full of surprises. Ben, open her up. Let's take a look." The hand that's been stroking me moves to pull my cheeks apart, revealing what's sitting snug between them.

Colin gasps; so does Mrs. Medlock. But Dickon just lets out a satisfied little sound, like he was right about something. Like he knew it all along.

"Ah," he says. He gives the flare at the base a little tug. "The missing item has indeed been returned. And so prettily. I'd love to take the credit, but tell us, who exactly placed it in there for you?"

No point in telling anything but the truth. "I did."

Colin shakes his head. "You have no idea what you're doing. This sort of thing isn't a toy. You can't just *do* stuff that you don't know anything about. That's how people get hurt." The urgency is back in his voice.

I twist around so I can see them better. "Your father," I say, making eye contact with Colin before I have to drop my gaze, "told me to put it there. And told me *how*." I'm wracked through by shame and heat, want and need. I hate them all looking at me with my ass stuffed full, but part of me wants to spread my legs wider, to let Ben's clever callouses punish me the way Colin's did last night. I wonder how differently he'd do it. Less remorse and more delight, I imagine.

Colin's furious with me. "I thought better of you.

All this innocence, but you lie as easily as you breathe."

Dickon clicks his tongue. "Are you so certain?"

Ben massages the tender skin of my ass, making me tremble with sensation.

"Someone taught her how to put this in, Colin," Dickon says. "Told her the right way, so that she *wouldn't* hurt herself with her inexperience. She must have made herself very slick, playing with that pretty little pussy. When she finally felt so close that she couldn't take it anymore..." Ben's thumbs brush near my entrance and I swallow the sound I want to make. "It would have slid right into this needy little hole. Oh, how the Garden would love her."

Ben lets go of my ass. Dickon comes behind me and kicks my legs open, and I can't hide the gasp I make. The air in the room is still chilled, and it feels glacial against the heat building in the seam of my cunt.

"She is our *guest*," Mrs. Medlock reminds him, the second time.

"I know. For now. But I wish Ben could train her," Dickon says, slowly stroking what Ben had just handled with far less appreciation. "She'd be exquisite, don't you think? Innocent as a child, but the body of a woman. He'd teach her all the things she likes. Then, once she's got a taste for it, teach her all the things others like. And how much our clients would pay for the first taste of each piece of her..."

He trails off, imagining. I want to follow him down that path, want to hear everything he's thinking.

"No." It's Colin who answers first, firm and certain. With that, he storms to me and flips my skirt down. "Get up."

I stand up on shaking legs. My face is pink with shame, and in the thin dress I'm wearing, without a brassiere, the peaked tips of my nipples are all too visible.

"My father has forbidden it." Colin has lost his sweet demeanor. He has Arch's chin and forehead. Now he has the powerful, commanding expression. None would defy a man like this.

"What happened between you two?" Dickon asks. "When did Master Craven tell you to plug yourself?"

"In the garden," I tell them. "Yesterday. After I ran off. He came to talk to me. He said...he said a lot of things. But he knew I'd taken the...the piece of silver. He said I could face punishment, or I could put it inside myself, exactly as he instructed. That he was going to prove to me that I fit here, one way or another. So I did. I was just trying to be good for him."

Dickon gives a low, filthy chuckle. "And how good you were," he says.

But the color has drained from Colin's face while I've been talking. His pupils are thin with anger, and so is his mouth. "Bullshit. You," he says, "cannot lie to me. My father hasn't been with a woman since my mother died. He hasn't *touched* one. This is the made-up fantasy of a repressed schoolgirl, and it is a vile, pathetic one. You do not fit here, and you never will."

I don't know how to convince him that I'm telling the truth. "He didn't *touch* me, exactly. He said I remind him of Lily," I try, hoping that Colin will see the connection and let me off the hook.

Instead, he gets angrier. "Don't you dare."

"I was to meet him this morning and show it to him," I say. "But he never came. Why else would I be sitting in the gardens with this thing inside of me?"

"He left this morning," Mrs. Medlock notes. "I'm not certain why he would have told you to meet him when this trip has been on his schedule for weeks."

So, he *knew*? Why would he tell me to meet him if he knew he wasn't going to be there?

Because he enjoys inflicting all kinds of pain.

Even Colin seems off-balance, now, though I can't say why. Is it so hard to believe that his father did what he did to me? I don't understand anything about this strange place, and I feel a brief shard of longing for the commune, where rules were strict but clear.

"He often punishes with absence..." Colin muses. But then his voice grows steadier, louder. "But I'm certain you have misunderstood him. It's not your fault, Mary. You're behaving stupidly because you don't know any better. But you simply do not have the experience to get more from the Cravens than we take from you. Whatever you think you're going to accomplish here, I can assure you that you will not."

"I don't think I'm going to accomplish anything," I say. Colin believes I'm trying to seduce his father to improve my station. Ridiculous. "I would never assume that he..."

But what did I feel, alone with him in the garden? When he spoke to me like an equal? When I had a stray thought about marriage? Even when he had me over the bench, it was terrifying, but at the same time...freeing. I felt unashamed with him. Taken care of. I could let myself melt into his capable hands, and he would give me what I needed.

Something his son refuses to hear, or even entertain. Suddenly, I'm not defensive, I'm furious.

"You know what? You were right about one thing. This *is* bullshit. I came here for one thing. The painting I was promised was being held in trust for me. It isn't me who's too busy to locate it. It isn't me who asked for a room here, and a list of rules to follow. It isn't me who decided whether or not I could be trained, or ruined. It wasn't even me who decided I wanted to stay so innocent! Every single person here has their orders about me, but no one has ever bothered to include me in the discussion. Just because I don't know about the hedonism that goes on here doesn't mean I'm stupid, or incapable. It just means I don't know. Tell me what I want to know about this place. Ask me what I want. Or just give me what I came for, and I'll *accomplish* going back to my repressed schoolgirl life and spend it forgetting you exist."

I'm out of breath and redder than ever, but Colin is worse. Color has spilled back into his face, turning it red with fury. Whatever hurricane rages inside him won't be calmed by my words.

"You will *never* have what you came for!" he roars. "None of it! Now go!"

I turn and run.

13

I RUN until my lungs burn in my chest, the mansion's grounds whipping by in a blurry tangle of green and gray. I pass the garden where last night's party was held and press on, further, deeper, letting brambles tear at my skin and the fabric of my new dress.

It's only when the muscles in my legs start to cramp that I slow down, tears of frustration still streaming down my face as I walk along an old stone wall. This part of the gardens feels more abandoned even than the rest of it: desiccated vines and sharp twigs crack under my feet with each step, and there's so much overgrowth I can barely tell what was originally planted where.

I want to find the edge of the property, I think. Climb the wall. Dig under it. Pass through iron and stone like a ghost, and then—then I don't know what. I need to be reminded that Misselthwaite Manor isn't all that exists in the world.

But the grounds stretch on, and on, and on. I turn one corner, and then another. I turn too many corners and somehow I'm back to the Garden, standing before its high, forbidding barrier. I follow the line of its walls, expecting to see nothing, but instead, around a corner, color catches my eye. It's a trellis covered in something that seems to be alive, for once: a climbing vine that's just beginning to bud with sprays of soft pink flowers.

I find a wooden door that's nearly rusted off its hinges. The slats are warped and decayed from years of rain, and when I nudge it with my fingertips, it swings open with a deep, echoing groan.

I'm in a private garden—a very different kind of secret from the one I discovered last night. The trellis continues overhead, here, so there are more of those pink buds dappling the sky. They're not the only thing growing. The grass is brittle and dry, and so are the stone fountains that dot the landscape. But I can scent the unmistakable greenness of lovage, the bright tang of crow garlic. I recognize a neglected paradise. This soil, this light...it's everything I'd dream about in the Kingdom of Love while I was pulling yet another dead vegetable from the thin soil.

A swing hangs from the tallest tree, but one of the ropes has come loose from the wooden slat, and it hangs, broken, swaying slightly in the breeze.

I brush aside a mass of brambles to find one of the walls covered in the climbing English roses from the trellis. They're budding, too, like the pink flowers are, but their vines are twined around old sticks and dead plants; when I try to clear them, a thorn scratches my palm. I blink back a fresh set of tears.

I can't even do this right anymore. I don't recognize myself.

I sit on one of the benches as another wave of weeping overcomes me. This time it's pure longing, not anger. I miss the commune—the people, mostly, who I'd known all my life. People who never confused me like these ones have. I miss the beauty I knew there, those small snatches I could grasp, anyway: my quiet mornings to myself. The purposefulness of my labors. I miss when things were simple.

I try to imagine going back and marrying one of the elders who excommunicated me, wearing a rough white linen gown to match the suit I'd have sewn him as a symbol of my commitment. It wouldn't fit me as well as Dickon's garments do. Neither would my husband's. But ours would feel better, because they would be a sign of my purity and devotion. Of how hard I've fought to keep myself righteous for my husband. Maybe I'll tell him how I thought of him while I was here.

Or maybe I'll never tell him what happened here. Maybe I'll spend the night before my return on my knees before the gates of my home, purifying my thoughts with prayer and pleas, before walking back in with my head high and my heart pure.

But there is no scenario for me that doesn't involve financial redemption.

I don't get to decide how to return if I'm not allowed to return at all.

It hits me for the first time—all the things that I just yelled at Colin, Dickon, and Mrs. Medlock about are also things that I could apply, albeit in different ways, to the Elders of the Kingdom. I didn't ask to be part of things. I grew up there. I never questioned the rules that I followed. Even the one that I broke was never one that I'd tested before. I hadn't been a bad girl. I had been guilty, most of all, of ignorance.

In the space I'm clearing around the roses as I fume, I can see that one of the buds is blooming early, pussy-pink petals bursting forth to lift a hopeful face up to the sun. I touch its fragile petals, letting it perfume my fingertips with its perfect early-spring scent.

This flower wasn't told what to do, where it was allowed to be, who was allowed to gaze at its delicate stamen. It became who it was all on its own. Instinct and habitat combined to produce this perfect, beautiful thing.

Even here, in the midst of desolation and neglect, miracles happen.

For a moment, I see the same sheen of divinity I used to occasionally glimpse in the meetinghouse.

I wish I had what I needed—gloves, a shovel, a rake, and a broom, for starters—to tend to these plants. I was never allowed to plant flowers on the commune, where they were considered a waste of land and resources. They probably wouldn't have flourished even if I had, in that terrible soil. But isn't beauty also one of God's gifts?

I rise to my feet, wiping the tears from my face. I need to take inspiration from the roses. I must be stronger than this. I can't keep accepting non-answers from everyone I question. To figure out what I can do—what I *want* to do—I'll have to look inside myself.

I walk to the other side of the garden in search of tools, but there are no further doors or gates there. No sheds or lean-tos. Just a blank stone wall. A dead end.

I hope it isn't a portent.

"Finding all your silver bells and cockle shells?" The sound of a man's voice in all of this quiet startles me, and I whip around to see who's found me. It's Neville, properly dressed for the weather in thick, black wool trousers and a coat. His hair is combed back from his face today and it makes the angles of his bones stand out in sharper relief, giving him an even more sinister aspect. He smiles at me as he crosses the space between us, though it never reaches his eyes.

He brings one hand up to cup my cheek. His touch feels like a spark against my skin: it's electric, but there's something scary about that charge. The contact crackles with static and a real, deep fear curdles in my belly, reminding me that this is not a man I ought to be alone with. I flinch from his heat.

"Contrary child," he says. "You shouldn't be here."

"I haven't wandered anywhere forbidden to me."

Not today, at least.

"You've wandered right into Lily Craven's den."

Oh, no. Why do I keep retracing her steps? She may not haunt the Manor, but Aunt Lily seems to be haunting me. "I'm sorry," I stammer. "I'll go. I can—"

But he doesn't move, and I can't walk with him in my way. He does step back, finally, giving me space between our bodies. He gestures to one of the low stone benches. "Come, sit."

There's years of dirt and grime on everything in this place, but he brushes the topmost layers of leaves off and leaves me room.

I sit alongside Neville and keep my eyes fixed on his long, lean legs as he talks.

"I come here quite often," he tells me. "It's very difficult to forget the late Mrs. Craven." He glances at me sideways before continuing. "Despite all efforts by my brother."

"He was heartbroken." I echo Mrs. Medlock's and Martha's words.

"He was a man who never knew how lucky he was until it was gone." There's a lewd edge to his voice that feels like the whetstone you sharpen knives on. And suddenly a few more pieces click into place—a rivalry between brothers, the desire to possess what resembles love in a funhouse mirror. This is what Colin meant about Neville.

He's never known happiness, so he delights in taking it from others.

Did he truly love Aunt Lily? Did he become twisted and angry when his feelings went unreciprocated? I prefer that idea to that of a man who was born unhappy and covetous.

"Every time I come out here," he says. "I wish I could turn back time. At least, if I could bring Misselthwaite back to its former glory. It feels disrespectful to her memory to neglect her favorite spaces. Lily was so vibrant, so full of life...I can't imagine what she would say seeing it like this."

For the first time, I feel like I understand both Neville and Arch. Grief is a terrible burden. I remember from losing my mother how much easier it is when shared. I also remember how long it took me to admit that the mere idea of her being in a better place wasn't enough for me to relinquish my sadness. I look at what surrounds us: the brambles and thorns, the weeds and overgrowth. It deserves more than the scorn born of sorrow.

"Why don't you have it tended to?"

"Arch is so weighted down by his version of the past that he can't see anything else. And he won't let the rest of us move on. So, I'm afraid this place, like the other Garden, is tacitly off-limits."

"Do you think," I ask, my voice hesitant, shy. I do miss working with my hands. I miss having something to *do*. I know Arch wouldn't approve of me even being here—much less gardening—but surely Lily would. And maybe he doesn't have to know. "I would love to make it beautiful again. Do you think, if I'm very careful, maybe I could honor her memory by bringing this space back to life?"

"I certainly don't care," Neville says with an elegant shrug. "Just don't let yourself get caught. My brother is a cruel man, even when he doesn't recognize it. I'll do what I can to protect you."

I imagine this space in the fullness of spring, the roses open and the benches and walkways cleared of debris. The fountains running so that the sound of water fills the air. Songbirds rustling in the leaves, chirping back and forth at one another. My own hard work reflected back to me; a beautiful place of my own making.

I won't be here then, I remind myself. I'll be long gone, back at the commune harvesting practical things: corn and beans and hearty greens.

But still. I would like the work, and I will like thinking of it after I'm gone. We're far enough from the house that I'll be left alone here. Arch doesn't come out to the grounds anyway, certainly not to the areas around the Garden. Who even knows when he'll be home again?

And once he sees it brought to life again—maybe the memory will restore a small bit of joy to his heart?

Another thought occurs to me. "Protecting me isn't a task for the Craven men."

Neville shrugs again, though this time, I can see the effort. "And whose task is it?" he asks.

"Mine."

Neville's look stops me cold. "Are you sure you know what's involved here?" he asks.

"I—"

He puts his hand on my jaw. There it is again: that sensation of danger, surging electric. I want to run from it, but I know I can't. I have to bargain with the devil if I want to get back into heaven.

"I can assure you that you do not know what you are asking for. But if you'd like—if you'd but ask—I could offer you something that might bridge the gap."

I have some idea, but I'm not exactly sure what that means. I bite my lip briefly. What I *do* know is that I am out of options, a rose growing with no gardener in sight. I'll have to trust my instincts to allow me to bloom in sinful soil without setting down roots.

"I'm asking. Even if I don't understand, you'll tell me. In detail. I need to know everything." My eyes never leave his, even when they light with lust and avarice. The hand he lays on my knee must be meant to reassure. It feels more like an anchor.

"Someone," he says, with a gentle caress, "maybe a man, maybe a woman, could buy your mouth for a night. If you chose to allow it. If you wanted the money they'd spend. Then you'd use that mouth in any way they selected. To suck a pussy, or take a cock down your throat."

I hadn't planned to react. I'd seen such filthy things in the Garden, and I'd learned the vocabulary between the men and the books. I still turn beetroot red just hearing him use these words so casually thrown together like they were simple things to do.

In this manor, with these people...there's nothing shameful.

"You'd suck and lick whatever they told you to. You'd take cock all the way down your throat, if called for," Neville tells me. His voice is even, like we're discussing how to prepare a roast chicken for dinner. "Of course, the fantasy you provide wouldn't suffer if you pretended to resist. Acted like you didn't know what to do. That's part of the lie. Regardless of how many well-trained whores they adore, our clients never seem able to resist the fantasy of the virgin who somehow knows just what to do."

My ass clenches around the bulb inside of it. I'd almost forgotten it was there, but I remember again now as I try to picture myself doing those things, and blood keeps rushing between my legs. It would be disgusting and degrading.

I'm wet at the thought.

"I'm not saying no," I tell Neville. My voice shakes. I hope he doesn't know why.

He stands up. "But you aren't saying yes." He heads for the exit.

I have to remind myself what's at stake here. Look

inside myself. What am I willing to do to leave? How much of myself am I willing to leave behind?

"Wait," I call. Neville turns to me. "If I just did the thing with my mouth. And that was all. Do you think I could earn enough money to leave?"

Neville considers this. "You could certainly *leave.* Whether you could buy your way back into your purity cult for the price of your mouth, I couldn't say."

For the first time, I'm actually thankful I am usually good at controlling my temper. It doesn't matter what he says. I know who I am. I know where I want to be. And if I can keep my firm line of virginity intact, then I have to try. Doors are closing all around me, and though I wouldn't have chosen this one before, I am now. This is the garden in which new seeds will grow.

"I want to try."

Neville doesn't take me seriously at first. "Arch would be mad," he says. "And you've never even tasted a cock before. I just can't be sure that the product would justify the price tag. Between an unsatisfied client and my brother…"

I gather all my courage in hand. "How hard can it really be?"

Neville narrows his eyes, but he walks back so he's standing in front of me.

"Open your mouth," he commands, and I do. The next thing I know, his finger is on my tongue. "Close, now," he says, "and suck."

It's different than the bulb was earlier: smaller, but warmer, tasting more salty than metallic. He pulls his finger out and pushes it in again, the rhythm of the movement matching the pulsing in my chest and between my legs.

"To become truly adept, the kind of innocent whore that would pay top dollar, your mouth has to be greedy," he says. "It sucks whatever you put inside of it. It swallows everything you give it." He adds a second finger. "Look at you. Are all your holes this hungry? Would you open up for as many cocks as you could take?"

With that, he pushes his fingers to the back of my throat, and I gag reflexively, startling him out of my mouth.

"Apparently not, but you'll want to pretend," Neville tells me. It had been easy up to that point. I swallow once, twice, and open wide so he can put his fingers back in again. He does the same thing: thrusts idly in and then out again, telling me to work my tongue, to get him as wet and sloppy as my empty cunt. And again, when he pushes too far, my throat twitches and my stomach heaves.

He's ready for it, this time, though, and he doesn't let up. "Relax," he commands, hand still shoved in my mouth. "Just relax and let me—"

Waves of nausea are rolling over me now, but the commune raised me to be tough and to do my duty. Even when it seems impossible to bear, I do what I must. Beyond that, though, there's a surge of something hotter, a fire I've been trying to put out since I was a child. So I let his fingers choke me. His hand moves to his pants while a damp stain spreads across them. I can't breathe, but I won't make him stop.

Because I can't let him win.

"I can learn," I tell him.

He looks me up and down again, and this time, he seems satisfied by what he sees. "Indeed," he says. "I bet you can."

14

THAT AFTERNOON, I find myself in a daze as I wander back into the house. My stomach is still heaving, and I can feel the phantom shape of Neville's fingers in my mouth, pressing down my throat. I feel dirty and used, but also oddly...hopeful. This is the first time I've had any control over my fate. Now I can stop sitting around waiting for Arch to give me what I want—what I need.

It will take longer than I'd hoped, but I will have money of my own, one way or another, and then I will have my life back at last.

I will reckon with the cost of the money after that. I can't afford to do it now.

The climb back up the stairs to my attic room is a long one, and I pause on one of the landings midway up to catch my breath. At first I think the noises I hear are my heart pounding in my ears, but even as my pulse calms, I still hear them: they clarify into growls and the sounds of floorboards squeaking rhythmically. Is this another ghost, like the one that drew me out of bed my second night here? Or will daylight reveal secrets to me now that I've decided to remake myself at the Manor?

I recall that last creep along the hallway, how those noises seemed to move around the house, as I do it again. This time nothing disappears. Lending credence to my fancy that Misselthwaite has accepted me, these tones just get louder and clearer. At the end of the hall, I see a door left ajar, and I tiptoe up until I can see what's happening inside.

The room is a bedroom, much finer than mine: there's a thick carpet on the floor, inlaid with a gorgeously intricate pattern, and a thick comforter is twisted up on the bed in a heap. One wall is entirely covered with heavy red velvet. Shelves are lined with books and knick-knacks—but what arrests my attention is the naked man on his knees in the middle of all of it.

It's Colin. Seeing him here in his own space feels more intrusive than looking at the hard cock in his hand.

"You don't deserve this," he whimpers, staring down at the pleasure he's giving himself. With his other hand, he flings a small, many-tailed whip over his shoulder.

It's a miracle I manage to turn back from the door as the gasp escapes my mouth.

He's found a way to punish himself for the sins he isn't even committing.

I should be inspired. I'm not. Pity overrides pious, horror pushes righteousness out of my mind. This isn't good. It cannot be the path to glory.

Colin needs to find his own way to allow new growth in, of that I'm certain. Whatever soil he is tending is full of nothing but sorrow and shame.

When I can bear witness to him no longer, I slowly walk to the bathroom. The pressure in my cunt and my ass is less insistent now, like it's found a home. Once I'm locked inside, I turn on the shower and stand under its hot spray. Now I can take my time: teasing my clit, dipping my fingers into my hole, pressing curiously against the bulb in my ass and noticing how it makes my cunt clench, how good it feels to be filled up this way. Telling myself that it's okay. That I'm fertilizing my own garden with joy and not sorrow.

When I come, it's a long, luxurious orgasm. One that rolls through me like a wave, crashing once, and then again, and again.

As I ride out the tremors, I pull the silver piece from its seat inside me. Again, I indulge myself by imagining again that Arch is here: that it's his hands between my legs, soothing my swollen pussy, the puffy edges of my asshole. Would he praise me? Tell me I'd been good for him? My whole body feels like pleading, and I'm glad I know he isn't on the Manor grounds. I want him in a way that feels too big, too dangerous.

Never, ever.

When I get up to my rooms at last, I fling myself on the bed, my legs falling apart automatically and my hands coming between them to stroke my again-soaking folds.

I've been on edge all morning, so it isn't surprising that I'm again ready to tumble into sweet oblivion, my breath catching in my throat. I hear my own little whining sounds, helpless and needy, and I imagine Arch catching them in the warm, broad expanse of his palm.

Thinking of him makes me come again, softer, this time, an aftershock quaking through me as I grind against my own palm and whimper.

I wash the silver sculpture and then myself, dressing carefully in the most modest outfit Dickon made before going down to the library to replace the stolen object where it belongs.

Hunger is starting to make itself known in my stomach, so I follow the smells of food and the noises of pots and pans banging to see if I can scrounge up something to eat.

It's the quiet period between lunch and dinner, so the room is nearly empty: a few serving girls are finishing up the washing in one corner, and Martha and Mrs. Medlock are conferring at one of the flour-dusted counters. I shrink when I see Mrs. Medlock, afraid that, despite my confession, she'll be mad at me for leaving my room, but she just waves me over with a smile.

"There you are," she says. "We've been worrying about you—when the Cravens have you in their sights, it can be difficult not to punish yourself worse than they can."

It's more astute than she knows, given how Colin Craven appears to be punishing himself as well.

"I needed to..." I start, trying to sound both contrite and confident. "I needed to clear my head. Put my hands in the soil. The Cravens have a way of making me forget who I am."

"And have you remembered?" asks Mrs. Medlock. I must look surprised, because she pats me gently on the shoulder. "We heard Colin's punished you for his own innocence," she says. "I do apologize for that. If we'd known, we would have stepped in."

"Colin gets carried away," Martha agrees. She shakes her head. "He hasn't been the same since Sarah."

I want to know more—*need* to know more—but my stomach is growling louder than any of the Craven men's demons. There are rolls in a basket on the counter; Mrs. Medlock sees me eyeing them, and pushes them towards me. "Have you eaten lunch yet?"

I shake my head.

"Oh, you must be starving. I'll get you some butter for those," she says, bustling across the room. "And Martha's right about Sarah—he changed, after her."

She sets the butter dish in front of me and leans a stubby knife against it. The roll must have been baked this morning; it's still faintly warm, and when I break it open, its insides breathe out a little billow of steam. I spread a thick wad of butter, and then another, before taking a hungry bite. We didn't have much white flour on the commune—the elders preferred that we eat millet and oats. I'm still not used to how soft and luxurious warm bread can be.

"He was happy," Martha says. "It didn't matter how his father was. At least this is what Dickon tells me. I came on afterwards, so. My God, I wish I could have seen the Garden in its prime, when Mistress Lily braided the rose branches and didn't stand for men's bullshit."

Mrs. Medlock swats her. "They've both suffered losses, and it improves nothing to make light."

I swallow and look up at them, glad to have something in my stomach to settle it. "What happened to her?" I ask. "Sarah."

Mrs. Medlock and Martha share a look, and I wonder if this is another secret they're going to try to keep from me.

But then Mrs. Medlock turns to me, and says, "It was a tragedy, and there wasn't anything he could have done. Don't you fall for his martyrdom routine. It's exactly as useful as Martha's gossip." Martha opens her mouth, then closes it again, having apparently thought better.

"Sarah worked in the Garden, and you know what that means now."

"But she had a thing for Colin," Martha interjects, getting a stern glare from the older woman.

"She didn't think he would love her if he knew," Mrs. Medlock continues. "Which says a lot about what she thought of him, not that anyone asked me. So she pretended to be a housemaid, and we all played along. They were sweet. Happy. He didn't attend the Garden parties and she wore a mask when she did. Didn't seem any harm in it."

"Well, *he* was happy," Martha adds without remorse this time.

"Martha!"

"I'm just saying." She takes a roll for herself, carefully spreading on only half the butter I allowed myself. "We all let him think he was the only one, but it's not like she wasn't taking her pleasure elsewhere." The look on her face as she bites the frugally-topped roll doesn't speak wonders for control. The irony isn't lost on me.

"The *pleasure* you speak of could have meant her employment." Mrs. Medlock glances at me, and I know with a sinking feeling she means that Uncle Arch was the source of the girl's fear. "It's not fair to suggest she was... Regardless. Sarah didn't know she was pregnant, so there's also no point in speculating on that. She'd never been regular enough to suspect something was wrong until the pain started."

"Ectopic pregnancy," Martha explains. "It's when the baby tries to grow in the wrong place."

"Colin's always had a difficult time of it—and who wouldn't, shut up in a house with a man who can't bear to look at him, but won't let him leave...but after Sarah died...he blamed himself. And yet still he and the Master can't find common ground. They mourn differently, for different women."

"Uncle Arch won't let anyone in, and Colin tries to keep everyone out. Maybe not that different," I say. My head is spinning—at the awful death of this girl, at this new insight into Colin's pain and Arch's desires.

"Of course, I expect you won't breathe a word of this," Mrs. Medlock offers me another roll.

It's nice to be included, to be spoken to as an equal and not like a child.

"I won't," I promise. But as long as I'm here, I need to gather as much information as possible, if I'm to set my new plans with Neville in motion.

I have to do *something* to ensure I can get out of here soon, and with my virtue intact. *I'm trading one bit of it for another*, I tell myself. As long as I remain a virgin, as pure and untouched for my future husband as possible...well, I will do what I need to do in order to get back to the commune. To earn my place. I can't let myself get distracted by thinking about Arch.

"Did Neville sell Sarah, too?" I ask.

Mrs. Medlock looks mildly scandalized at my

suggestion, and Martha narrows her eyes at me. "Where did you get that idea?" she asks sharply.

"In Arch's study, I heard them talking about selling parts...parts of bodies...for use, at Garden parties," I say as quickly as I can stammer through, hoping she wasn't really listening to what all they were saying as they inspected me.

"Do you understand what that entails?" Mrs. Medlock asks. I nod, although I'm not completely sure that I do.

"It's asking a *lot* of a girl," she says, finally taking a roll for herself.

"To stay a virgin around here, where hiking and sex are basically the only things to do? I'd say so." Martha earns another swat for that one.

"It's bigger than ignoring one's...urges. It means letting go of any notions of romance. Sex is vulnerable enough without having your first time in public. Your virtue becomes some rich man's trophy, just another night for him, but a lifetime's memory for you. Selling first times largely fell off at the Garden while Mistress Lily was here, unless a girl really wanted it."

"Wanting it can be a kink, you know." Martha says it in a way that makes it clear it isn't hers.

"Neville was always fond of sales. The money, of course, but he also likes the power. I would stay far away from him if I were you, Mary."

Of course, it's rather too late for that.

The commune's compulsion to truthfulness

resurfaces, and I hear myself saying, "I saw him just now," I admit. "In the gardens. We talked about it. And he…" I barely know how to say it. "Tested me out, a bit."

I expect them to be mad, or shocked at least, but Martha's not concerned with propriety.

"Did you like it?" she asks.

I don't know how to answer that question. I liked parts of it—the heaviness of his fingers in my mouth, and the way he put me on display for him. I didn't like *him*. Didn't like the look in his eye as he measured me up, or the lingering suspicion in the back of my mind that he's already three steps ahead of me.

But I don't know how to put all of that into words that won't upset them, so I just nod.

"I know it's wrong. Only…that's the part I like, too."

"It *is* your kink! I love it," Martha says. "Imagine the outfits my brother could make you!"

"You forget yourself, Martha," Mrs. Medlock says sternly. "Neville's opinion is one thing, but Master Arch forbade her from being touched. That is the end of the discussion."

"He's the first to say a woman's body is her own," she reminds Mrs. Medlock.

Here, in this manor, with these people…

"Name me a time that disobeying the Master has ended well for the willful one."

Martha waves a hand dismissively. "That's staff. Neville, on the other hand…"

"He is *not* to be trusted!"

Martha has been sitting between me and Mrs. Medlock, the three of us arranged in a half-moon shape around the counter. Now she turns her back to Mrs. Medlock, so she's only facing me. "Mrs. Medlock can't stop you, and neither can Arch, or anyone else, for that matter," she says. "It's your choice to make, and if you want it, you should have it, Mary. Though I *would* take advantage of the Master being away, and do it before he gets back." She smiles at me, and she looks genuinely happy. "I think it's exciting you're taking control of your own sexuality."

I imagine walking out of the gates with the money I made in my pocket, and no one owning me. Owing the world nothing, and even having taken something I want from it on my own terms. I imagine a cock in my mouth, in my throat, giving me as much as I can handle, and then more, more, more. My imagined self looks up at the man stroking my hair.

His face is taut with unreleased pleasure.

The man is Uncle Arch.

"It *is* exciting," I agree, streaking more butter on my roll.

15

THE NEXT MORNING, I'm up with the sun. This time, rather than dreading anything shameful, twisted, or strange, I'm eager to begin reclaiming a piece of myself.

Maybe it will help offset the other pieces I've given away.

It doesn't take long to find the shed where Colin spanked me, which, as I'd hoped, turns out to be full of useful tools. I drag long-forgotten rakes, brooms, buckets, and shovels out to Aunt Lily's long-dead garden and set to work. There's much that needs doing. I rake up piles of old leaves and then sweep the dust underneath them, unearthing a flagstone path that winds in undulating curves around the space. I separate what was planted intentionally from what's volunteered, and what's still early-spring dormant from what's dead and never coming back.

The routine is familiar and calming. For the first time since I arrived at Misselthwaite, I feel at home.

I'm just starting to untangle one of the rose bushes—with gloves on, this time—when the groan of the gate announces Neville's arrival. He's smartly dressed, as usual, in a prim black suit, and I realize in a rush that I'm dusty and sweaty, my hair curling wildly at my temples and where I pinned it back at the nape of my neck. The very picture of the innocent farm girl I swore to everyone that I was done being.

"Mary," he says. "Hopefully you'll work as hard at our lessons as you have at...this."

"I will," I promise, shedding my gloves and wiping my hands nervously on my skirt.

"Good. Today will be your first lesson." He inspects me carefully, his gaze stinging like a nettle where it passes on each part of my body. "You'll have to learn several techniques, since there's no telling who will end up buying you, or what they'll want when they do." He steps in closer to me and casually hauls the hem of my shirt up, tucking it so that my breasts are exposed. The sun is hidden behind a thin layer of cottony clouds. The sweat I worked up gardening is suddenly very cool, and my nipples stand at attention under his gaze.

I like it, but I thought we had agreed to a different kind of deal. "You said," I begin, but then my voice falters.

"What did I say?"

"You said my mouth."

Neville's grin is predatory. "Nobody wants a mouth alone," he says. "Any street whore could provide that. The Garden sells fantasy. I'm not simply auctioning off a sucking. I'm auctioning off a girl who is so desperate to suck that she can hardly stand it. That merely the thought of her mouth filled with sex causes a physical reaction."

He strokes one of my exposed breasts with the back of his hand, and I feel my spine straighten. I was right to fear he was planning to push me further than I'd intended to go.

"They're lovely," he says. "I cannot wait to show off how hard these get." He tweaks my nipple before giving it a firm tug. I can't help the whimper that escapes me. "So responsive," Neville says before taking a step back. "Now, take off your skirt."

I do as he commands, the soft cotton whispering down my legs and puddling in a heap around my feet. As I watch, Neville strides over to a particularly tangled section of vines and tugs them aside to reveal a metal loop anchored in the wall's stone. "Come." He snaps his fingers. I do, marveling at the ease he has in this place, how he seems to know instinctively where to find what he's looking for.

When I'm close enough, he puts my back to the wall and tugs my arms over my head, using his belt to tie them together—suspending me from the loop like a fish on a hook.

My shirt is still up and over the swells of my

breasts, and it's somehow more humiliating than
being naked, I think: there's an innocence to nakedness, or there can be. But now anyone who comes in
here will think I was in such a rush to get touched
that I couldn't even undress properly. The shirt
frames my breasts like they're meant to be on display,
and I can feel my cunt getting needy and wet
between my legs.

Neville tweaks my nipples again, and this time,
when he runs the back of his hand down the side of
my breast, it keeps going, stroking across my ribs, the
curve of my waist and then the jut of my hip. He
kicks my legs apart and laughs at me when I gasp.

He inspects me like livestock, like he did in Arch's
study: he touches me everywhere. It's cursory, and
not at all affectionate. I've just begun to wonder if I'm
not measuring up—if my body disappoints him—
when he catches my gaze and says, "You look like
your mother. I always intended to find out what she
tasted like."

My mouth falls open, and he hooks a thumb in
my bottom lip. Instinctively, I go to suck on it like he
taught me, my eyes falling closed in pleasure because
his other hand reaches around to stroke my ass,
proprietary, and when he squeezes, I fail to hold in
my groan.

"Shush," he says, smacking my ass so hard I startle. "That's right," he continues, pulling his hands out
of my mouth and stepping away from me. I feel the
loss of contact immediately. "Look at you. I've

barely touched you and you're already begging for it."

He slaps my pussy, this time, and my knees give at the sensation. I'd fall over if the belt wasn't holding me up. The hand that slapped me slips between my legs, briefly, and I flush, knowing he can feel how slick I am for him.

Does every girl like this as much as I do? It seems impossible.

"Oh," he says. "You like pain. Good."

In a move so fast I barely register it, he lifts the belt from the hook, and I stumble down to my knees.

Neville surveys me as if I'm an object. "Now," he says, "you're going to learn to take a cock."

I watch wide-eyed as he undoes his trousers and draws himself out. He's hard, of course, and big as I'm discovering all Craven men are. Thick and rude, swollen with want, ready to fill my mouth and my throat…only that would spoil the sale. My eyes drift back up, to where he's pulled a banana from his pocket.

"Don't worry," Neville says. "We'll work up to my size. Now open." I do, and he taps the fruit on my tongue, a brief tease, before pulling it back again. I've tasted them so rarely in my life. I want more. He laughs when I give chase, reaching out a hand to grab my hair and hold me still. "That's precisely the hunger I'm selling," he says. "Don't worry, you'll get what you need."

This time when he slides the soft, delicious fruit

onto my tongue, he leaves it there. His other hand rests gently on his cock as his hips move idly back and forth. I keep perfectly still until he taps the bottom of my chin, letting me know I'm allowed to close around the treat, to start taking it in.

The noise I make is a wordless, helpless question. If he wanted to train me to crave this, he chose exactly right. This taste is overwhelming in the best way: obliterating, almost. I forget about the commune, about the money, almost even about myself. The only thing I know is this moment, on my knees in the spring dirt, taking pleasure and watching his. I swallow helplessly once, and then again.

"Leave a mark and you'll pay for it," Neville purrs.

My throat is empty now, but it won't be for long. The delicate nature of the banana will show any marks I leave, so I'm careful to use nothing but my tongue.

"Breathe through your nose," Neville instructs curtly. "And open your throat."

With that, he's pushing it further in, past the gag reflex he triggered with his fingers, deeper inside of me than I thought I could go. I make a protesting sound and he pulls back just slightly before pressing another inch in. Tears prick my eyes, hot and sudden, and I try to blink them back, try to breathe, try to stay still. *In through my nose*, I remind myself.

Focus on the taste, focus on the pleasure in a job well done.

"You'll soon be able to throat a man without complaint," he says. "Without even thinking. Any time, any place, your body will know what to do." I moan a little at the wanton thought and I feel my throat work around the banana. Something inside of me settles. It must be obvious. I'm blossoming, becoming the slut everyone seems to see in me.

"Fuck." His hand is actively working his cock now. "Oh, fuck, you were born for this, weren't you? Who wouldn't spend a fortune to see your blushing tits, your wet, pink little pussy, and to get to fuck— wider, now, take it—fuck your sweet mouth?"

His praise is making me woozy, or maybe it's the fact that I keep forgetting to breathe. I sneak a hand between my legs to relieve the pressure, stroking my clit firmly while he fucks my face with the fruit. I sneak in one orgasm, a brief rush of release. But he notices, of course, the way I twitch and squirm when I come.

"None of that," he says, taking his hand off himself and slapping my hand away. Then he smacks my cheek. His shaft leaps in excitement, and cold dread starts to override the wonderful taste, the task it represents.

He likes the power.

"Don't get distracted. You have a job to do." With that, he grabs the back of my head and forces me down so that I'm impaled, all the way down, choking on the sweetness and pressure, unable to catch my breath.

It's too much. I'm crying freely, now, tears leaking out of my eyes, spit pooling in the corners of my mouth. I try to pull back, or push him away, but my hands are ineffectual against the ropy muscles his suit covers. Darkness is pricking at the corners of my vision when he lets go to grab his cock. It pulses in his hand and he comes on my face, groaning with satisfaction.

Something shudders through me, and I can't tell if I'm going to come again, untouched, or pass out from lack of oxygen.

He pulls the banana out just as suddenly as he pushed in, and I cough and sputter, trying to wipe my face with my hands as he inspects for bite marks. I must pass, because he smiles.

"Don't fight this," he says from above me, tossing the banana into the dirt as though it's one of a million. I suppose it is, but the waste of something so precious still brings fresh tears to my eyes. He tilts my face up and away from his discarded tool and strokes a hand against my cheek, still red from where he slapped me. "You are a natural. A mouth that soft —and on your first time—with just a little practice, the bids will be outrageous. It's a pleasure to oversee your training personally.

I'm panting, still, my chest heaving, my pussy aching and soaked. I want him to leave and never come back.

I want him to teach me more, show me how to master this so that I can leave and never come back.

I want to make myself come again, and again, and again, the exotic taste still lingering in my mouth, as I imagine it was Arch I was choking on.

Neville runs a speculative finger through the mess I've made of myself, the spit and tears running tracks down my chin to my throat. "I can't wait to see my brother's face," he says, smiling that predatory grin, "when he realizes someone's fucked yours."

16

AT LAST, my days at Misselthwaite Manor fall into a predictable pattern. I rise with the sun and wash myself. I eat a small breakfast with Mrs. Medlock in the kitchen, and then I head out to my little garden to work for a while.

These mornings remind me of the best parts of my life on the commune: watching the light change and feeling the air warm; having time to myself to take in the world and its pleasures. The first day I see grass starting to shoot up from a piece of ground I've cleared, their little stalks so tender and green and hopeful, I feel like crying.

Finally, I have something to myself.

Finally, the world looks as I wish it to.

Neville comes for me in the afternoons, a cloud across the sun.

He's always crisply dressed, as if to make a

mockery of how dirty I get in the gardens. His cock doesn't seem to mind, though: he's always as hard for me as he was on the first day, capable of filling my mouth and my throat and making me think forbidden thoughts about what it would feel like if he broke the rules and actually did it.

After the first day, he started bringing cucumbers instead. Each time, they get a little larger. The only things that change are the lessons.

One day he'll make me sit against the wall and shove the length into my mouth, the sensation of stone against my skull reminding me that I have nowhere to go, that all I can do is relax and take it. All the while, he murmurs filthy things that take me to the very edge again and again before finally allowing me to relieve the pressure in my throbbing clit and come when he does. The next he'll insist on teasing me, brushing his cockhead against my lips while I play with my pussy, never letting me suckle before pulling away and replacing himself with the cucumber.

He makes me try different combinations of tongue, lips, hands, and trains me how to feel the way he twitches before he comes, to know when he's on the verge of losing himself. He has me on my hands and knees like an animal when I'm not strung up by the hook in the wall. And every time I think I'm used to what we're doing, he shocks me again.

One day, instead of having me in the dirt or at the

wall, he seats me on a stone bench and has me pull my skirts over my knees.

"Do you like sucking cock, Mary?" he asks idly, stroking himself through his pants.

I'm already wet, eager for the moment I'll be allowed to release the pressure that's building up low inside my belly even before we begin. "Yes."

"I know you do." His smile is still poison-edged, equally beautiful and cruel. "I've been dropping hints about something special to the men who frequent our little parties, you know. Just enough to whet their appetite. It's been so long since we've had a proper sale. Between your hard work here and mine there, I'm certain you'll fetch a pretty price."

"I'm glad."

"I'm sure you are. Though I can't help noticing that your pussy is looking a little neglected this morning." I fight against the urge to close my legs together, the old shame at exposure creeping up the way it always seems to when he's around, and I can feel the way he delights to watch me squirm.

"So wet, so eager. I bet even the breeze feels like a lover. It feels so good to make men feel good, doesn't it, Mary?"

He's right about the breeze, blowing chill air across my most delicate folds and making my clit swell impossibly more. I imagine that it's Arch's mouth. There's no way I can respond with words, but I let out a whimper of agreement.

"Do you touch yourself, at night, imagining what it will be like? On display like art. All those eyes on you, all of them so desirous that they'd give anything at all to be the one to claim you."

I whimper again, rocking back and forth on the bench.

"Show me," he commands. "Show me how you touch yourself, crammed up in your little room, trying so hard to be a good girl. You probably don't even put your fingers inside yourself, do you? Imagine the auction, the relief you'll feel at finally being able to stop pretending you don't love this."

Neville cups my tits in one warm palm; I slide my fingers over and around my slick, plump little bud. I do love this. I do.

A whore is a woman who knows how to enjoy her body.

Not for the first time, I wish it was his knee I was learning to enjoy it at. When Neville continues, I pretend his brother Arch is the one guiding me closer to heaven.

"You'll be so happy, won't you, when you're finally allowed to open your mouth and practice all these skills on a real, heavy, thick cock. So proud to show off all you've learned, letting everyone who didn't win see what they missed out on. What wouldn't they give, after they watch your pretty little performance, to have more? To maybe taste your sweet, virgin pussy?"

He pinches my nipple at the same time I pinch my

clit, picturing the forbidden, impossible scene of Arch's tongue buried within me, and the next thing I know I'm nearly crying with the pulse of my release.

"Good," he says. "Again. This time, while you suck on the cucumber." I do. It feels so good to give myself up to him, to not think for as long as he has me on my knees.

He makes me come until I can't anymore, until my body is so wrung out and useless I can barely make it back up the stairs to my room. My throat is so sore even a full pot of Mrs. Medlock's chamomile tea with honey doesn't soothe it. But the next day, I'm ready to do it all over again. My orgasms are becoming inextricably linked with my fledgling abilities to pleasure a man, with the fantasies I indulge in more and more where the man of the house is the one receiving my ministrations.

Each time I come, thunderously pulsing around the emptiness where I'm imagining Arch's fat cock, I tell myself it's the last time. I swear to myself I'll stop once he returns. That this slutty little interlude doesn't really count, and that I'll soon replace his face in my mind with that of an elder—of the husband I will soon have.

But it gets harder to pretend I'm not playing a dangerous game once I start getting the letters.

Mrs. Medlock hands them to me sealed, but they don't have a postmark on them. I don't know where Uncle Arch is, and what he writes offers me no clues, for he doesn't talk about himself. Instead, he instructs me to do things for him.

The first letter is curt: *Your debt remains unpaid*, it says. *Tonight, follow my instructions again. Make yourself come while you wear the plug.*

When I do, there's no question of thinking of anyone else but him. In my mind, he's standing at the end of my bed as I writhe, ass in the air so that he can see both of my holes: the one filled with his wife's silver sculpture, and the one dripping with desire for him to fill himself.

The next letter is longer, more detailed. More cruel. He instructs me to use my sheets to tie my feet to my bedposts, so that I sleep all night with my legs spread wide.

Anyone could come in and see the most secret part of you as you sleep, he says. *But you're all alone in that attic, and no one will. Are you lonely up there, Mary?*

I've been lonely my whole life. Even surrounded by my sisters in God, I was always alone. It's only now that I've discovered what it is to be wanted that it aches.

So does my pussy. When the sun finally goes down, I use the showerhead in the bathroom on myself until I can't come anymore, until I'm sitting on the tile dripping and shaking in a post-orgasmic daze. Does Arch suspect what Neville and I are doing? Would he care if he did?

No, I tell myself. I can't think that thought. Arch may toy with me, but his only care is being obeyed.

Whatever his purpose is in sending me the letters, is for his benefit alone. My head swims trying to work out what game he's playing, though I follow every new rule he sets without question. He starts to touch and control new parts of my life with each one.

He instructs me on which dresses to wear; he writes that he's told Mrs. Medlock what to feed me, and for a week every time I see a bowl of fresh berries with breakfast it feels overwhelming and unbearable, for a man who I can't see, who's barely touched my skin, to be in my life so intimately and totally.

The only sign of Arch's body that I have is the knowledge that his hands touched the paper I'm holding. Sometimes I press it against my nose while I touch myself according to his instructions, trying to inhale the last lingering traces of his scent, my body wracked with pleasure and somehow, at the same time, more and more and more need.

Surrendering to the Garden, even for this one thing, has awakened an unquenchable fire within me.

As if he senses it, Arch's letters continue to expand and unfold. Opening up about the past, he tells me how to braid a whip out of the vines of a climbing rose plant. *The first one of these was an idle fancy of Lily's*, he writes, *but it became a specialty of our Garden parties. She would open the night by whipping the new girls on stage, and you've never seen anything lovelier than blood kissing the tips of those thorns. The way they would blush and holler and wail. They were hers forever,*

after she'd done that to them. There was no one else who
could hurt them exactly like Lily could.

I wonder what sort of exquisite hurt could allow
someone to own you.

What is he hoping to grow by planting these seeds
in my mind?

In Lily's old garden one morning, I cut some
green vines and braid them as she once did. Her
fingers were more skilled; I'm sure she didn't bleed
all over her own whips. Despite the pain, both of the
thorny pricks and the constant reminder that I am
merely an interloper at Misselthwaite, I find the
work calming. Again, I feel close to Aunt Lily.
Whoever my mother was when she painted here, she
must have been joyful also. Who wouldn't be? This
space is only a shadow of what it once was, and it's
already becoming so lovely it nearly hurts me to
look.

I make sure the whip is hidden from Neville when
he comes for my lesson that afternoon—I don't trust
him with it—but when I leave in the evening, I bring
the braid up to my room with me, coiling it around
one of my bedposts. That night I drag it carefully
along the inside of my thigh.

As the thorns scratch my tender skin, I imagine
what it would feel like if Arch bent me over one of
the Garden's benches and whipped me with this.

I don't write back to him—how could I? What
would I even say? But he answers my questions
without me having to ask them. He writes of the past

he seems to live in: of meeting Lily and marrying her, and trying to satisfy her appetites. *I loved her as myself. She needed everything in the world: every experience, every sensation,* he says. *And she needed it all so badly, and beautifully. What else would a good husband do, except provide?*

She was as insatiable for beauty as she was for sensation. The shows she put on in the Garden were art, as beautiful as any of your mother's paintings. Meanwhile, I traveled the world looking for antiques and sculptures that would make the Garden feel opulent. We wanted it to be paradise.

I pause briefly, wondering at his words. A good husband must provide. It's scripture. Of course, so is the role of a good wife to be submissive and chaste. But Arch loved Lily—loves her still. Somehow, the paradise they created allowed her to be both a good and loving wife, and also a famously creative whore.

I wonder again about my mother and her choices. She was peaceful at the commune, poverty and simplicity and hard honest work making up her days. I resented her constant warnings against my selfishness. It never occurred to me to wonder if she'd resented me for forcing her decision to leave all of this. Surely it was the right choice. This is not a righteous life.

But it's growing harder and harder not to wish, for my own sake, that she had never left.

The end of Arch's letter has a command, as usual. *One of my favorite objects in the Garden was a wooden rocking horse*, he says. *It's in the library now, tucked into a corner near the fireplace. Bring it up to your room.*

Night has fallen, and I know it's only a matter of time before Mrs. Medlock comes up to ask me if I need anything before she goes to bed, so I hurry downstairs before she can. If anyone's noticed that I take things from the library occasionally now—the second bulb he had me wear in my ass, a book he wanted me to look through and touch myself to—they haven't said anything. *And anyway, the Master commanded this*, I think, as I located the horse exactly where Uncle Arch said it would be.

It's large but thankfully not too heavy; its saddle is wooden, textured but carefully sanded smooth. There's no paint on it, and I stroke a curious finger against its carved mane. What does Arch want me to do with this?

I hear a sound behind me and whirl around to find Colin watching me, a sad smile on his face.

"I was going to bring it up to my room," I blurt out, too tired to tell anything but the truth.

"Of course you were," he says. "You know, sometimes I forget how sheltered—how *young*—you are. You really shouldn't be here. This place will ruin you."

I don't know what to say to him. Can't he see how hard I've been trying to keep that exact thing from happening? I know I can't stay. My bargain is simple: I will do what I have to do, sell what I need to sell, in order to get back to the commune.

From there, I can only pray that God will forgive me. It's growing more difficult to imagine though. Forgiveness requires repentance. And long after I'm gone, I know the memories of what I've done here— what I've seen, and felt, and wanted—will always be with me. Every day, and especially every night.

17

I'M ATTUNED ENOUGH to the rhythms of the house now to sense a night of entertainment coming. One morning I wake up and see a servant in the gardens, patiently pruning back new growth along one of the pathways, and I think: *ah-hah.*

Tonight, then.

Tonight, all my practice will be put into action. Every hypothetical made real. I will play Magdalene, and hope to be redeemed afterwards as she was.

I go down to my garden, but I don't start gardening my secret spot right away. It's the last chance I'll have to enjoy this place. I hope Uncle Arch will see what I've done. I hope he'll continue my work. Though it's easier to picture him naked than in a pair of gardening boots, perhaps he could also feel close to Lily here. The pang of hope that he'd feel close to me here too drives me to my feet and then to work. I've barely gotten started on the weeding when Martha appears in the doorway. "Mary," she says. "You have to come with me."

I've also been here long enough now to know that I'm allowed to be cheeky with Martha, so I straighten up and put a hand on my hip. "Do I?"

"I'm sorry," she says. "But you do. Colin's orders. He doesn't want you wandering around with all of this going on."

"I'm not wandering around!"

She rolls her eyes. "You know how he is."

I have a flash of Colin berating me; I remember what Mrs. Medlock said about Colin's punishments. I don't know if he'd extend them to his employees, but I don't want to chance Martha getting in trouble.

I follow her back to the house and up the stairs to my room. I'm only half listening to Martha's chatter about the festivities tonight—what treats the kitchen is preparing, what color Dickon is dressing the girls in—most of my mind is on what's going to happen to me.

I assume Neville has a plan to distract Colin, and will come get me when his nephew is otherwise occupied. Once I'm on the auction block, no one will be able to stop me from selling myself to the highest bidder. I can only pray that my mouth fetches a good enough price to get me what I need—my path back to the commune open again at last.

And maybe some real good will come of it, I tell

myself. With a truly substantial dowry, I'd make a good match. And whoever I do marry, well, he'll be getting more than he bargained for if he likes having his cock sucked as well as Neville promises all men do.

Of course, I'll have to pretend he's my first. But I can do that.

I wonder if he'll have a care for my pleasure as well. The Song of Solomon is the only indication in the Bible that a woman is capable of enjoying anything beyond her duties. Perhaps it's a topic the other wives will discuss with me as I'm prepared for the ceremony.

I wonder what I should do to prepare myself for tonight's ceremony.

I linger by the windows, watching the preparations as the staff swirl around the grounds. They mark out the paths that tonight's guests will take to the Garden before carefully brushing each flagstone clean along the way. With winter no longer fighting the encroachment of spring, there is grass to mow and budding branches to tie back.

Pulling away from the view isn't easy, but I force myself to read until Mrs. Medlock brings me an early dinner tray. She's secured me some treats from the kitchen's party preparations. I would have sworn I was too nervous to eat, but the scents are too tempting to ignore. Besides, this will likely be the last time I'm ever offered frivolous little delicacies. A demitasse cup's worth of a creamy soup. A single wedge of cheese tucked inside yet another fruit I've never seen before. The tiniest bite of seafood served on a crisp slice of cucumber—I wonder if Neville ordered this dish—and topped with little flower petals.

Each taste is more dazzling than the last, but once I'm back inside the Kingdom of Love, plain fare will ensure our caloric intake, not our tastebud's delight. I sigh at the thought of brown bread and stew.

Then it's time to bathe, something I'll miss far more than French cheeses. Yet, each drop of hot water, each perfumed oil takes me closer to my sale. Closer to my home.

I've never felt further from it than now.

Outside, I note the processions of servers bringing bottles and trays of snacks along the Garden path where candles are being lit as the sun starts to sink in the west.

It's dark outside and the first guests are trickling in when I hear a man's voice through one of my bedroom walls. He's so muffled I can barely make out what he's saying. I draw closer, but the words are still obscured. The Manor ghost again.

Except now I know better. Now I know that what truly haunts this place is guilt. I know, because it's haunting me too. So whoever I can hear is flesh and blood. It could be a member of staff, but I doubt it. Almost everyone still working now is outside.

There is another possibility. A guest, straying out

of curiosity or mischief. Who could he be talking to? Martha? I know she'd as much as told me, that day in the kitchen with Mrs. Medlock, that she believed in enjoying her sexuality. Still, from what Neville has intimated about the kind of men that frequent these entertainments…

Besides, Uncle Arch would certainly not stand for it.

So I knock on the wall where the sound seems to be coming from. A brief silence, and then, "Who's there?"

"Mary." I pause, but there's no acknowledgement from him or Martha or anyone. So who is it? And why's he up here? "Is everything okay?"

The next time the man speaks, he sounds clearer, like he moved closer to the wall. Maybe it wasn't deliberate, before, but he wants me to hear him now. "Always so considerate."

Is he mocking me? "Colin?"

I still can't say for sure who it is, though this is my best guess. Dickon would come right in if he wanted something, and so would Neville; Arch is still out of town. But Colin is as likely to stay in as attend tonight's event. I've witnessed him talking to himself before. But tonight, despite needing him distracted for my plan to work, I want to know he's all right. I may not see him again, and knowing what I now know about Sarah, the girl he loved who died… I can't just walk away.

"I can't," he finally answers a question I didn't ask.

If he's trying to tell me something, I don't understand what it is.

"Is there something I can do?" Another silence, a few more quiet words unintelligible from my side of the wall.

"Do you have the rocking horse in your room?" he finally asks.

If it is Colin, I don't understand the game he's playing with me tonight. He carried it for me after he caught me with it in the library. But no guest could possibly know about the horse, so I relax. "You know I do," I remind him.

"Bring it close," he commands. "Straddle it."

Oh. I understand the game now. Like before, unable to bring himself to be with a woman, he'll pleasure himself with me as the untouched object of lust. Anticipation sparks in my chest as I drag the horse over to the wall and take a seat. I'm already damp beneath my robe as I press myself against the knobby surface.

Once he hears the groan of wood—"Now put your cunt against the saddle, and ride it."

I hitch my hips back and then forward again, the horse rocking as I move. The grooves and bumps in the wood rub against my cunt unevenly, and I lean forward to press my clit against where the carved saddle rises up, moaning in relief at the contact. The planks of the floor underneath me squeal with every rock of my hips, and I hope Mrs. Medlock is in the kitchen, where the noises might cover the ones I'm making.

"Tell me how it feels," he demands. *Come in here and you could see how I feel,* I want to tell him, but I don't. He's so careful to separate himself from my pleasure, I assume to ensure nothing bad could ever happen to me the way it had to Sarah. It's that impulse towards kindness that puts the lie to his claim that he's not a good man.

That he's like his father, his uncle. The Craven men are so different, and certainly not all good. But not all bad, either. One thing they all know inside and out, though, is how to make me come.

"It feels—ah—it feels good. But I want more," I tell him, still rocking, still needy.

"Of course you do. Little slut. With a cunt like that —you want to be held open and fucked until you cry. You want everyone in the Garden to watch you beg for cock, so that they know how badly you need it. And then you want to let them fuck you like the whore you've always known deep down that you are."

Every word out of his mouth is so filthy, so sinful, and it only makes the sensation of the saddle's bumps against my cunt stronger. "I do," I whimper. "I —please—"

"Yes," he says, his voice getting deeper, rougher. "Don't you wish I was in there with you, watching you? Telling you to go faster and harder, making you come without even touching you, over and over again. And only when you were exhausted—your pussy aching, sure you couldn't possibly take any more—then I would bend you over your bed and pull out my cock, and fuck you with it until you screamed."

I moan helplessly, my hips moving in a frantic rhythm, now, the floor underneath me groaning in counterpoint to my every thrust. I feel crazed with need, stripped naked and terrifyingly seen. From the other side of the wall comes a single grunt, an almost painful sound, and that's what does it for me—I come hard, shaking, my clit twitching and my cunt spasming as I cry out in ecstasy.

I'm still sitting on the horse, catching my breath, when Dickon pushes the door open. I hear the voice on the other side of the wall hiss with displeasure when Dickon says, "Let's get you into your party clothes, Mary."

Neville will have his work cut out for him keeping Colin from spoiling my sale.

I stand up, straightening my robe.

"Take that off," Dickon says. "I need your pretty body naked, now." It feels less shameful, now, to undress in front of Dickon; in part that's because I'm growing used to it, but also it's in part because he's so cheerful about it. It seems impossible to be ashamed around someone like him.

I step out of the robe, leaving it on the floor by the horse.

His hands are gentle but firm as he outfits me:

first in a device made of butter-soft leather straps that slides up my legs and just barely covers my pussy and my ass. It's trimmed in gold, and he padlocks it shut when he's done, placing the key on top of my dresser.

"To guard your virtue," he says, grinning up at me from where he's kneeling between my legs. He glides his hands up my thighs as he stands, his touch making my skin feel molten wherever it passes. He does my arms next, pulling them behind me and securing a matching leather and gold cuff around each wrist. The tension forces my chest out slightly, so it looks like I'm presenting my tits, with my nipples hard again at their peaks.

Dickon tweaks one before stepping back to see how I look. His gaze is hot against my skin, and I want to see that wicked smile on Arch's face, want him to be the one inspecting me.

But I can't let myself stay in that thought too long. Dickon snugs a collar around my neck, careful to make sure it's not too tight before he attaches a long leather leash. Then, the last thing he puts on me is a pair of ankle cuffs. They're not attached to anything, so I can walk freely, but I see the hooks there, and imagine my legs being chained apart while I'm up on stage tonight. How will it feel to suck someone's cock with my pussy spread and aching, and knowing no one is going to touch it? That with this belt on, no one can?

"Time for your debut, darling," Dickon says.

"You're going to be a star."

I blush at the praise. As he walks me out of the room, the leash held lightly in one hand, I can't help glancing at the wall one more time, where the horse is still sitting. But it's silent and still, and no one stops us as we make our way down to the Garden.

18

Walking into the Garden feels so different than last time I came, though it's only been a few weeks. Then I was a scared little mouse, trying to sneak her way in, cowering under her stolen mask and out of place in her shabby nightgown. Tonight, though, I'm not just invited, I'm part of the show. I can feel the excitement in the crowd as people watch Dickon parade me through the gates.

I pause for just a moment to take it all in, and he lets me. There's so much to see: the trees are strung with fairy lights tonight, and they look like their branches have caught a shower of falling stars. The color scheme tonight is all gold and brown. Flowering branches of forsythia in huge gilded urns offer a perfectly seasonal backdrop for Robin. The piano has been swathed in brown silk scarves, and it's being played by her. She's nude of course, except for tonight's necklace, a huge garnet on a silk cord that hangs between her tear-shaped breasts.

There's so much to look at that I feel like a child in front of a buffet: I don't even know where to start. It's almost a relief when Neville comes and takes the leash out of Dickon's hands.

"Come." He tugs me forward roughly.

He walks me around the party, showing me off. Though the point is to be seen, I still get a front-row seat to all the different activities that are underway. There are people being flogged on the benches and people being fucked up against the walls. Their hands are lashed to the hooks so they can stay standing even when their knees buckle with need. I watch as a woman is strapped to an elaborately carved wooden X. As soon as her legs are secured, a man emerges out of the crowd, takes his cock out and starts fucking her without a word. The woman cries while the man thrusts in and out of her, but they seem to be tears of pleasure, and she has several keening orgasms while I watch.

There are no braided rose-thorn whips, but behind one of the urns, a woman's skin is being stroked with stinging nettles. Around a corner, I watch as a man ties his cock and balls up with a piece of silk ribbon.

I still don't quite know what to make of any of it. My initial rush of arousal is edged with curiosity. There's darkness here, things I don't understand, but there's so much pleasure, too. We pass a cozy nook where three people appear to be re-enacting the story of Adam, Eve, and the snake—well, if the snake was a woman, ropes tied around her in elaborate diamond patterns, who loved to lick pussy. As far as blasphemy goes, it's intriguing.

And I seem to be just as intriguing. Guests stop Neville to ask what treasure he's putting up for sale tonight.

"A natural talent with a virgin mouth," he says to a middle-aged man with a generous paunch and thick moustache. "Open your mouth, dear slut."

I do as I'm told. Neville unceremoniously slips his fingers in. "Now your throat." I press down my tongue and he gets three fingers past where I would have gagged and choked a month ago. A tight little crowd has gathered.

"You're going to get a pretty penny for this one," Moustache says.

"I hope you bid more than a few pretty pennies."

The man looks me up and down.

"The cunt?"

"Untouched," Neville says. "And for tonight, untouchable."

Neville decides the crowd has seen enough of me and starts the show. Another girl and I wait at the side of the stage. I try to make eye contact with her, but she keeps hers cast down toward her bare feet, adorned with delicate gold ankle bracelets. What was it that Martha had said?

It can be a kink, you know.

But before I have a chance to spend much time wondering why someone would ask for this—comparing her motives to my own—Robin has stopped playing, and Neville is tapping on a champagne glass.

"Ladies and gentlemen, you may have heard the rumors about tonight. I am here to confirm their truth. It has been such a very long time since our last...so welcome, welcome our girls to the auction block!" There is a round of applause and much excited chatter before Neville cuts it short to begin.

"Allow me to introduce you to tonight's first auction item: Mary, Mary, quite contrary, but eager to see how your cock grows. She's never before put one in her mouth, and it's all she wants." He grabs me by the cheeks, forcing my jaw to drop, and holds me there for their inspection.

"I've overseen her training myself," Neville continues, dropping his hand from my jaw. "As you see, she's quite lovely. But I assure you, she's also very talented. You, there, show her your cock."

A man strokes himself through his pants, grinning at me. He reaches in and draws his cock out, and I bite my lip.

"Look how she blushes. How her tits are hard for you. She loves cock," Neville tells the crowd confidingly. "She's desperate for it. Day and night, she imagines what it will be like. She wants to feel the sensation of cum down her throat so badly she'd be on her knees begging if I wasn't here. But there can only be one, only one lucky man to be the first to fuck her face. So come up and have a look. Don't be shy, now. Mary certainly isn't."

The next thing I know, there are four or five men surrounding me, watching Neville demonstrate my abilities. If I thought being watched by the men in Uncle Arch's office was overwhelming, this is another level entirely. Neville pulls out a fake cock, wrapped in leather, and tests my gag reflex. The soft material shows them, like the banana did on my first day, how soft my mouth is, no marks from my teeth left behind. He smacks my ass and pulls my hair to show how I'll react to pain. Vaguely, I can hear him talking to them, playing up my virtues, but the words run together in a shifting sea of sensation and pleasure.

I am wet, like Neville promised. But I'm also scared. It won't be long now until a perfect stranger offers me his hard length, and I must treat it like I've never dreamed of anything better if I want to earn my escape money. But of course I've dreamed of something better. Every single time I come, it's Arch's face in my mind. The reminder of my forbidden fantasy causes another throb between my thighs. My bare cunt rubs almost uncomfortably against the leather of the belt. I must squirm a bit, because that becomes the focus of his spiel.

"See how she wants it? Her sweet, virgin pussy, dripping wet at the very thought. Play with her nipples, if you'd like, see how she reacts. Imagine how delicious they'll be, Mary, yes, I see you pressing your little clit into your cage."

"When will that be available?" one of the men asks. "How much would it run me to own that cherry?"

"I'd outbid you," another says. "Nothing in the world like a virgin's pussy. Especially one who wants it as much as this one does. Don't you, sweetheart?" I'm freezing, my blood running cold. This wasn't part of the plan.

"We could split her," the first man says before I can answer. "I could fuck her ass, while you fuck her cunt. How many times could you come on two cocks, do you think, Mary?"

"Gentlemen," Neville cuts in, to my immense relief. The deal was that I'd sell my mouth. Not my virginity. That belongs to me, and to the man I'll someday marry. What they were offering was beyond obscene.

And grotesquely arousing.

"Our little virgin Mary isn't the cherry on the auction block today. All in good time," Neville says to the disappointed men. "It seems everyone's gotten a look. More than a few have felt how sweet the prize is. And you all know I wouldn't promise something I couldn't deliver. So, who's ready to bid for the best first blowjob they've ever gotten? The right to use Mary's mouth the way it was meant to be used?"

In the moment, I'm so caught up by the sensation of all that praise that I forget to be nervous. I expect a cacophony—all the men who just discussed my virtues will be fighting—and paying handsomely—for the right to fuck my mouth.

But instead, there's an awkward pause, and then someone calls out an amount that even I can tell is insulting.

"That's a start," Neville says. He sounds uncertain, and I shrink inside of myself.

More bids trickle in after that, but they don't sound enthusiastic, and Neville seems to be urging them on rather more than I thought he'd have to. I stand on the stage, hands still cuffed behind my back, and shame and doubt start to sweep through me. Was I not enthusiastic enough? When different men put their fingers in my mouth, I moaned—perhaps they couldn't hear me over the noise of the crowd? Or if they did, did I not sound enthusiastic enough? Could they all tell I'm doing this because I have no choice?

Or am I just undesirable?

I can hear in Neville's voice that he's angry, and I can only pray it's not with me. But no one's raised a new bid in a few minutes, and he's running out of ways to say that I can suck cock like a very good whore. Finally, I hear him say reluctantly, "Going once."

Silence.

"Going twice."

The sum he's about to settle on might buy me cab fare and a new dress. It won't take me away from here. The gates of the Kingdom of Love will remain closed to me. And this thing, this trick I've spent so many hours learning, promising myself it will be okay, worth it, ends justifying the means…it's for nothing. I'm nothing but a common whore after all.

Here, in this manor, with these people…

I can't believe I was so foolish as to believe Arch. I let his letters blind me to the truth of the Craven men, the truth Colin told me from the beginning. The truth I knew before I ever even got here.

Never, ever trust Archibald Craven.

Just before Neville can declare me sold, another voice cuts in with another, higher bid. It's not much more, but maybe he will have reinvigorated the bidding? Maybe the last man will want to raise his price, now, too? I scan the crowd, willing them to fix this. Praying, though I know how wrong it is to pray for such a sinful thing.

Please don't let me be stuck here forever.

Please let someone else buy me for the money I need.

They don't. No one else breathes a word until Neville asks my buyer to come up to the stage, and I see who's won me. The one who will use me, the very first cock I'll taste, the man I'm whoring myself to.

Colin Craven.

19

I'M SO overwhelmed that I wouldn't know where to begin even if I could speak. Neville moves on to the next girl he has to sell. I'm ushered off to the side of the stage with my new owner. I glance at Colin, wondering what possessed him to buy a public sex act when he's so scared of his own desires that just an hour ago, he had to hide behind a wall to make me come. He doesn't want to make eye contact any more than the other girl had, though, and I can't blame him.

He knew what that money meant to me, even if I hadn't exactly told him this was how I'd decided to earn it. And even though he wants me to leave perhaps even more than I want it myself, he still offered this paltry sum.

He is the heir to Misselthwaite Manor, to the Garden, to all the Craven clubs around the world. I know he can afford more.

And as bewildered and frustrated as I am, I'm still touched that he found a way to make this easy for me. My first time sucking a man and not a vegetable, and it's a man I know would rather die than truly hurt me. He will be gentle and patient with me. No threats—or promises—of sharing my other first times with some other stranger.

"I can tell that everyone's held onto their wallets for something special tonight," Neville says, and I don't know if anyone but me and Colin can hear the chill under his performer's smiling tone. "And our next item will not disappoint. Susan?"

The girl doesn't move from her position at Colin's other side.

"Susan, darling, everyone's waiting for you." Neville holds out his hand. Susan finally looks up, surprise on her face. She points to herself as though she cannot possibly have heard him right. He nods over-emphatically, playing to the crowd. They are eating it up already.

Besides the fine golden chains around her ankles, Susan wears more at her wrists and around her hips. There's a sparkling jewel in her navel that catches the candlelight. She's everything I'm not in this moment: confident, and clearly at home here. Around her neck is a leash like mine. As Ben picks it up to lead her over, she winks at Dickon, lounging on the side of the stage. He grins back, that easy confidence I've admired reflected in Susan. When Ben hands her leash to Neville, she pretends she's being given in marriage to him—grabbing his hands and turning them both back to Ben as she steals a flower from his tux jacket to hold as a bouquet.

Who wouldn't be charmed? Susan's putting on quite a show.

"I'm afraid I'm not your intended, my dear," Neville says, unleashing his wolfish smile on her. "In fact, I'm not going to take care of you at all. Instead, I'm going to sell you to the highest bidder, and let him do whatever he wants to that pretty little untouched cunt of yours."

"Sell me?" Susan asks, feigning shock. She turns to the crowd, a look of faux helplessness on her face. "To them? You can't! What will they do with me?"

"Fuck you senseless," Neville says. "If you're lucky."

"But I'm a virgin!"

The crowd roars with laughter, and when Neville invites them up to the stage to inspect her for themselves, the rush is instantaneous. They're just as handsy as they were with me as she's put through her paces. The difference is in her face. She seems confident throughout, knowing exactly when to part her legs and when to play shy. Even I can tell from the tones the men have talking amongst themselves that this is the fantasy they want to be sold.

I shrink back even further into myself. Why didn't I come here with that kind of confidence? That's probably why my price was so low: who would want to fuck a scared little girl, unsure of herself, when he could have a woman as beautiful and brave as Susan?

I deserved my low price twice over. First for boring them, and second for having the hubris to believe that I knew better than everyone who told me my soul was worth more than my body, that this place was not for me.

What a stupid girl I am, believing maybe I did fit here, or could if I tried hard enough.

Of course Colin had to buy me. And I'm sure he's furious about it. He wasn't thinking about his pleasure at all. He probably felt sorry for me.

Finally, the men are sent back into the crowd. Someone brings a chair onstage, and Susan sits in it, spreading first her legs and then her secret folds. Dickon holds up a small light and Neville invites the crowd to see for themselves that she's intact. Susan plays it up, her thighs quivering as she holds herself apart, her fingers clearly itching to touch herself even as she pretends she's all innocence.

"I don't know what's happening," she says, when Neville points out how wet she is. "Do you think it would help if you touched it for me?"

Despite my bitter disappointment, I can't help but feel a renewed rush of desire myself. If I did fit in here, if I knew how to ask with the right combination of begging and cheek, I could choose how to come. The man in the green mask's thick fingers, or the haughty older woman in blue's tongue.

Arch's cock.

Foolish fantasies. Even if I belonged, even if I could hold a laughing crowd in the palm of my hand and plead beautifully for my orgasms, abandoning any thoughts of a good and godly life or marriage... he never comes to the Garden. His desires may not have died with Lily, but they grew as twisted as the vines. It's time to uproot him from my imagination.

The crowd can hardly wait to start the bidding, though Neville does his best to continue building excitement. When at last, he asks for an opening amount, the price for her hymen begins at five times what Neville assured me the price of my mouth would fetch. It's a much larger thing to auction off your virginity, I know this, but I can't help but feel slapped at the reminder that none of this money means a thing to the men bidding.

From there, the numbers fly up so fast even Susan seems a little surprised. She goes for a number that could buy me my very own commune, and everyone seems pleased when she stands up to be claimed. Even me. It must feel good to know your worth, and for it to be large.

Neville has us both stand in front of the crowd for one last look before we're sent off to make good on our offers. They're buzzing, now, speculating heavily on how much—or little—was spent and whether we'll be worth it.

"Good work, Susan," Neville murmurs. I expect her to bloom under his praise, the way she did while she was being auctioned, but instead she recoils slightly, like now that the show is over she's not sure she likes him after all. I don't have time to think about it before Neville is turning to me.

"Mary, I'd expected you would whet their appetites, but the idea of Susan seems to have kept your price low. Unfortunate circumstances. Let's discuss alternatives later." Alternatives? What alternative can there be, except the one that Susan just demonstrated?

And I cannot do that. I will not. I will never spread my legs for a man who's not my husband.

Not that there is any indication someone would want to buy me anyway.

As I watch, I see the man who won Susan hold out his hand for her. When she reaches to take it, I can see that she's trembling just slightly. Maybe the way she was on stage really was just an act. Not a kink at all, not something she begged for. Is she just as scared and uncertain about all of this as I am?

Did Neville convince her, too?

I don't have time to ask her any of this before she's whisked away. And then Colin is taking my leash in his hands and leading me off the stage, tugging hard enough I'm certain to be bruised in the morning.

Colin, who told me himself that I'd be ruined if I stayed, is now the one leading me further into the Garden.

20

I'M LEASHED, nearly naked, and at last, I'm allowed to be like this. The satisfaction is bitter in my mouth. But there's nothing I can do about that now. Colin leads me away from the crowd at the front of the stage. I both want to be as far away from them—and the reminder of my worthlessness—as possible, and worry that I don't want to see what happens in the darker corners of this place.

What happens in the light is disturbing enough.

Traditionally, Neville has told me, the winners of the auction take their prize in the Garden; it's meant to remind the losing bidders of all they missed out on, and hopefully tempt them to spend more at the next party. I'll have to stay until Colin is satisfied that he got what he paid for.

I must not be moving quickly enough for him, because he stops and drops my leash. For half a second I do consider running, but what would be the point? I have nowhere to go. And if I've learned anything from my time at Misselthwaite, it's that the Craven men will always find you. He unlocks my handcuffs, letting my hands fall, finally, to my sides.

And that's something else I've learned. Nothing is ever done for kindness, but for their benefit.

Colin takes my leash back into his hand and starts walking me again, now that I can move freely enough to keep up. Behind him, I see Susan being led into a patch of lavender, above which hangs an enormous brass birdcage. I crane my head around to keep watching as the man helps her into the cage. He has her legs spread and his cock between them before Colin and I even turn the corner of the path. Not a single reassuring touch first, or even an erotic one. I listen to hear what she sounds like—is she experiencing pleasure? Pain? Excitement? Regret? But the party is loud again and I can't see her face, just the way the man is thrusting into her.

Now I see, in part, why Ben's training is so invaluable. If her body wasn't taught to be prepared at the drop of a hat, Susan's first time would be nothing but agony. He's seeming to enjoy himself plenty. No thoughts for the cost to the woman he bought.

I look away when I realize Colin has brought us to a halt. We're underneath the curve of a weeping willow tree, its branches enfolding us in a small space that feels quiet, if not entirely private. No one seems to have followed us here, and I feel guilty all over again. Was I that unappealing, that no one even wants to watch me perform for free?

He sighs, and I can see now that he isn't angry the way I'd assumed. He's conflicted, sad. Frustrated. All the same emotions churning in my own chest, but I don't understand why. He didn't have to do this. And even now, he could walk away, leaving me saved from the act, though not from my sin.

He swallows hard, gazing at my body and not my eyes.

I've been trained too, so of course, like Susan, my body responds. My skin flushes and my nipples pebble.

I drop to my knees, and at the familiarity of the gesture and the moment—Colin's cock, thick for me, the knowledge that I can throat him as deep as he wants, even my knees in soft, damp, dirty ground— my mouth waters and my pussy gets wet. I open for him, offering my mouth like a gift.

He won't be sorry he chose me. I will make it worth it for him, and then maybe he'll feel better.

Maybe I will, too.

I look down to see that Colin has pulled his cock out of his pants. He doesn't give it to me right away though. "You don't have to do this," he says instead.

"You paid."

"And it's the buyer's right to say you don't have to."

I consider his offer. With no one watching to know the difference, I don't have to do a thing. I could let him touch himself the way he prefers, let him come on my tits or my face. We could both walk away the same as we walked in, never having crossed the lines the auction seemed to obligate us to. But in this position, my body reminded of the sensuality of having my mouth invaded, it's less tempting to leave. Staying will feel good. Sucking him will feel even better.

"I want to," I tell him. It was, after all, the point. And he's bought me, even if it wasn't for much money. Fair is fair. I will make good on my bargain. I will taste my first man. Yes, it's a sin, but my body's want is overriding my mind's concerns.

"I don't want you to want to!"

I don't have time to figure out the puzzle of Colin's feelings right now. I'm already humiliated enough; if he doesn't take the prize I'm offering, I don't know what I'll do. I reach for his cock with one hand, massaging the tip, and his hips tilt forward into the touch. My confidence blooms, just a little. I've learned how to do this well, even if no one bidding believed it.

"You look like you want me to," I say, my voice coming out husked and raspy, even though he hasn't touched my throat yet. "So tell me. Why did you do this, Colin?"

He looks down, meeting my eyes for the first time, and says, "It's better that it's with me."

What a gentleman, I think, shame heating my body all over again. Did he really sacrifice his own ideals to make sure I would be comfortable? That the man who bought me would treat me with some measure of respect? I am glad it's not a stranger who's here with me. I'm anxious to please, to get this exactly right. It will be easier with him. He may be a Craven, but he is the kindest of them.

I want to thank him, and I don't hesitate: I pull him closer to me, swallowing his cock before he can protest or decide to resist, or do anything at all but let me suck him.

He melts as soon as I start, groaning low and rough every time I take him down to the root. His hands find my hair and after a while he sets the rhythm, pulling me back and forth along his length as he pleases. "Mary," he says, and my name sounds like a plea, almost like a prayer.

Spit and slick are pooling at the corners of my mouth, running down my chin and neck. My cunt is so wet against the leather of the chastity belt, and I can hear myself panting and whimpering, making little needy animal sounds. So this is what it's like. This is how it feels, with a real cock. The actions are the same, but the taste, the sensation, the excitement —they are all brand new and thrilling.

I am certainly a whore now, in both senses. The biblical one, the one I scorned, the one I became when I sold my mouth to the highest bidder. Maybe more than that, the sense that Uncle Arch meant.

A woman who enjoys her body.

Colin is fucking me so perfectly, and I love having

him in my mouth. Whatever those other men thought, however they interpreted my anxiety and reticence, I *was* made for this. Every bob of my head is echoed by a throb in my pussy. I keep my hands on his hips so that I don't reach down to try to touch myself. I have to keep my focus on him, and nowhere else.

He draws it out for as long as he can; a few times he seems to get almost to the brink before he pulls his cock out of my mouth, holding it tight at the base, making me wait, with my cheeks red and my mouth aching. He'll give me a little slap, then tug my hair before he shoves back in, and I see stars every time: the pain, and the pleasure, and the way he takes over my body, using it, like Neville said, the way it was meant to be used.

When he's finally ready to come, he holds me down the way I imagine his father would, so that he's thick in my throat, so that there's nothing I can do but swallow around him as he moans above me. I can't cry out with my mouth so full but I would, I know, as an orgasm explodes between my legs with no warning, leaving me a trembling mess when he draws himself out and wipes the corner of my mouth with one tender thumb.

"He was right," Colin murmurs, mostly to himself. "We both needed this."

I'm so cum-drunk it takes a moment to sink in, but then it does and I'm clearheaded again. All traces of lingering pleasure fade away in a heartbeat as I replay what he just said. My legs are shaking as I rise to my feet.

"Wait a minute," I say. He ignores me and starts to leave our little bower. I grab him by the arm, as hard as he held me only a moment ago.

"Wait, Colin—who is *he*? *Who* was right?"

21

"Who was right?" I repeat when Colin doesn't answer.

"What are you talking about?" Colin asks. He tries to shake me off with a little smile, but I won't be deterred that easily.

"You just said, he was right. Who is he?"

Colin has gone from blissed out and feral to looking shut-up and guilty as fast as I've gone from orgasm to fury.

"No one," he says. "Lots of people have told me I need to stop holding myself back. And they were right. That's all. Thank you for the...you know."

I imagine lots of people probably have told him to stop holding back. To go out, to have fun, to get laid. At the very least, simply to stop blaming himself for something he couldn't have done anything about. But how many of those people—men—also know me? Would suggest me?

The answer is already dawning, but I want him to admit it to my face.

"I'd say you're welcome, but you just got what you paid for. And at a bargain price." I can match the haughtiness of his tone. So much time around disdainful men has taught me more than how to swallow a cock.

"Don't be like that. Just forget I said anything. Go collect your part of the money, and maybe we can try to work out some sort of loan to get you the rest of what you need. Or you could work around the house maybe..." He trails off and leans back against the tree's trunk.

"I don't want to work as your housemaid, Colin. I want to work on my commune. And we both know I'll never repay a loan from there. Please, just tell me the truth."

But he's back to not meeting my eyes, and I know he won't say anything more. He doesn't need to. His desire to save me will always take a back seat to the priorities of the crueler Cravens. And I can see now that Neville was never going to be content with selling my mouth. He all but told me as much, and insinuated it again to the men inspecting me tonight.

My position had been clear—I would only consent to this, only what I had to do for the money I needed.

Stupid, stupid me. Of course he would arrange for my price to stay low. He's trying to force me to agree to more. He wants my virginity on the auction block, and it's not just the money.

He enjoys the power.

By insisting that I could never, ever allow myself to have sex with a man who wasn't my husband, I'd all but guaranteed his interest. I made myself a challenge. And unlike Lily Craven, I didn't know any better than to walk right into his trap. He's already made me a whore, now he means to make it my career.

Colin's leaving the garden and I'm glad to see him go. The gentleman he wants to be isn't strong enough to stand up to the men that control his inheritance; I resent him for it.

I glance around to see if anyone's paying attention to me. They aren't. But I can see Susan again, out of the birdcage and sitting in a plush chair next to it, being brought a glass of champagne. She accepts it with a laugh and a smile, and whatever happened while she was being devirginized, she seems happy and comfortable again. She's still naked, and her skin seems to glow with contentment and pleasure.

What will it be like for me? I can't help wondering.

Before tonight, I was so certain. I'd go back to the commune, having renounced worldliness, demonstrating it by having sold my one earthly valuable possession. Of course, once Arch left town without my securing it, I was still prepared to tell them I had.

The lie would stop mattering once I was home. Then surely elders would select someone for me to marry.

I'd hoped for one of them, to be important there. I can admit that now. There would be a small triumph in not just re-earning my place, but a better one. It had been a comforting thought during my first days outside.

No matter who was chosen, we wouldn't live together—cohabitating encourages valuing partnership over community—but we'd spend our first night in the same bed so he could perform his marital duties and finalize our bond in the eyes of the Lord. Then, in the morning, among the women again, I'd be teased a little, like Susan is now.

It wouldn't be bad. It's what I've been expecting my whole life. I shouldn't even think to want more, or different. But…I can't help wondering how similar that deflowering would be to what Susan's just experienced. It would also be with a stranger, as men and women are kept as separate as possible. And I couldn't expect them to know the things I'm only just learning myself about my own body—what it likes, how to make it wet and ready.

It's a terrifying thought, that my salvation might not be the heaven on earth I've dreamed of.

So I push it down, alongside the fear about what Neville expects next, and turn my wicked imaginings to what it would be like if my first time was here, with one of the men I've come to know. The idea of it being Neville makes me shiver, like somehow his skin wouldn't feel like skin, but instead like a snake's cool, dry scales slithering over me in bed.

It could be Ben, with his legendary cock; he's trained enough girls that he would know what to do with me. Gruff, but pleasurable.

Colin wouldn't want the responsibility, but if I took it from him? If I begged, or tricked him somehow... *He'd be shockingly rough and even more shockingly gentle in turns*, I think. He'd be a first time to remember fondly, and often.

Dickon, too, would be wonderful. His clever fingers. That devilish tongue. I shiver a little at the very thought.

Or, I think, giving in to that itch in the back of my mind, *it could be Uncle Arch*. He would tell me exactly what to do, the way he has in his letters: he'd be demanding and rough with me. He would fuck me hard, and mercilessly. He'd make me come until my throat was raw from screaming.

He would take what was his, and make me his own.

I'm wet again, my cunt starting to throb, but I'm still belted. I wonder if I could wriggle enough, pay enough attention to my nipples, to steal another orgasm as I watch the ongoing entertainments. I'm about to try when Dickon appears at my side.

"That's enough excitement for one night, eh, Mary?" he says slyly. "Time to go back into the Manor."

I don't want to, but there's nothing to be done but

follow him. I try to drink in the last little bits of the party as I walk out of it: the strangeness and the beauty all around me, so many bodies seeming to feel everything as intensely as they can. I hear a woman cry out in pleasure and I can't help being jealous of her orgasm: the way it seems to hold the promise of more, not the ending that mine did.

"I'm sorry about how things shook out," Dickon says once we're outside the gate, removing my leash. "But you were spectacular. You remember where I set the key to your belt?"

I nod, and he leaves me, the gate swinging closed behind him as he plunges himself back into the Garden and its pleasures. I look up at the high walls, listening to Robin's song drifting out. For a moment I feel like I'm being kicked out of the commune all over again: standing at the edge of something, longing to be let back in.

Except this time I no longer know where I belong, or where I should dream of going next.

The only place I can reliably escape is into the throes of passion. I start trudging back towards the Manor, eager to get the belt off and touch myself in bed until I can forget all my fears and anger, when I spot two familiar figures talking outside of the house. It's Uncle Arch, in the middle of an animated conversation with Neville.

When did he get home?

As I draw closer, I realize that they're not talking —they're arguing.

Neville has his back to me, so all I can see of him are his broad shoulders, his long black hair hanging loose and free over them.

Is it me they're arguing about? Surely not. Arch can't possibly know about my disobedience. Not yet.

I try to creep closer discreetly, but my attention is too much on the men and not enough on the path. A twig snaps beneath my bare foot. As though that sound wasn't enough, I let out an involuntary hiss of pain that draws Arch's attention.

He looks up, over Neville's shoulder—and he sees me. Neville keeps berating him—I can't quite catch about what—but Arch's gaze is locked on my body, my skin so vulnerable against the black straps that barely cover it. I'd felt warm in the Garden, but now I can feel the shivers rippling through me as his cold eyes chill each place they land.

Arch's staring is interrupted by someone else coming out of the Garden, not bothering to move stealthily as I had. When he sees who it is, his face changes all over again. He'd looked angry when he saw me, and hungry again, the same way he was the first time I met him.

But now his mouth breaks into an irresistible smile of triumph.

I glance back to see Colin, still looking disheveled, eyes wide as his gaze bounces between us.

When I turn back to Arch, certain puzzle pieces start to rearrange themselves. He looks like he's won a victory. And Neville—manipulative, calculating Neville—looks unmoored.

He didn't do this to me. He didn't see it coming any more than I did. Arch is the only man the whole Garden would listen to—the only one who could decide before an auction how it was going to end, who was going to win, and for exactly how much.

In short, he bought me for his son. On clearance.

I fly at Arch, my self-possession forgotten, caught in a furious rage. It doesn't even occur to me what a reckless risk I'm taking as I pound my fists against his chest. He doesn't flinch or back away even minutely. My fists don't affect him at all. Why would they? Nothing else I do does. When I stop hitting him, it's to conserve my energy, not because I've given up.

"What have you done?"

"What have *you* done, Virgin Mary?" He grabs my wrists in the vise of his fingers. "I don't recall giving you permission to enter the Garden, much less to sell yourself there."

"She didn't need your permission," Neville reminds him silkily.

I expect Arch to take up the argument—to say that everything on this property is his, or something like that—but he ignores his brother, gaze fixed directly on me.

"I asked for what was mine," I say, pulling my arms free. "If you would have given me my mother's painting, I never would have had to do this. You gave me no choice!"

Arch steps sideways, putting space between us without quite giving up ground. I realize I'm pink-cheeked from shouting, and as the initial heat of my anger leaves me, a new fear bubbles up to take its place. *Arch could kick me out right now,* I think, *send me into the night dressed like a whore, with a belt I can't unlock.* He might do it. I have to be careful.

He doesn't, though. Instead, he shrugs, letting my accusation slide off his broad shoulders like water. "Neville," he says. "Colin. Leave us alone."

"I don't think—" Colin starts, but Neville grabs his arm.

"Leave them to it," he says. "It's none of your business what he does with her mouth now."

Colin must be furious at being belittled, or at the reminder that his father may want me after all, because he storms back to the house. Neville aims his oiliest smile at both of us. "Good night," he says, heading back towards the light and warmth of the Garden's interior.

"I made it clear that your painting was not my priority," Arch says when we're alone. "Yet you showed no patience. No consideration. The moment I turned my back, you thought to take advantage. I needed to teach you a lesson. You were instructed to stay far away from the Garden. Since you chose to disobey me, I ensured you would not be rewarded for your behavior."

"You cannot control me, the way you control everything else at Misselthwaite Manor."

His eyes narrow; he looks at me like a cat assessing its prey. "Oh," he says. "Is that so?"

My decision comes over me like a revelation. "Yes. I'm not going to play your game anymore, or your brother's. This knife's-edge I'm balancing on—you won't let me leave, you don't want me to stay—I'm done. My time and my body will be my own from now on." And just to twist that knife into him this time, I continue. "And if I so choose, I'll speak to Ben and Dickon about continuing my training with them."

He grabs my arm and hauls me until my face is pressed up against one of the Garden's outer walls, nestled among the ivy leaves. I smell the mineral of old stone, and the slight dampness of the earth below me. My ass is mostly bare, and there's barely a pause between the sound of Arch's belt sliding from its loops and the whistle it makes as it arcs through the air and lands, hard, on the backs of my thighs.

I cry out, my voice splitting the air between us, pleading, almost desperate. But I know no one will hear. On the other side of the wall, the party is still in full swing, and if anyone catches an echo, they won't think twice about it. Just another girl getting exactly what she wants, they'll think.

I'm not scared. I knew what I was asking for. But it still hurts like hell, worse than last time by yards...

also somehow better for the increased pain and shame.

"I just gave you a lesson in going behind my back," Arch growls, the belt flying through the air, lashing me relentlessly. "But apparently it didn't take, so here's another. Maybe this one will stick."

I feel a tear trickle down my cheek, and I realize I'm crying. It's hard to keep track when everything is so overwhelming—the ache of where Arch is spanking me, and the way it's making me wet all over again, my cunt aching for some tenderness as he unloads on me. Everything below my waist feels swollen and hot, and though he can't see my face, I know he can sense what he's doing to me—how he's making me feel so completely undone, even though he hasn't actually touched me yet. I want his hands on me so badly, his skin smoothing against mine, tender where he's hurt me, and the thought just makes me cry harder, sobs shaking my back.

The spanking ends just as abruptly as it began.

"Look at you, you whore," Arch says. "Legs spread like you're begging for it. That's what those men in the Garden didn't know: you'd give it to them for free if they knew how to ask."

My legs did slide apart, I realize; my back arched, shamelessly presenting my ass to Arch. I stand up and wipe the tears from my face before turning around again. He's just buckling his belt again. The thin strip of leather around his waist looks so innocent, but the skin of my ass and thighs is on fire, and I know I'll have to sleep on my stomach.

I expect him to leave, but he doesn't; he walks over and turns me around one more time, running a hand over the skin he just hit. "Mmmm," is all he says, his voice breaking over me like a wave. He looks more peaceful than I've ever seen him.

I hate him for what he's done to me, but I'm also a little proud.

There's so much pain at this house. It's filled with hurt people who continue to hurt each other. This time, by letting Uncle Arch hurt me, I think I took a little pain away from him. And just maybe, that was worth it.

22

I'M in my room when the door opens. I expect
Martha to have heard about my sale and come to
gossip, or maybe Mrs. Medlock is bringing me some
tea. Instead, surprising me for the third time tonight,
it's Colin. He's changed out of the formalwear he'd
donned for the entertainment, trading it for a pair of
casual pants and a soft dark sweater. His face looks
softer than it did down there, slightly younger,
maybe.

I took my outfit off as soon as I got up here,
unlocking the lock with the key Dickon had left me.
Then I showered in the coldest water I could stand.
When Colin walks in, I'm lying on my belly, naked,
wondering if I have the nerve to rub some ointment
into the welts, or if it would even help enough to
make it worth the pain.

"My God." His voice is soft, but serious. "I should
never have left you alone with him."

I stand up hurriedly, grabbing my nightdress and pulling it over my head.

"Neville was right. It's none of your business."

"It is," he says. "I walked away. Again. Let me see."

"No!" I meant what I said to Uncle Arch to earn this. My body is my own now, and I won't let the men of Misselthwaite Manor tell me what to do with it. Not anymore. The choices I make now will be between myself and God. I'm prepared for a fight, and not for his useless kindness.

"I think I have something in my room that will help. If I go get it, will you let me help you put it on? There are other ways for a body to be touched than for pain or pleasure. Sometimes, it's for comfort."

I eye him warily, but if it will really help... I have lots to do in the garden tomorrow, now that I'm not leaving. I don't want soreness to keep me away. I find comfort in the touch of sun on my face, the scent of dirt in my nose. Perhaps it's Colin who needs the comfort of skin on skin, maybe even especially after what happened between us tonight. So...

"Okay."

When he returns, he's carrying a small unlabeled jar. He has me lie on my belly again before he lifts up my dress, smoothing it carefully up my legs. I remember how I spread for Arch unconsciously and will myself to keep still. Colin's hands feel huge and cool on my skin, rubbing his ointment into the bruises and welts. It smells of arnica and mint—not beautiful, but soothing and familiar.

"He isn't allowed to hurt you." His voice is nearly as soothing as his hands. "I'll tell him so."

Of course, he can't tell his father anything. Nor was this entirely non-consensual. Even while it was happening, when I knew it was going too far, I didn't truly try to stop it. But how can I explain that to Colin?

"He didn't hurt me," I finally say. "Or, he did, but...it felt good, too."

"Of course it did. That's what worries me." Colin sighs. I turn around to look at him.

"Why?" His touch feels like a scorch on my skin, but when our gazes meet, he doesn't look like he's trying to turn me on. Instead, his lights are out: his face is shuttered, haunted.

"Sarah liked the pain too."

Sarah. The name that Martha and Mrs. Medlock invoked in the kitchen. The one who died, tragically, when she didn't realize she had an ectopic pregnancy, something I'd looked up later in the library. *God works in mysterious ways.* I heard that phrase over and over growing up. It's still reflexive for me in situations where God's will seems more cruel than anything else.

Regardless of God's hand in any of it, Colin seems to have decided that he alone bears the blame. He rubs the last of the cream into my skin before gently pulling my dress down so that I'm covered. I'm afraid to break the spell, but I want to hear more.

"What did she look like?"

"An angel," Colin says. "I thought she was the most beautiful thing I'd ever seen. Most of the help wear their hair up—it's more practical—but hers was always down in these long, soft blonde waves. The first time I saw her, she was up on a ladder in the library, dusting the top of the bookshelves, and the sun was streaming in through the windows, and I really thought—" he laughs at himself. "For a moment, I thought she was flying."

I lay my head down on my folded arms. I know it has a sad ending, but I feel like he's telling me a bedtime story.

"She had a mouth made for sin, though. Christ, those lips. So full and red. The first time she sucked me I thought I'd die. Couldn't think about anything but covering her face with my cum."

Colin is saying something else about her cunt, but all I can hear is Martha in the kitchen, implying that Uncle Arch had slept with her, too. Jealousy rolls through me, hot acid. I know now that my low price at the auction was Arch's fault, but all of my self-consciousness from earlier reappears. I shift uncomfortably on the bed.

"She didn't need it as badly as you do," Colin says, as if reading my thoughts. He pinches my bottom experimentally, and I wriggle at the pain, and the zing of sensation that goes straight to my clit. "But she liked to be tossed around and manhandled. So I did. Even though I knew she hadn't been feeling well,

I believed her when she said she was fine. And I was rough. And then..."

And then it happened. The rupture that killed her. Oh no. It all clicks together, and I see now why he blames himself. He's quiet for a long moment.

"I'm worried that my father will hurt you far more than Neville will."

He's right to be concerned that I don't know my boundaries. I'm not experienced enough to know how much is too much. And if I'm being honest with myself, even knowing it might not be enough to make me pull back if an orgasm is within my grasp. Selfishness has always been my favorite sin.

"I won't taunt him again. He won't spank me if I don't talk back."

"Even if I believed that, there are many other ways to inflict pain on someone. And when I see the way you look at him..." He trails off, and I feel like a fool. How did I expect no one would have guessed my fantasies? I touched myself to thoughts of his father so many times a day that they must be written all over my face. All I can hope for is that Arch himself hasn't noticed.

But of course he has. Why else would he have written me those letters? He's encouraged me at every turn. The shame and humiliation of it could drown me if I let it. I can't let it. I need to make a new plan for what to do, and I will hold my head high until that plan is executed.

So instead, it's Colin that I taunt. I roll gingerly

onto my back and spread my legs for him, watching the way his face changes from pitying to worshipful.

When he lowers his mouth to my pussy, I gasp. With his tongue tracing long, slow lines around my clit, I can feel my climax building already. Finally, he gently sucks my swollen bud into his mouth. My thighs clamp around his head as I ride out the waves of my first orgasm on his face.

The shame and humiliation are gone, as I'd hoped they would be, chased off by satisfaction.

After my second orgasm, I think Colin is feeling better. After my third, I'm certain he thinks I'm better, too. That his compelling argument against the painful pleasures his father offers was convincing.

"I won't let anything happen to you, Mary." He sits up after a final soft kiss. His voice sounds wild, like he means it so much it hurts him. "I won't. I'll make it right. I'll fix everything."

But for the first time since I came here, I don't feel broken.

23

I DON'T KNOW if it's just my mood, but in the morning, my garden surprises me with its beauty. Now that I've cleared away all of that debris, there are clear walking paths, and though the fountains are still dry, they look graceful amid the explosions of spring blossoms. The climbing rosebush is so thick against the wall that all of the hooks and chains are nearly invisible, and their perfume greets me as I take my first tentative steps across the velvet of the grass.

There's still work to be done, just like there always is. I wonder if there's anywhere on the Manor grounds I could find seed packets, or if Martha would help me buy some—*that's a more likely use of last night's winnings than freedom*, I think ruefully.

I'm knuckle deep in the earth, turning it over where it's been trampled and packed down too hard over the years, when I hear someone walk into the garden, humming tunelessly to himself. I know without having to turn and look that it's Neville.

He doesn't seem to care that I'm busy; he comes right up behind me and tucks a lock of hair behind my ear with a single finger. The touch makes me shiver.

"I have a new plan," he says.

I get up off my knees, standing so that I can look him in the eye. I'm so used to being on my knees with him now that it feels strange to realize that, as tall as he is, he's not actually a giant. He doesn't get to tower over me if I don't let him. "If it's for me, I don't want to hear it," I say.

He laughs at me, the same incredulous tone his brother had when I said I was not going to live under Craven control. "Is that so? Why not?"

"I don't feel like it." I shrug. "I was in the middle of loosening soil. Once I've finished what I'm doing, then maybe I'll talk to you. Or maybe not. Your last plan didn't exactly do me any favors."

"Did you misunderstand last night?" he asks. He looks confused to see me in an open rebellion. "You didn't earn what you needed. You're never going back to that commune you miss so much. Unless I help you, Mary, and that's what I'm offering now. Help. Don't you want that? Don't you want to go home?"

Do I? Do I want to sell myself again here, risking Uncle Arch's fury, only to sell myself back to the Kingdom of Love?

Is that love? Really love?

It's not so clear anymore. I turn back to my task, and keep my tone even and light. "I said not right now."

"Leave her alone, Neville."

I whirl around to see Arch striding through the garden's gate, his face like a thunderhead already. Whatever peace he found whipping me last night seems to have disappeared, and he looks furious all over again.

"I told you last night," Neville says. "She's not yours to command."

"And she's not yours to sell." Arch is talking about me, but he's barely looked at me; his attention is fixed on his brother, the two of them glaring at each other like dogs about to fight. "Mary's a guest, and you had no business dragging her into one of your auctions."

"He didn't drag me," I remind Arch. "I didn't see another choice to earn the money. And actually—"

"You think you know what's best for everyone," Neville says, cutting me off without a thought. "But the world doesn't turn at your whim, Archie Craven, or your command."

"You're still a little boy," Arch shoots back. "Kicking your feet and breaking your toys."

I don't even hear what Neville says in return. This is clearly a fight the two of them have been having since they were children; it started before me, and it will keep on going long after I leave Misselthwaite Manor. I'm just the thing they're arguing about today: a pretext for the power struggle that's defined their lives together.

There's so much to do here, and on such a nice day, I'd like to get on with it. But I don't want to stand here and listen to these two men talk about me like I'm just a pawn in their game. *Maybe I'll go to the kitchens*, I think, *and find Martha, or to the library for something to read.* Surely they'll finish while I still have daylight left for work. But when I try to go, Arch stops me, and all the ire that he turned on his brother comes blazing onto me.

"As for you." His voice is thick with disdain. "What do you think you're doing here?" He doesn't give me time to answer. "I did not give you permission to come to this garden, let alone to touch it. In fact, I told you to stay in your room, did I not?"

"Yes, but—"

"I've tried to be kind to you, and understanding. Out of respect for your mother. But everything on this estate," Arch growls. "Is my property. The ground we stand on and the roots in the soil. The play Garden, this garden, and the wall between them: they are mine. You are mine. Every petal on that rosebush belongs to me, Mary, and if I want to pluck them—if I want to make you tear up every vine until your fingers bleed—that is my right. Do you understand that?"

Did he really expect me to stay shut up in that attic for weeks on end? And I haven't harmed this place. I've tried to make it beautiful again. I've honored this garden, as no one else apparently has since Aunt Lily died. He doesn't seem to care. He doesn't even look around to take it in.

"I should punish you," he says. "It'll have to be crueler, this time, since I see a good spanking doesn't deter you. What would teach you a lesson, Mary? Maybe, since you like to sneak around outside so much, I should leave you here. You could sleep on the grass and get up with the sun. I could keep you like a dog out here. You'd be grateful, then, to remember your room in the Manor."

He looks me up and down, his gaze seeming to penetrate my clothing, to lay me bare before him. "No, you'd like that too, wouldn't you? I could show you how to respect me by using you like an animal, but you'd just beg for more. Slut."

I realize I'm shaking, my whole body trembling with anger and want that churns and seethes under my skin. I imagine myself the way he's describing, kept on my knees for him, and how it would feel to let him sink his cock into my throat. My pussy. My ass. I'm as turned on as I am repulsed, and now that I know how transparent I am—how easily he can read me—I don't want to show him any more.

Instead, I turn, and run.

I haven't gotten very far before I run headlong into Dickon, who's been taking a stroll around the grounds with his morning coffee. He wraps a large, warm hand around my arm to stop me from trying to escape. "Mary," he says. "Mary, is everything all right?"

I keep my eyes fixed on his shoes as I gasp out, "No."

"What happened?"

I don't know where to begin. Everything has happened. My ass is still sore from last night's spanking; my cunt is wet for things I shouldn't want, I've involved myself in a war between brothers by accident, I sold my mouth and have so little to show for it.

I have no idea what I'm supposed to do next.

"Everything feels wrong," I tell him. "It's a mess. I've just made a mess of everything. I just…if only I hadn't been so curious at the commune, I never would have thought to want anything more. But it's getting harder and harder to imagine going back. I don't think the Kingdom of Love is home anymore. I can't stay here, but I don't have anywhere else to go. If Arch would just give me the painting my mother left for me, maybe I could find somewhere brandnew to start over."

I blink up at him, trying to smile through my tears. His face is somber, like I've never seen it before, as he puts his arm around me. I sink into his embrace, pressing my face into his broad, firm chest and thinking that Colin was right, some touch is meant for nothing but comfort.

"There's something you should know. Come with me," Dickon says.

He leads me to a part of the property I've never been to before: it's past the gardens, where the land spreads back out into its natural self. The landscape is dotted with small, rolling hills, and as he leads me to the base of one I realize there's a house built into the front of it. It's much smaller and more modest than the Manor, but undeniably charming.

"Is this your house?" I ask.

"In a manner of speaking. This is where the Garden staff lives," Dickon says. He walks me to the heavy wooden front door, and I follow him inside.

The interior is cozy and beautiful, not lavish but clearly well-made and well-cared for. The furniture is handsome but sturdy, and everything is decorated with a mix of woven blankets and silk sheeting, like the house's inhabitants have taken some of the Garden's luxuries and combined them with practical necessities, too.

Then I notice the paintings that cover the walls. Each one bears a signature in the corner, the name signed with a graceful, girlish flourish: Grace Lennox.

My mother's work.

I've never seen any of it before. Mother gave up painting entirely when she came to the commune; before she left Misselthwaite Manor, she once told me, she burned everything she hadn't sold—except the painting she gave to Uncle Arch for me. But here they are, paintings I didn't even know existed.

All of the oversized paintings take the Garden as

their subject. They depict various entertainments, things I could never have imagined my prudish mother knowing about—much less considering a fit subject for art. The living room holds a series of portraits of couples engaged in different acts with one another: the first one I see shows a man standing behind a woman, one hand around her throat and the other between her legs. Her head is thrown back so you can't see her face, but you can tell from the lines of her body that she's in ecstasy, being held still so she can be given exactly what she wants.

In the next painting, a different woman is on her knees for a different man. His hand is fisted tightly in her hair, and you can see the glint of something silver between her ass cheeks. *A bulb like the one Arch made me wear*, I think, and flush.

I never could have imagined her talent; each brushstroke feels like a miracle, outlining the curves and angles of a body or describing the light that illuminates skin. Her colors are pure, vibrant, luxurious, and her subjects feel alive on the canvas. I can almost hear their moans, smell their sweat. Imagine their impossibly, trembling pleasure.

But for all the attention she gave her human subjects, she reserved an equal amount for the flowers. Each couple is surrounded by the most gorgeous overblown roses and peonies, sensual irises and languid lilies. I'm shocked all over again by how much my mother must have loved this world. How hard it must have been to devote herself to the meager existence she brought me up in.

Despite the privations of the Kingdom and the constant corrections of my behavior, she must have loved me beyond measure.

It's already brought me to the edge of tears again when Dickon brings me a glass of something amber and sweet-scented.

"Ben was here when Lily was alive, did you know that?" I take a sip of the liquid. It's fiery like the kind I drank from the Petersen boy's flask, but somehow bright on the tongue like champagne at the same time. I take another.

"He remembers how it was when she died. The unimaginable grief Arch Craven suffered. He was like a man possessed, Ben told me. He destroyed everything that would remind him of her, though of course you can't simply throw away a broken heart."

I drain my glass, hoping against hope that he isn't about to say what I think he is.

"I don't think the painting exists, Mary. I can't imagine it could possibly have survived his sorrow. I'm so sorry."

My tears are falling freely now. "Why wouldn't he tell me? Why wouldn't he just pay me what it's worth?"

"I can only wager a guess. He was probably ashamed to admit what he'd done. What would Lily think if she knew he'd failed to do right by her best friend's only daughter?"

I never knew Lily, obviously. Even in my mother's mentions, she was vaguely drawn. But living in her house, working in her garden, having seen the sinful glory of her Garden, I feel now that I do. And the Lily I've come to understand wouldn't be proud of a single thing Arch has done since she fell from the bower and out of his life forever.

And I don't think she'd be wasting her tears on it, either. I dry mine on my blouse. Aunt Lily would be making plans, deciding her own place in the world. If it didn't already exist, she would invent it.

God helps those who help themselves.

Mother had that one right at least. I turn to Dickon and allow myself to be buoyed by his easy smile.

"Do you think I could have a new shirt?" I ask, gesturing to the tearstained one I'm wearing.

"I think I can find something. Silk would show you off to your best effect. Am I right in thinking perhaps you'd like to try something a bit more flattering today? Marvelous. Take this off and wait here for me, would you? There's a good, brave girl."

He walks off and I take the opportunity to refill my glass before wandering closer to the paintings. The detail is remarkable, down to tiny ants in the roses. How could Grace Lennox have been two such different women in her life? The one I never met, who could see every facet of a beautiful moment and recreate it larger than life; the one who steadfastly turned her face from worldly pleasures to be an example of righteousness for me.

But the biggest question of all might be—how could God make such beauty, such pleasure and not want it to be enjoyed?

24

I'M SO deep in the paintings, I don't feel someone come up behind me.

"Beautiful, aren't they?" a woman's voice says.

I turn around to find Susan standing in the doorway, holding a mug of steaming tea. She's dressed in a silk slip the color of spring roses, a pale, beautiful pink; it reminds me of Robin, the woman in red who I met on my first day here. Though this garment is hardly as scandalous.

"They are," I say. "I didn't know—do you work here?"

"I do," she says, folding herself to sit on one of the other overstuffed couches. With her soft blonde hair, the generous shape of her breasts, her taut, flat stomach and long, lean legs, she rather resembles the way Colin described Sarah. "I was training before, but now that I've been deflowered, I'm officially a member of the staff."

I follow suit, tucking my legs up under me and setting my glass down. I'm glad that she doesn't seem alarmed that I'm wandering around her house in just my bra and skirt. I keep thinking I'll get used to the way people live here, so casual and louche, but it hasn't happened yet.

"How has that been?" I ask.

Her laugh tinkles like bells, and I remember how charming she was up on that stage. "Fine," she says. "I think I'll be popular enough—lots of men asked after me after the auction last night. And that's what we're hired for: we're supposed to be the fulfillment of everyone's fantasies."

"Is that your kink?" The drink has made me bold.

"Oh goodness, no. Other people's fantasies are certainly interesting to me, but I've never gotten off on getting other people off. I just knew that it would be the smartest way to raise interest in me prior to joining, and the large bonus helped. No, my kinks are much smaller. More like fantasies."

"Don't you get to ask for those too? Shouldn't someone give you what you want?" I don't truly understand how it works, when this is your job. Is it like Martha says, where you get to explore your desires? Or like Mrs. Medlock's warning, where your desires have to be locked away?

Susan's smile turns predatory, considering. She puts her mug down on the coffee table.

"My fantasies," she repeats. "Those...those I have to take for myself."

I realize that she's looking at me like a man would: her head cocked at an angle, her gaze hungry on my face, my tits, the stiff peaks of my nipples. I don't know what to say. Nothing about being desired upsets me anymore, but this is still a new experience.

Dickon comes back in just then with a silk shirt for me. He can see immediately the choice before me. Rather than interrupt, he drapes the shirt over the back of a chair and takes a seat in a corner, crossing his arms and raising an eyebrow at me.

My response is wordless and subtle.

Can I?

With a slow blink and a nod, he answers.

You may.

Do I want to?

He can't answer that. Only I know what I want.

I turn back to Susan. She reaches out and touches my knee, checking for a response. When I don't stop her, she flattens her hand against my thigh.

"Sometimes," Susan says, "we have to take what we want."

"And sometimes, we have to let it be taken."

She thumbs at one of my nipples gently, toying with it through the thin fabric of my bra. I feel a line of sensation between her touch and my clit, and my lips part almost unconsciously.

Then her hand comes up to my throat, my jaw, and the next thing I know, she's tilting my head and moving in to kiss me, her mouth soft and plush and hot against my own, her knee tight between my legs.

I'm too surprised to do anything but shove her away.

Because for all the things I tried here, all the boundaries I've been pushed past and limits I've willingly broken...

I've never been kissed before.

"Is that not okay?" Susan has immediately withdrawn her hands, awaiting my consent. I appreciate that as much as I feel suddenly cold at her departure. I didn't expect kissing to feel...like that. So intense.

"It's okay."

Her smile is delicious, but her kiss is better. She seems to know that I need guidance, and she takes control, plundering my mouth, dominating me in exactly the way the men dominate my mouth with their cocks. She draws me into her lap and I go willingly, my knees sinking into the couch on either side of her hips as she undoes the clasp on my bra and lets it fall to the floor.

She's all softness underneath me; I cup my hand around her breast and swallow her moan with my mouth. I miss the hardness of a cock between my legs, the way I imagine a man's body might fit with mine, but I don't mind this, either, especially not when she skates her hands up my legs and under my skirt. She finds the crotch of my underwear and strokes me there, long, languid touches that melt me into a puddle. I forget how to kiss; I'm just breathing into her mouth while she touches me.

"No fair," Dickon calls from his chair. "Let me see."

"What do you think, Mary," Susan asks. She's speaking softly, just in the space between us. "Should we give him a show?"

Oh. The thought of Dickon watching me—while Susan touches me—while I fall apart—my cheeks are hot, but I'm determined to follow my pleasure where it leads me, so I nod a silent yes. Susan has me stand up and take off my panties and skirt so that I'm completely naked; then she has me turn around so that I'm sitting between her legs, my back pressed to her front.

"Now this is a fantasy," she says against my throat. She's playing with my nipples again, pinching and teasing me, and she has to hold me still so I don't get too restless with want. "When I came in here and saw you with your tits out and your mouth open, staring at those paintings. Have you done any of those things, Mary?"

"Not..." I gasp. I want her hands back on my pussy so badly. "Not...not most of them."

"Would you like to?"

"Yes." It's only a murmur the first time, so I say it again louder. "*Yes.*"

Dickon isn't touching himself, but he's hard in his chair, his legs spread so I can see his cock straining against his thigh through his pants. Susan urges my thighs apart, spreading me so that Dickon can see my trembling empty center.

"Look how perfect she is," she breathes. "Shall I lick that perfect, pink little pussy for her, Dickon? Do you think she'll like the way another woman knows how to work a clit?"

My moan startles both of us. Susan doesn't take long to adjust, though; she slides out from behind me and comes to kneel between my legs. Now Dickon *is* stroking himself through his pants, clearly enjoying every bit of the performance we're putting on for him. Maybe this is his fantasy. Maybe getting other people off *is* my kink.

Or maybe I'm just so keyed up that the idea of other people enjoying my pleasure too—*oh*. Her tongue laps at me now, and yes, I do see how different this is than when Colin did it. I'm writhing beneath her like a crazy person, even daring to grab a handful of those beautiful blonde waves and tug her even closer.

"She likes it so much," Susan moans, then she applies her mouth to my cunt in earnest, and every illustration in those filthy books comes to blazing, aching life between my legs.

I'm making a steady stream of noises now, wordless, thoughtless questions, pleas for more, *please*, more of this. Her tongue is warm against my clit, relentless as the waves of the ocean; the fingers on one hand spread me wide so she can taste me. The other delves a finger inside me, just a little, just enough. It's almost too much to take, but when I try to move away from the sensation she holds me firmly in place, forcing me to give in to the exquisite torture that is her tongue and her lips taking me apart.

I can't help imagining what might happen if Arch walked in and saw us: Susan between my legs while Dickon watches us. Would it set his rage off again? Or would he like it?

Which of those would please me more?

A fantasy spins itself around me while Susan touches me. I can almost feel it happening: Arch hearing the noises I'm making. He'd come storming into this room. He'd be livid. He might pull Susan away from me; he might turn me over and spank me again, turning last night's bruises into more fresh red marks. And if he was really, really mad—powerfully out of control—he might pull out his cock and fuck me with it.

The thought sends me over the edge, into an orgasm that takes me over from the inside out. When I come, it's convulsive, keening; my body shakes and shakes and Susan licks me through it, nuzzling my pussy until I'm finally back in my body again.

Colin was right. I need the pain; even the thought is enough to take me higher than I can go with kindness. I've never felt this good in my life. But Arch isn't here, of course. He didn't come.

And I need to remember: the hole inside him is shaped like another woman.

25

THE NEXT DAY I work in the garden all morning, tempting fate, but no one comes. Luckily, not Neville, but regretfully, also not Arch.

After that, every hour of silence feels like punishment. And not the kind I enjoy.

I find a hose that allows me to fill the fountains so that they burble and sing; it also makes it easier to water the plants, since this spring hasn't been very rainy so far. I watch the water cascade out from the nozzle, a steady, even flow, and imagine going back to the commune, where I'd be carrying buckets again, doing everything by hand, the hard way.

It doesn't sound appealing. Though it hasn't truly been so long, I've changed too much out here to ever go back and fit in the way I used to.

No matter how hard I pray, I can't un-bite that apple.

The thought should terrify me, but somehow, it doesn't. I don't *feel* like I've fallen from grace. All the warning bells my mind kept ringing never found an echo in my soul.

The Kingdom of Love taught me so much. I learned hard work from them; I learned how to tend land and make it bear fruit. I tried not to be selfish, with mixed results, but I always believed in putting the whole ahead of the self. Maybe it's because I feared I couldn't survive without the structure, support, and discipline that the elders provided—and sometimes mandated. *But it turns out I can*, I think, surveying the scene I've created here with satisfaction.

But I'm learning something else here, too: that pleasure is as God-given as pain.

Here, in this manor, with these people...there's nothing shameful.

If only "these people" were more forgiving. *You can't stay here*, I remind myself. *And you have nowhere else to go*. My mind turns to daydreaming about the possibilities as I weed. Perhaps Mrs. Medlock would know of another estate like this one that wants a gardener. Or Dickon could teach me how to tailor.

Or I could seek work in the Garden. I push the thought away, despite the instant jolt I feel between my legs. I will not align myself with Neville. And despite my recent revelation about my virginity on the auction block and the realization that my virginity at the commune are both loveless transactions, I still can't quite picture that most intimate moment happening with a stranger.

Besides, Uncle Arch forbade it.

The thought makes me contrary all over again. I can't keep him out of my head, and I can't figure out what's in his. I can't believe he destroyed my painting. Actually, I *can* believe it, it makes more sense than almost anything here has so far.

What I can't believe is that he didn't have a plan.

I'd hardly have known the difference if he gave me a different painting, one not of Lily. I can't imagine the selling price would be that different. Given what I was told about the scarcity of her available works, one would surely be the same as another. Or, as I told Dickon, he could have simply paid me for it. If he's still stringing me along, leading me to believe that the painting is in storage somewhere, he *must* be planning something.

Arch doesn't want to sell me. He doesn't want Colin to save me. What, then, does *he* want of me? It both chills and excites me to think of what he said yesterday, right where I'm standing now. That he'd keep me like an animal, using me at his will, whenever and however he likes.

What if that was honesty, rather than a threat?

Never, ever trust Archibald Craven.

I breathe a silent apology to my mother. Then I formulate a new plan.

After lunch, I go to the smaller staff house to find Dickon. He's lounging in the living room, drinking tea with Robin and another girl I recognize vaguely from the Garden.

"Mary, Mary!" Robin says, sitting up straighter when I walk in. She's in the same red dress from my first day, and it still thrills me to see it, despite the more salacious things I've seen since. "Did you come to see how *my* garden grows?"

"Actually, I came for Dickon. Would you be able to dress me *completely* like you did with yesterday's blouse?" It earns me one of his large, sensual smiles.

"Oh darling," he says. "I thought you'd never ask."

He takes me back to his studio, which is a small building adjacent to the servants' house. It seems to be a converted barn, and I'm surprised by how lovely it is: light falls in thick, pale shafts through the skylights he's installed in the roof, and the floor is warm, worn-in wooden planks. Stacks of fabrics and cabinets full of notions catch my eye—I see sequins and feathers, gorgeously patterned silks and satins. It's like a dream factory, which makes sense, I think, since this is where the Garden's girls come to become fantasies.

And now I'll become one, too.

Dickon gestures for me to stand on a raised pedestal in the center of the space, where light is falling. He pulls his measuring tape from an inner pocket. "Clothes off."

The first time I got undressed before men here, I was petrified. Now, it's routine. I remember how Susan played with the men on stage, and try her pretend innocence on for size as I shed my clothes. He watches appreciatively as I feign reluctance even as I continue to expose myself to him.

The light coming down is so sweet and warm on my skin, and I let myself bask as Dickon wraps his measuring tape around my ribs, and then around the fullest part of my breasts, pressing the fabric against the peaks of my nipples. He already has my measurements from when I first came here, but I've filled out a bit since then. Food eaten for pleasure and not simply for fuel has made my breasts larger, softened my angular hips. It feels nice to let his hands discover and record my growth, his fingers skimming down my back to my waist, tracing the curve of my ass before giving it a squeeze that makes me gasp.

"Is there something in particular you'd like? A favorite color, or pattern, perhaps. Your wish is my command."

Even though I've turned this idea over and over in my mind like fresh soil, I still hesitate before saying it aloud. But it's Dickon, and I trust him. Or at least, I trust that he'll be amused enough to go along with me.

"What would Lily Craven choose?" I ask. As I'd

hoped, he wags a finger at me with a roguish grin before launching into a recitation.

"What an extremely naughty thought!"

My face tingles with shame. I've gone too far.

But Dickon smiles. "I love it. Mistress Lily was fond of rose. Silk, of course, but also linen. She wore shades ranging from nearly scarlet to palest blush—even mauve—but always pink. She liked empire waists and cap sleeves, simple lines with exquisite draping. For you, we'll update a bit, but keep the style classic. And I think we want to stay in the lightest range, with accents of blue. Emphasize your virginal nature."

He holds up a bolt of fabric so thin it looks like gauze. "It will feel like heaven," he promises. "And it'll make him want you like hell."

"Thank you," I say, not bothering to pretend I don't know what he means. I may not know what game Uncle Arch is playing, but I know that I'm more than a pawn. This is me making a move.

"You're welcome." He looks me over, his gaze passing like a touch over my entire body. "Now go, I have work to do, and lots of it."

I put my clothes back on and let myself out of his studio before crossing back through the staff house, half hoping that Susan will be there, and she'll offer to touch me again. I don't see her, but I do hear a woman whimpering, a sound that just a month ago I would have associated with pain. Now I know it for a sound of pleasure, and I follow its path without thinking, listening as the cries get louder the closer I get.

I find a room that looks like the library without all of its books. There are shelves filled with bulbs and belts like the one I wore to the Garden; the walls are mounted with hooks and chains. Some things I've learned the use for—a padded bench, an X like the one that woman was strapped to—and some I still don't recognize.

In the middle of all of it stands Ben Weatherstaff, fully dressed except for his bare cock, which is at full attention as he strokes it in his massive palm. Before him stands a woman whose hands are held above her head in wooden stocks chained to the ceiling.

As I watch, Ben kicks her legs apart and pushes into her. She cants her hips forward, begging for more, and he smacks her ass. "Be still, greedy slut," he commands, pounding her.

"Your favorite slut," Robin gasps back, the effort of holding herself steady making it hard for her to breathe. Ben fucks her ruthlessly, pumping into her body like she's just a doll, a plaything made for his pleasure. One hand is on her throat and the other grips her ass to keep her still. She seems to love it, crying out every time he spanks her, begging wordlessly until he says *"Now,"* and she falls apart, her orgasm ripping through her like a wildfire. Ben waits until she's done to follow suit, pulling out beforehand to decorate her red silk with his cum.

It's electrifying to watch.

I thought maybe they hadn't noticed me. But Robin looks up and catches my eye, gives me a knowing smile that only makes the ache between my legs feel more brutal and urgent. "Look what you made me do," she says. "I had to go find some cockleshells."

Ben looks around to see me and chuckles.

"Don't tease our little virgin Mary." He unlocks the stocks and lets her down gently, half carrying her to a soft couch towards the back of the room.

"What did you think, Mary?" He sits, and she lays her head on his lap to be petted. "Robin here's one of our best girls. You saw her hold her orgasm—not many can, when they're getting fucked like that. Incredible self-control."

"I'm his favorite," she reminds me, practically purring under his touch.

"It was fascinating to watch," I confess, twisting my hands in my lap. "I'm sorry. I get so curious. I'm sure I'm not supposed to have seen that, and I don't want to get in trouble…"

"What we do here is not for everyone," Ben says. "But there's nothing wrong with a healthy curiosity."

He sighs and looks off into the distance, remembering something far away from where and when we are now. "I do miss Lily. A rarity, that one. The Garden was her life. She was so welcoming, and everyone found their place around her, shy or bold."

"And which was she?"

"Feisty and demanding—not a submissive little

wallflower. I loved watching Lily in the Garden. She needed it so badly—her eyes would go glassy when Arch fucked her in front of everyone, and she came like a wildcat. Not at all what you might have thought a man like Archibald Craven would like, knowing him these days."

Just as everyone says. Aunt Lily must have been a true force of nature. What else could tame a man like him?

"Rather like you, in fact. Watching you on the auction block the other day—well. And I've seen how you speak to the Master. To anyone who crosses you. You've got a temper on you." He smiles, moving his massage down Robin's upper back.

"When I lived on the commune, they called it sinful. Just like this." I gesture at the room, symbolic of so many forbidden things.

"Of course they did," Ben says. "Men always want to control women's pleasure. It's how they keep you small. Mistress Lily…she was powerful. And terrifying. Do you know the story of Lilith?"

I shake my head.

"Of course they didn't tell you about Adam's first wife. She refused to be subservient. So she was replaced by Eve and erased from the stories. Now most godly men never even know that there was a time where women were equal, though they spend all of theirs making sure you'll never try. A woman like you, with a body like yours, and an appetite like yours—it should be celebrated and indulged. Flowers don't bloom in darkness; God didn't mean for you to live there either."

He leans to the side table and grabs a tub of ointment to rub into Robin's muscles.

"You have more power than you think," he says. "I hope you learn to use it."

26

___

THREE DAYS LATER, I still haven't seen Arch.

I've been good, for once, staying in my room and only coming out to go down to the kitchens with Martha and Mrs. Medlock in the afternoons. I'll behave myself while my new wardrobe is being prepared. Besides, it turns out I like to be with them while they work; it reminds me of the best parts of the commune, when the women would quilt together, singing as we sewed.

So I spend my days kneading bread dough or sorting through produce deliveries and listening to them talk. I don't go to the gardens. I barely even touch myself. My own body feels off-limits to me as I wait to know how the next part of my life begins.

But Uncle Arch doesn't seem interested in whether I'm being obedient or not. Maybe he took it for granted that I'd give in and do what everyone else does here: let him rule me.

He shouldn't have.

The waiting rankles me, every day lasting longer and longer. I can feel impatience growing inside of me, curling around my bones like a kudzu vine until, on the fourth day, I wake up and see the sun shimmering on the grass outside.

When I go to the bathroom to wash up, a sweet breeze blows through the window, and I can tell it's going to be a beautiful day. I can almost feel the way the flowers in my garden will be blossoming, spreading their petals and releasing their fragrances; I can sense, too, the weeds that will be taking advantage of this weather to put down strong roots.

I'm dying to be outside again, breathing fresh air, with my hands in the soil. I can't leave my garden half finished, all my work abandoned to be swallowed up by willful neglect like everything else "under his control" on this property.

When I get back to my room, my bed is covered in brown paper packages. I rip open one after another. Each item of clothing is softer and more finely made than the last, and I can't stop running my hands over them. It seems wrong to wear any of these beautiful things out to play in the dirt.

Finally, I settle on a pale pink linen dress with blue edging around the neck and sleeves. It's flowy enough to pull over my knees when I kneel, hopefully avoiding the worst of the grass stains.

After putting on the clothes and pinning my hair, I slip out the back door and into the sun. If Uncle

Arch wants me to stop restoring Lily's garden, he can just come and stop me himself.

And if he does... The idea sends a shiver down my spine, between my legs to the aching, lonely nub of my clit. *I'll make him make me. Show me how much he wants to be in control of me, and what he'll do to ensure that he is. I'll force him to reveal the game, and then I'll rewrite the rules.*

There's plenty of weeding to do, so that takes up most of the morning, but the flowers are heartier now, and once I've cleared away everything around their bases, there's not much left for me to do. The fountains are still going, water singing sweetly as it tumbles into their stone basins. So I set my sights on the last thing in the garden that needs repair: the swing.

The branch it was hung from is still sturdy and strong. When I examine it more closely, I can see what happened: dampness got into the rope and rotted it away, fiber by fiber, until all at once—it snapped. The board for the seat is still intact, though, so all I have to do is cut away the part of the rope that's not good, cut away the same length on the other side, and re-attach it to the branch. My gloves are back in the shed and I don't want to go get them, so my hands sting with the work—the coarse fibers of the ropes, and tiny splinters from the board making their way into my palms.

I imagine them as penance. This blister, for my original sin at the commune. This splinter, for staying away from my tasks here so long. This cut, for being foolish enough to believe in Arch, and this callous, for everything I want to do with him, even now.

When I'm done, I sit down gingerly on the board, testing to see if it can take my weight. It's a little shorter now, but still languid. The branch above me creaks, and the wood offers a long, low groan, but it holds me up, sturdy and strong. I listen to the breeze rustling through the sparse leaves overhead, spring still slow coming for this ancient oak.

We had a swing like this on the commune, another selfish secret I kept for myself until I couldn't anymore. It was in a far corner of the land, leftover from previous owners; I used to sneak away when I was a child and glory in the moments I could steal to spend flying through the air. One day I arrived to swing—after all my chores were done, of course—and it had been taken down, the tree it hung from chopped to a stump.

No one confronted me about it, but I prayed extra hard in the weeks and months that followed, begging forgiveness from the elders as much as from God. God never seemed as swift with His punishments as they were.

That was years ago, but my body remembers what to do. I push my toes against the soil to get the swing moving, pumping my legs and leaning my torso back and forth to build momentum. I'm much stronger than the child I used to be, and the swing flies gorgeously through the air, tossing me up high before we tumble back towards the earth together.

It's the most beautiful this garden has ever felt to me—with every swing I can smell the roses blooming and the soil's damp mineral scent. Sunlight dapples through the tree's leaves, brushing my face as gently as the breeze. I put all of my pent-up energy into the movement, letting the frustration and want and need and hurt that's been building inside of me send my back arching and my body flying. I try to forget about everything but soaking up all the beauty God has made. From up here, I can see it all.

I can see out of the garden too, now, I realize: up to the top floors of the house, where my little attic room is.

I'm trying to pick out which one it is when a movement in another one of the windows catches my eye.

There is no forgetting this man, especially on his property. I know his shape instantly. Arch is standing there in an upper window watching me, brooding like a gargoyle on a castle corner.

I expect him to do something. I wore this outfit to be provocative, to force his hand. But he doesn't. He just stays there, his eyes fixed on me, his gaze suddenly making my body feel hot all over. His shirt is white, stark against the gloom that surrounds him. My childish glee at capturing his attention turns into something sharp-edged as I watch him watch me.

I've had enough of this man and his mysteries and

his orders, of living in his house without choices, but never told what to expect. I want him to *do* something. Anything.

I want him to come here and confront me.

The next time I swing down, I lift my hips up to hike my skirts up over my thighs, and when I come up again, I spread my legs, letting him see my sweet, spread center, the part of me that no man has ever had. I want him to see it tempting him, taunting him.

Maybe I even want him to take it.

He turns away from the window, and my heart thumps madly in my chest. Did it work? Will he come?

What will he do if he does?

I stop pumping my legs, letting the swing slow down of its own accord, until my feet can drag through the soil below to stop me. My pussy is wet, my breath coming quickly. I feel blissful, both completely in and out of control at the same time. I've made myself clear, goaded and provoked Arch as much as I can. Now I find out what he'll do next. When I hear the gate groan open, my breath almost stops.

But then I see who it is.

It's not Arch at all.

Instead, it's Mrs. Medlock, tendrils of hair escaping from her practical bun and her face damp with sweat like she ran all the way here from the Manor.

"Master Craven wants to see you in his... Oh

dear," she says, surveying the state of me. My skirts are still around my waist, baring my knees and thighs; my hair, too, is disheveled from the wind, and my skin is pink from exertion and excitement. I hop off the swing, brushing off my skirts. I don't bother to smooth and re-pin my hair. It's no use—and anyway, he knows what I was just doing. There's no point in trying to hide it.

"He's quite upset," Mrs. Medlock says, all but wringing her hands. "You won't have time to make yourself presentable, but at least keep your eyes down. He'll calm down when he's said his piece, he always does."

That would be an unfortunate outcome.

"Thank you." It's an acknowledgement. Not a promise to obey.

I know he wants me to feel cowed and terrified, but I harness the impulse that encouraged me to goad Arch in the first place. Soon it takes over, making me feel dangerous and unpredictable as I follow Mrs. Medlock up the stairs to his quarters. It's more than that, actually: my anger starts to build anew as I consider my position here, and what's likely to happen to me next.

So instead of taking her advice to be meek, I'm in a temper when she lets me into Arch's bedroom.

It nearly covers my surprise at discovering where he sleeps.

An attic room, just a door down from mine.

His space, though, feels darker and heavier than

mine does. His windows are flanked by velvet curtains that cut the sunlight in half, and his furniture oversized to the point of intimidation. It doesn't matter, though. Once I see him standing in the center of the floor, everything else falls away. He commands every room he's in, and this one is no exception.

I take my fury-born courage in hand and speak first. "I can't wait to hear the reason you disturbed both me and Mrs. Medlock."

I can see that he's hard, his cock so big it looks like a threat. His eyes on my skin are as hot as a brand, and I can feel that his temper is as inflamed as mine right now.

"I've been lenient with you so far, but from now on, I suppose I will have to be strict," Arch growls.

"Are you done?"

"Are you?"

"I haven't even begun."

"Since you seem to have forgotten who's the Master of Misselthwaite, allow me to refresh your memory." He begins to pace around me, a tiger in the cage I've willingly entered. "It is not my brother, and he will not touch you. It is not my son, and you will not touch him. It is not Susan, or Dickon, or Ben. You belong to *me* as long as you're in this house. You're *mine* to share at my discretion…or not."

I can't hide the way my body reacts to the idea: my nipples pricking up through the top of my dress, and the shudder of want that shakes through me. My pussy is wet, radiating heat between my legs. It would be so easy to say *yes*, to let him master me. To get on my knees and beg him for mercy, for pain. To make me his, to make me come. To make me stay.

But just because the fantasy turns me on doesn't mean I'm truly ready to concede. Men have dictated the terms of my entire life. I want some of the power Ben saw in me. So I make another move.

"What do I get in exchange?"

Arch's reaction is furious and instant. He grabs me by the hair and pushes me down on his desk, face-first, so that I'm pressed against the polished woodgrain. He kicks my legs apart and pulls my skirts up, the way they were on the swing, only this way I'm twice as exposed.

"What do you *get*?" he asks. "Little brat. You want me to tell you?"

My heart is hammering again, and I can feel my pulse everywhere: in my throat, my belly, my cunt. I can't believe what I'm about to say, but then again, how could I swallow it? I have to admit to the aching, scorching truth.

"I want you to show me."

27

THE AGONIZING PAUSE that follows is filled with self-recrimination.

Never, ever trust Archibald Craven.

Then he's moving: his belt is being unbuckled, whipped out of its loops, and it whistles through the air. A long, hot sting that makes me gasp. He pinches the reddened skin between two fingers until I squeal.

Oh, I've waited so long for this.

I expect another spank, but instead that hand slips between my legs, rubbing against my wetness. I arch my back and he slaps my ass with an open palm. "You needy little whore."

I let out a choked sob, and he starts to work me harder, one hand on my pussy and the other on my ass. He spanks me while he finger-fucks me, and I become an animal in rut: chasing the pleasure of his hands at the same time I'm trying to escape the pain they inflict. It's so good, and then it's so bad, but it's good again and I'm chasing that fleeting, pulsing moment of reconciliation.

But he won't let me come; every time I get close, he takes away his hands and goes back to the belt so that I'm left panting, cunt twitching with need, my orgasm building behind my eyes like a wave. My own wetness is dripping down my inner thighs, and tears fill my eyes every time another smack comes against my tender skin.

"Of course you like this," he says, chanting like a prayer. "Only a slut like mine could get off on being punished. You need this. My bratty little whore. Mine."

I try to keep my mouth shut, but eventually I can't anymore, and I hear myself beg. My voice is hoarse already from all the cries I've swallowed. I never begged God for anything the way I beg Arch for my orgasm.

"Please," I say. "Please, please let me come. I'm so close and I need it so badly."

"Yes, you do. You need this. Need *me*." He tugs me back, pressing my bare skin against the front of his pants, and I can feel how hard he is for me. He's so *big*—bigger than Neville, than Colin, than any cock I've seen or tasted. I whimper when he grinds against me, and I cry out when he pushes me forward again, leaving me feeling cold and lonely and more desperate than ever.

I'm ready to give it all up for him, to throw away the last sacred piece of me, if I can only make this agony end. My body is in charge now; there's no arguing with it. The need to feel Arch inside of me is a physical fact.

"I need it." I can hear the animal whimper in my voice. "Please, please, please."

Inside my head, the plea is so much dirtier. Sinful. *Cock, cock, cock.* If he takes me now, it wasn't my fault. Not really. If he takes that fat cock and feeds it into my wet, wet pussy, if he pushes up farther than Ben's fingers, than Susan's fingers, if he takes that one shred of grace I have left...

"No." His hand is back between my legs, working mercilessly at my clit. I'm panting open-mouthed against the desk. All thoughts of becoming a player are gone. This is a game he'll always win, because I have no idea how to turn off the want he inspires. I can hardly come without his name on my tongue.

Where do I go from here? If I don't fit here, where *do* I fit?

"I'm begging you. It hurts too much. *Please.* Can you—will you let me?"

He circles around to the other side of the desk, so I can watch as he takes his cock out. There's no possible way he'll fit, not that massive, throbbing thing in my tiny, unused pussy. My cunt is soaked; there are tear tracks down my face. I feel like a river, flowing inexorably. My body is dissolving into pure, sheer desire.

"You know nothing of the pain of need." Arch fists his cock, his fingers flexing around its swollen length. His hand is large enough to fit around it, but mine would never. "*This* is need. *This* is longing."

He's so hard it looks like it must hurt him, swollen tip glistening with wetness of its own. I imagine the plush head of it on my tongue and down my throat, how it would gag me until I could barely breathe. How it might break me. His brother trained me to crave that, and I pulse at the thought. I don't understand why he won't give us both what we want. What we need.

"So show me." I breathe it more than say it, pressing up onto my elbows, willing my breathing to slow, my heart to calm.

"I can't. I can't take that from you, I can't."

And I know, with a ferocious, undeniable intuition, that the game is over. I've done it. Uncle Arch has admitted that I'm the one with the power, that force Ben told me I had, the one Dickon dressed and Martha longed for. I have it, not only aching between my spread thighs, but in my very temptation of him.

The knowledge Eve tasted was that she wasn't less than Adam; the original sin was always showing a man how unworthy he is.

I let myself back down onto the desk again, so that I'm prostrate in front of him, my legs still spread, my cunt still bare. The emptiness of it is agony, regardless of my victory.

"Yes, you can," I offer, as much for my sake as his. "The Master of the house can take whatever he needs."

All I can see is the dark wood in front of me, but I hear his sharp intake of breath and the sound of his footsteps as he circles back around behind me. I expect another smack from his belt or a slap from his palm, maybe another round of torment with his fingers. But instead, his fingers smooth and spread me, exposing my glistening clit to him.

When I feel the head of his cock brush against my entrance, I have a stab of fear that I've miscalculated, that he'll take what he wants, thinking I offered. It feels even bigger than it looks, and as wet as I am, it's too big, too much.

I let out a ragged cry as I prepare myself, but he doesn't push forward. Doesn't claim what's his.

"Soaked," he murmurs, his voice gravel and smoke. "You need something too. You want this."

His cock is resting against my entrance now, his heat just touching mine. My breathing is frantic; my hands keep clenching and unclenching at my sides.

"I want this." It's hardly a whisper, words shaped on a sigh, but it's enough.

"You can't have it."

Before I can protest, he hauls me up to standing and turns me around. I'm in a daze while he pulls my dress over my head and unclasps my bra, so that I'm naked before him, just like the day we met. His gaze passes over me, and even if I couldn't see his cock still leaping for my attention, just the way his eyes feel on my skin tells me he's as hungry as I am for this.

"Sit down on the couch," he says. "Legs spread for me, there's a good girl."

I don't know what's about to happen, but I don't care as long as he'll touch me again.

There's a small table next to the couch; he pulls open one of its drawers and takes out a small vial of clear liquid. He drips some on his fingers, and then he comes to kneel between my legs.

I wait for him to taste me, dying to compare reality to fantasy. He doesn't touch my pussy, though. Instead, he pulls me forward so that I slide down the couch, my legs splaying further and further. Then, when he has me where he wants me, he slides his slick fingers between my ass cheeks and starts to circle my hole.

"Remember when you plugged yourself for me, Mary?" he asks. "I didn't see it myself, but I heard that you did exactly what I told you to do. Heard you looked like you had been made for it, to have something filling up your tight little asshole." He smacks me with his free hand, and slides the finger inside of me at the same time. "Oh, you must have been so ashamed, when everyone saw you and realized you weren't such a good girl after all."

"I always knew." All of the tension that gripped me earlier has fallen away; I feel myself melting into his hands, letting his words unravel me as his hands stretch me open, getting me ready to take his enormous cock.

"And I always knew I would have to fuck some

sense into you. You're going to take it so beautifully."

I can feel my inner muscles fluttering around his fingers, getting used to the intrusion. Trying to draw him further, deeper in.

"Yes," I breathe. "Yes, please, I'll be so good."

"No you won't. Naughty girl. You can't help yourself." He reaches his free hand up to brush the hair from my face and I turn into the touch helplessly, letting his palm cup my cheek. My eyes flutter closed, and in the darkness that descends on me, the world is reduced to almost nothing: the fullness of Arch's fingers sliding in and out of my ass, every thrust in counterpoint to the deep, empty ache of my pussy.

"Your tits are so gorgeous," he rumbles. "Play with them for me, won't you?"

I open my eyes again, and the look he gives me scorches straight through me. I cup my breast in my palm, circle my nipple with my fingertips. I pinch one hard peak, and then the other. My mouth falls open at the mix of sensations: my hands are cool compared to Arch's, dry where his are wet, working between my legs.

"Look at you. You can hardly believe your own body," he says. "How much it can feel." He bites at my inner thigh, hard enough to leave a bruise, and the thought of it—his mark on me a claim, a reminder that this happened, that I'm his.

Words finally fail me. *Yes*, I want to say. *I want to feel everything.*

But he's moving, now, rearranging me so I'm on

my back on the couch, putting more of the clear liquid inside and outside me. All I can do is strain upwards into his touch, trying to get as much of his hands on me as possible.

Then, when he has me where he wants me, he presses the head of his cock against the rim of my hole.

"Mine," he says. One hand cradles my face as he starts to press in, and in, and in. The cold, hard metal of the plug was nothing like the heat of a cock, the sense of being breached and plundered, split open and taken over. I'm crying again, tears leaking from my eyes, and Arch brushes them away with his thumb. I turn my head so that I can kiss his palm, tasting his skin at last.

"Mine, mine, mine." His low chant is a hymn to pleasure.

He lowers his head so that he can breathe against my neck, and I can feel the even rhythm of his inhales and exhales go ragged as I tentatively allow him more, those last few inches inside of me. I wonder if he's going to kiss me, and I want him to—I want his tongue to fuck me while his cock does, I want to let him inside every part of me—but he doesn't. Instead, he pulls out and presses in again, agonizingly slowly, making sure I feel every second.

"Oh," I hear myself saying. "Oh, oh, Arch—"

"Tell me," he says. He's still moving shallowly, barely thrusting, and I feel like I'm going to lose my mind. "Tell me what you need, Mary."

I've thought these words, but never said them. I can't hold back any longer, though. "Fuck me," I beg him, my voice breaking in the middle of the word. "Fuck me, please, Uncle Arch."

Whatever self-control has been holding him back finally snaps, and he drives his hips forward cruelly, filling me to the hilt. He starts to fuck me in earnest, folding my knees up to my chest so that he can force his cock deep inside of me, and make me feel him everywhere. He's moving like an animal, and I am, too, clutching at his back, my nails scoring his skin as I urge him to give me more.

His face is back at my neck again, and when he speaks his words are so close to my ear it almost feels like he's speaking through me, like they don't even have to pass through the air before they get to me. "When I fuck your pussy," he says. "You'll fall apart, won't you."

I'm falling apart already, and I can feel my orgasm spiraling closer and closer, the combination of my pleasure and his pushing me over the edge. The room smells like skin and musk, like the flowers of my garden and the salt of Arch's sweat, and he's so thick inside of me, so *fucking* big.

"I'm going to," I tell him. "I have to, I can't." I expect him to smack me again, to punish me for how helplessly needy I'm being, but he doesn't. Instead, he kisses the hollow of my throat and pinches my clit.

"Come for me," he commands, so of course, I do.

Usually when I'm orgasming I feel outside of

myself, like I'm just a conduit for whatever sensations are coursing through my body.

This time, though, with Arch still inside of me, I'm pinned in place, and all I can do is watch as he slams in one final time, his face contorting with pleasure as he finally lets go, too. Instead of feeling flung out into space, it's like being part of a circuit completed, his body and mine joined the way they were always meant to be.

Now I'm marked everywhere, inside and out, by this gale force of a man.

He's careful when he pulls out of me, but I still gasp at the suddenness of it, of being empty again. Something on my face catches Arch's gaze, and he pauses, looking down at me. For just a moment I'm self-conscious. My body is pink and white from exertion, damp with sweat and sticky with fluids.

Does he look at me now and see a ruined plaything?

Then he kisses me, a searching, ravaging kiss that destroys me just as easily and thoroughly as his cock did.

I press myself against him, my bare breasts rubbing against the fabric of his shirt, my hips lifting up to seek his yet again. I'm a wildcat in his arms, and he holds me close while I squirm. He strokes the bruises he left on my ass, my inner thighs, examining the mess he made of me. I remember a sign that Mr. Petersen kept in his store: *anything you break, you must buy.*

Arch has broken me. There's no one else for me after this. But that doesn't mean he'll keep me.

"Oh Mary," he murmurs, almost as if he can hear my thoughts. "What are we going to do with you?"

I have no idea. All I know is that I want him more than I've ever wanted anything before—more than sleeping in on cold winter mornings at the commune, more than the first orgasm I chased, my fingers busy against my clit in the shadows of the barns. I want him more than the painting or the money, more than a new life somewhere that's never heard the rumors about Misselthwaite Manor. I want to feel these sensations bloom over and over.

There's a knock on the door, and Mrs. Medlock's tentative voice calling Arch's name.

"I'm aware of the time," he calls back to her, his voice gruff again, all business. He stands up and snaps a few wipes from a dispenser. They're not for me. To me he says, "Go clean yourself up."

My legs are still spread, and I bask in his satisfaction as he takes one last look at me while he cleans himself. His cum is leaking out of my ass; my tits are rubbed raw and my legs are still spread, so he can see where he's going to fuck me next.

I'm not a broken toy. I found my power somewhere inside my surrender, and I'm wielding it now.

"You will stay in your rooms until I come for you," he continues. My heart flutters in my chest. That doesn't sound like a threat.

It sounds like a promise.

28

I WAIT ALL EVENING. When I wake the next morning, he still isn't there. But there is a note on my night table in his handwriting.

Picking it up makes me remember all of the letters he sent before, with instructions, and I wonder what he'll command me to do now. Debase myself in the garden, like he'd threatened before? Ask me to play with another toy from the library before he fucks me? I'm wet already, imagining how what happened between us yesterday has changed the game he's playing.

But when I open the letter, that's not what it says at all.

Mary, it begins.

No matter where I am or what I'm doing, you are mine.

You are mine. I stroke my fingertips over the letters, feeling where his pen pressed deep into the thick paper, leaving grooves I can still feel. I imagine him writing this, his handsome face open for just a moment as he tells me, at last, how he feels.

Obey me and my rules. By now you know that whether I am home or away, before you even came to Misselthwaite, I always know what you have done. So while I am gone:

Listen to the help; they know how I like things to run. If you must wander from the attic, do not leave the house. Under no circumstances do you venture anywhere near the Garden. If you do these things, you will have earned what I give you—my trust.

I remember my mother's warning and imagine a different look on his face now. *Never, ever trust Archibald Craven.* This time I picture the smirk of someone who believes he knows just what to say to keep my feelings growing while his own remain dead on the vine.

I'll take something from you as well. When I return, I will claim your virginity.

You were told to protect that hot, soft flower between your legs; I will make giving it away much, much sweeter than abstinence could ever be.

If there is a God who made these gardens, the sun that warms them, the water that helps them grow, why would you think He gave us these things with the intent that we should never enjoy them? God made your cunt, and he made my cock to fuck it. I'll honor Him and honor you with pleasure so sinful it becomes sacred.

I'm going to make you come so hard that there will be nothing and no one but me for you, forever.

You'll beg and plead and promise, do anything I ask, because you are mine to command, and you need my fucking cock. You were born to take it. To take me. For us to fit our broken edges together and become something greater than we were alone, praising His creation with our bodies.

I use my free hand to trace small, tight circles on my clit. This sacrilege is so lovely, so tempting. I imagine him buried in my pussy, the first man to ever explore me fully, as a blessing. A holy sacrament in our very own Garden of Eden.

It was never the shadow of Lily that made me take notice of you. It was your own innocence and your own spark: how unfamiliar you were with this world, but how you took to it all the same. I watched you come on Ben's fingers and whimper when I gave you the belt. You were timid, but you wanted to explore, and when you did, it was ecstasy. You reminded me of happier times. I told myself that was all.

It wasn't.

I want to be the one to guide you, to make sure every first time shatters you as completely as you have shattered me.

First, I'll bend you over and spread your legs; make sure no one has touched my property while I was away. I'll spank you the way you need. Keep you on the edge with pain, so you stay with me until I'm good and ready. I won't touch you anywhere else, but I'll watch you rub your swollen clit on the blankets until you beg, until you promise me you'll die if you don't have my cock buried inside of you.

Only then will I fuck you: slow, and deep, watching your eyes go wide, your mouth fall slack. I'll make you come on my cock over and over again, until each orgasm has to be ripped from you, until you beg me to stop. I'll feel every twitch and spasm of your sweet cunt, hear every noise you make. I will own your body, every exquisite inch of it.

I'll make you my whore, Mary, and it will be bliss for both of us. Don't disappoint me.

Arch

I fold the paper up with trembling fingers, only to immediately unfold it again. If I can trust this—if I can trust *him*—then his cruelty has always been about his desire. The idea that he wants me like I want him is overwhelming on every possible level. If owning me has been his goal all along...perhaps we aren't playing on opposite sides after all.

Am I willing to give up the idea of a new life for one at his side? The orgasm that wracks my entire body at the thought says yes.

And still it isn't enough.

I want to touch myself over and over to this idea. Open the letter again and stroke my folds while I imagine every sinful, depraved thing Arch is going to do to me when he gets home. But if he wanted me to do that, he would have told me. Probably as explicitly as possible. Instead, he said to wait.

If that's his first real command to me, I will obey it. I force myself to put the letter down on my night-stand and then go to the bathroom to take a cold shower, which Martha once mentioned to be useful for when one is…overheating.

By the time I'm dressed and heading downstairs for breakfast, the heat of desire has left me, and instead it's been replaced by an empty, aching loneliness. If he really wanted to do all those things to me —and as urgently as he claims—couldn't he have stayed another day? Even a few more hours? My ass is sore from yesterday, and it's hard not to feel a little ashamed of how easy I made it for him.

Maybe I'm a fool after all. Maybe he wants me as badly as I want him, but none of this means anything to him at all.

Is he capable of more?

Or does he simply play with his toys once and then discard them?

The kitchens are empty when I get there, but Martha left me some oatmeal on the stove, with instructions about where to find fruit, cream, and sugar to sweeten it. There are even small, early strawberries in a ceramic bowl on the counter. I'm cutting one into pieces, admiring its firm red flesh, when I feel someone coming up behind me.

"Mary." His voice is silk-soft on my skin, but somehow it doesn't feel right. It never does.

"Neville." I turn around and face him. His hair is loose today, shimmering black framing the angles of his face. He looks...satisfied, like a well-fed tiger. Somehow, it makes me more nervous than when he looks hungry, when he's still on the hunt.

I pick up my bowl so I can take it to the table to eat, but he doesn't move out of my way.

"Now that my dear brother is gone on business, do you suppose you can make time to discuss our plans? Don't disappoint me, Mary." He uses the same words as Arch's letter, but such different intent. "Not after I went to all this trouble to invent a crisis for him to solve."

His words uproot me. He sent his brother out of town in order to hold another auction? How can he be so certain that Arch won't know? Unless he *does* know, and this is merely another test for me.

"I don't need the money anymore. I'm not going back."

"Everyone," Neville says, a sneer creeping into his voice, "needs money. Especially pretty little girls like you. Sure, Arch enjoys looking at you this week, but he'll get tired of you eventually. And then where will you be? Nothing of any value, no skills to speak of, and a well-used cunt. Your only recourse would be working in the Garden, offering it to anyone and everyone." He blocks me when I try to get past. "Don't be silly, Mary. That isn't the life you want. The smart thing to do is turn your remaining asset into a nest egg."

I clench my bowl tighter to keep my hands from trembling. Is that what would happen? Has it happened before? Neville misunderstands my silence.

"Don't worry. My brother won't be able to cheat us again. I opened the books on you a little early, just to make sure we wouldn't get fleeced like last time. I made certain to ensure that I only approached buyers with whom I have a personal relationship." My blood chills as I wonder what kind of men enjoy spending time with Neville Craven.

He likes the toll it takes. How much of a toll would his "friends" exact?

"Excuse me." My voice is too tense. I don't want him to think he's affecting me. "Please."

He doesn't move.

"This is your chance, Mary. Your one chance to have everything you've ever dreamed of. The starting bids are already higher than what Susan sold for. Your tight little pussy is going to make us both rich."

I bite my lip, using the pain to try to keep my mind from spiraling out in a million directions. Is there any possible way for me to get in touch with Uncle Arch? Beg him to come back and save me?

But if he did, what if Neville is right? Would he fuck me until he's bored and then leave again?

He spelled out exactly what he plans to do to my body in that letter, but he didn't promise me anything resembling a future together. He didn't promise anything more than a single night. Only that I'd be ruined for anyone else forever. I had assumed he meant that no other man would compare. But what if he meant the ruination that taking my virginity would do to my value as a sale?

What if the letter that gave me such tentative hope was simply another blow aimed at Neville?

And this could be so much money. Enough to buy myself a life outside of Misselthwaite Manor and the Garden, however unimaginable that seems.

All it will cost me is my virginity.

But I can't make myself accept it. This auction is not what I want.

"No. I don't want to give that to a stranger." My voice is hesitant. I don't want to anger him. But I can't let him put me up on that stage again. No matter what happens with Arch, at least losing my virginity to him is my *choice*. It's a freedom I no longer want to give away.

"You thought you didn't want to suck cock, either," Neville reminds me. He seems to think this is a simple case of cold feet. "And look how you learned to love it. When you finally taste the full scope of how your body can be used, you'll be insensible from pleasure. You'll speak in tongues."

"No." My voice still quavers, but it's getting louder now. I cannot be auctioned while Arch is away. I will not choose money over my fantasy. "I don't want to, and that's that."

"The thing is, no one cares what you want. I have made powerful men promises. And they have already made me opening bids."

He advances on me, and I back up until my ass

hits the edge of the counter as he looms, filling my field of vision. "You are going to be sold by me. You are going to be fucked by the man who buys you. And you are going to make both of us more money than you can imagine."

When he grabs my wrist, tugging me forward and sending the bowl crashing to the floor, I think that someone will hear it and come running. But the sound gets lost in all of the manor's enormous, empty rooms, and no one intervenes. Not even when I start screaming. Maybe no one is left to hear.

Neville drags me bodily up the stairs to my room and throws me on my bed. He smirks at me.

"You'll thank me when it's done."

And then he locks me in.

29

AFTER POUNDING on the door until my hands are bruised, I end up slumped against the wall between Arch's room and my own, crying softly. I'm wrung out and exhausted; every part of my body hurts, even my bones. *Maybe no one will want me*, I think, *if I arrive in the Garden with tear tracks down my cheeks, my eyes red and my palms full of splinters. Maybe I can make myself too ugly to be desirable.*

But then will Neville just punish me more?

I let myself drift away into a fantasyland: that Arch finds out, somehow. That he hears my cries, even with all of the miles between us. That he runs into the house and up to my room, heart racing, cock hard, and throws open the door to free me. To claim me. He takes me in his arms; he cradles me against the broad, firm lines of chest, and tilts my head up to kiss me, and hitches me up so that my legs can wrap around his waist, and then—

My weeping is interrupted by a faint knock on the other side of the wall. I can't help it: for one shimmering moment, I let myself believe that it's all happening, that he has arrived to save me.

"Arch?"

"No," the wrong voice responds. "It's Colin."

My heart sinks, but I can't let myself get bogged down by disappointment. Colin can open my door, which is all I really need now. The rest is for later.

My words tumble over one another in a rush as I try to explain. "I need your help, please, Colin. I told Neville I wouldn't do another auction, so he locked me in. He's arranged a private sale, and I don't know how long I have. Can you get me out of here?"

He doesn't answer, but I hear the heavy sound of his boots on the wooden floors, and a moment later, my door swings open. He isn't his father, but the shape of his silhouette in the doorway still makes me swoon: broad shoulders, the same jaw. The fact that he's coming to my aid. Relief has me boneless.

I fall into his arms.

He lets me stay there for a few moments, my face pressed into his shirt, pretending everything is all right again, pretending he is someone else. Then he untangles us and steps back, regarding me with serious eyes.

"You can't stay here. You have to leave," he says. "Tonight."

I glance back at the letter on my bedside table. "I

can't leave now. I just need to hide from Neville until Uncle Arch gets back and straightens things out."

I have to know. If I don't see Arch, talk to him, find out if he truly wants me or if he's only acquiring a new piece for his collection... I'll wonder for the rest of my life. I'll be as haunted as the men of Misselthwaite. But Colin shakes his head.

"You don't understand. There is no hiding from him. He knows these grounds inside and out, and he won't walk away from a purse as big as the one you're about to net him. If you stay, you won't be safe. I can't protect you, Mary, and I can't watch him destroy you."

And I can't be Colin's next regret. For my own sake, as well as his.

"What should I do?" The problems of *where* and *how* remain as large as they've always been. I have no home but this, no money but my body's worth.

He sighs. "I'll give you money. Not a loan, a gift."

"I don't want charity, Colin. I've imposed enough in my life. I was a charity case at the commune after my mother died, and I've been a charity case here. I can't take money from you as well."

"Consider it payment for the work you've done, then. My mother's garden looks like it used to again. I like to go out there at night and look at your progress. I think she would be happy to know it's not abandoned anymore."

"I—thank you." A wave of grief passes over me,

that neither of us ever had a chance to know this woman who has defined our lives in so many ways.

"I'll take it over now," Colin says. "And I'll take good care of it. I promise."

"Oh, but I'll be back in a few days, it will be fine until then."

The determination on his face softens. "Mary, you don't understand. If you disappear tonight, you remain intact. But once you leave, you can't ever come back. Neville will be furious. Dangerous. He won't take to losing this money kindly, not to mention that the damage to his reputation will never heal." He must see the stricken look on my face, because he touches my cheek gently before continuing.

"Believe me, I don't like it either. Having you here —it's been a breath of fresh air. This musty old pile needed you. I didn't know how much I needed you until you came." For a moment it seems like he's wavering, and I pray that he'll offer me some compromise: a way to keep myself safe from Neville without leaving Misselthwaite forever.

It doesn't come. Colin puts his hands in his pockets, as if to guard against even the idea of touching me again. "I told you this place will ruin you. The only place I can be certain you'd be safe, maybe the only place Neville wouldn't go...is the Kingdom of Love."

It's all I've been asking for since I arrived here. He has no reason to know how foreign the idea of going back has begun to seem to me. But he does know that the money he's offering would be my dowry.

If I walk out this door, if I go back to the commune, I'm walking through a door that locks behind me. No other possibilities. No more dreams. No more pleasure.

I don't know if I can leave with things between Arch and myself so...unfinished.

All I can say is, "Uncle Arch doesn't want me to leave, and I want to stay. Neville won't cross Uncle Arch so directly."

"Even if I knew how to reach my father...he knew Neville was planning to hold a private event. He had to have at least guessed what would happen. He left anyway. Because that's the kind of man he is. His business is the only thing he will ever let himself love." Bitterness flavors his words, the unloved son of a man who can't bear to be hurt again.

"I can't believe that. He wrote to me—" I start, but Colin cuts me off.

"Mary." He looks at me with pity, a foolish child with a schoolgirl crush. "He *left*."

I deflate entirely, like a pricked balloon.

Actions speak louder than words. Yet another adage from my mother.

How can I argue with that? Arch did leave. And Colin knows his father better than I do. There are a lifetime of disappointments behind his words. I've let my emotions cloud my judgment. It was stupid. I have to muster control again, think this through. I spent the first eighteen years of my life not dreaming, not wanting, not needing anything or anyone.

It wasn't a good life, but maybe it was good enough. Maybe it's as good as I'll get.

I can't let myself think about what might be possible in this world, the world of the Cravens. I can't wait for the dream of Arch. I have to be practical. I have to put myself first.

If I stay, I risk being auctioned off to the highest bidder against my will. Losing control of my body, just as I was finally learning how to enjoy it. And giving something I've kept my whole life to someone who sees it as nothing more than a prize to be won. But if I leave...

If I weren't being forced out, I wouldn't be leaving. *God works in mysterious ways.* What if this is a blessing in disguise? Is this a sign, a final chance at redemption?

If I go back, I know what will happen every day for the rest of my life. Rising with the sun, the satisfaction of a hard day's work, the subsequent exhaustion chasing me from the dinner table to the dormhouse. Formal prayers morning, night, and before meals. Maybe I'll find my power again in the marriage bed. Maybe I'll be given to a husband with kind eyes and rough hands. Or maybe I'll be given to a cruel man I'll goad into giving me the pain I find so much pleasure in.

"Okay," I say. I can't seem to lift my head up enough to look Colin in the eye. "I'll go."

"Thank God." Colin hugs me again, pressing me tightly against his chest for another brief moment before pulling away.

"I'll call you a taxi while everyone's busy with the preparations," he says. "Pack anything you want to take with you, but be quick. Come down to the study when you're done. I'll meet you with the money."

I open the wardrobe's doors and then close them again. There's no point in bringing my beautiful new clothes with me. I'll never be allowed to wear them on the commune, and I couldn't bear watching them be torn up for rags or sold for some modest profit. They'll stay here, and I hope Dickon can find another girl they'll fit. The thought of all the work he put into them... I hope he'll understand that I never intended it to go to waste.

I stand in the doorway of my room for a long moment. Every inch of it feels like it's suffused with memories: the corner where I rode the rocking horse, listening to Arch—of course it was Arch—touch himself behind the wall. The bed, where I brought myself to even more orgasms, where I looked through the Manor's library books and learned that bodies could do things I'd never thought possible. The windows, where I watched the Garden's parties come alive.

It's hard to tear myself away, but I know I have to. I'm running out of time.

I walk down the stairs to the study as empty-handed as I arrived here. I will have the money with me when I go, but that isn't really mine, either, since I'll have to hand it over to the commune as soon as I arrive. Nothing in the world belongs to me except my body.

Well, until it's given in marriage, anyway.

At least they can't take my memories. My heart aches with longing and my lungs flood with sorrow. It's only years of habit—of knowing how to make myself do things I don't want to—that moves my legs, puts one foot in front of the other, until I find Colin in his father's study. He's holding a large brown envelope, which he hands to me.

"It's too much," I tell him, after peeking inside.

"The painting would have been worth twice this. I'm sorry I wasn't able to get you more. Quickly, now —the longer you stay inside the house, the more likely it is that Neville finds you. Your ride will be here shortly. You should go wait for him at the Manor gates."

I nod, and follow him obediently to the front door, far from the bustling kitchen. Colin hugs me one last time, but I don't feel anything anymore. There's no comfort in his touch, the warmth of his body seemingly as far away as the sun's in winter.

"It's for the best," he says.

As soon as I'm out the door, I hear it swing closed behind me with a heavy, final *thunk*.

I feel exposed out here, too visible; I can't help imagining Neville looking out the window and seeing me against the drive's pale gray gravel. I try to keep my mind empty and my feet light as I hurry the long, winding path to the gate. *Remember Lot's wife*, I tell myself. *Don't look back. Don't look back.*

But Colin's words keep echoing in my head. *It's for the best.* I've been told that various unpleasant things were *for the best* as far back as I can remember: the early mornings, the back-breaking labor. The death of my mother after months of painful illness. That's what they said when they kicked me out, too, shoving me out of the only home I'd ever known with no help, no resources, no nothing. They might as well have left me to die.

And if I had? *God works in mysterious ways.*

I try to imagine the version of me who lived her whole life in the commune's confines, bound strictly by their rules, and she feels like a stranger. She ate for fuel, not for the taste. She prayed with words and not with joy. She didn't know joy at all.

I don't know her. I don't want to have to be her again. And I'm not sure that I *can*.

Will I truly be able to swallow down every desire I have, now that I know how delicious fulfilling them can be? Not merely the pleasure I once believed to be a secret only I had discovered. When a handful of herbs can take a dish from plain to tasty, when flowers can brighten a sad day, will I be able to accept that godly women shouldn't covet?

When I have a child of my own, will I be able to look her in the eyes and tell her not to be selfish when she asks the same questions?

I don't think I can.

And what happens when I refuse, when I'm kicked back out? It wouldn't be giving my virginity to Arch that would ruin me, it would be leaving him without a word and knowing that as a result, this place won't be here to break my fall.

As soon as I think of it that way, the sadness that felt like a yoke on my shoulders lifts. I want this life, at the Manor. I want Arch. Maybe he can't love, maybe he's a cruel, broken collector. But maybe he just needs a second chance…like I have so many times before. I want to offer that to him, and I'll take my chances with what I get back. All I have to do is wait for him.

As soon as he's here I'll be safe.

Then a hand closes around my arm, cold and tight as an iron shackle. This time, not for a single heartbeat do I believe my fantasies have come true. I know this touch, icy and precise, for whose it is.

"I told you not to make this difficult," Neville says.

My voice is too hoarse from the screaming I did earlier, and then the crying, to imagine it would help to yell again.

He throws me over his shoulder like a ragdoll, where any blows I strike with my aching hands will do nothing at all. This time, he doesn't take me into the Manor. This time, he takes me close to the gate, close enough to see the taxi give up its idling and drive away.

I throw my envelope as far as I can in that direction, praying Colin will find it and know I didn't leave, knowing that it's an impossible hope.

We turn down a short path to a small, coldly modern guest house that I know immediately was chosen by Neville. He's going to keep me in his home, where no one will find me.

I put up a fight once at the door, and again when he brings me to a room with cuffs on the walls. But there is no fighting this. We both know it's too late for me, and I'm glad that at least he doesn't speak as he clicks my wrists in tight.

He washes me with clinical precision, adorns me with jewelry and a collar with a leash, just like last time.

But he adds a final accessory—a gag.

This time, when he leaves, he doesn't bother locking the door.

And I wish I'd never let myself dream of anything at all.

30

A HIGH WINDOW is visible to me from where I wait. Through it, I count the minutes until the sun goes down and the festivities begin. My heart still feels broken inside of my chest. I can't allow myself to escape to the fantasy of Arch rescuing me.

Even if he knew what was happening—even if he somehow arrived in time—he hasn't set foot in the Garden in decades.

Never, ever.

No, I will spend this time in contemplation. Not the way we did at the commune. Tonight, I want to pore over each memory of my time here, reliving each exquisite agony and bliss, and then let each of them go. After what happens tonight, they'll be too wrenching to bear.

Once another man takes the virginity I've guarded my entire life for the man I intended to commit myself to, how could I ever recall Arch inside me again? After I've become a victim of his uncle, how can I ever think about Colin's kindness? And when this last shred of innocence is taken from me by force, will I be able to enjoy pain given with the intent to arouse again?

Somehow, I doubt it.

The sky pinkens ahead of the coming darkness. It's going to be a magnificent sunset, which feels exceptionally cruel.

God works in mysterious ways.

Each degree of fading light is a reminder of how little time I have left. The road is being paved for my execution.

The Mary I was in the commune, the one I will leave in the past... I don't mourn her. I shed her slowly, piece by piece, molting into the me I am now. The me who decided to stay, to fight, to take a chance. To offer a chance. To take the lessons in pain and comfort I've learned and offer them to someone who needs them more than I do.

That me dies tonight on a stage, surrounded by the cruel, brilliantly-dressed masters of this cruel and brilliant universe, toasting one another with champagne as gold as the last rays of sunlight. I try to remember what it felt like to be among them, how magical the Garden seemed to me on my first visits.

Will this experience make me one of them?

Perhaps everyone who comes to play here at the

Manor once believed their lives would be different. Maybe this is the biggest surrender of all, and in the end my power will come from having survived the change.

That's what I pray for while I wait for Neville to bring me to the Garden. Not an impossible salvation, but a lesson I'll recognize in the clarity of hindsight.

I pray that God is working in a mysterious way.

When it isn't Neville that opens the door, but Ben, I stupidly allow myself another moment of hope. But with this gag in place, there's nothing I can say. His face is somber as he removes my cuffs from their attachments to the wall and links them together. Then he pulls something new out of his pocket: another delicate gold chain, but this one with a clip on either end.

"This isn't the power I hoped you'd find." His voice is just a shade deeper than it normally is, belying his disappointment in me. I blink back the tears that form. His brusque manner hides a generous heart, and I know he'll blame himself once the truth comes out.

"This belonged to Lily," he says, running the chain down my sternum. The metal is cold on my skin, brushing me where I'm sensitive, and I feel my nipples prick up with interest at the sensation. He opens the clips and attaches them to each pink peak, where they squeeze my tender skin. The little yelp I make is deep in my throat, muffled by the gag.

My nipples sting but the pressure is delicious, and no matter how my head and heart feel, my pussy is immediately wet and ready, pulsing as Ben sighs and leads me out of the room. The clamps shift as I walk, and the combination of friction, nerves, and hunger makes me woozy.

The dizziness lends a dreamlike feel to the dusky evening, as though this isn't happening, not really.

If this *is* a dream, Arch will come. The gates get closer and closer, and once I pass through, I will know for certain that this is real, that he isn't coming to save me. Ten steps, then five, then two, and then I'm inside and my mind no longer has any deep-seated reserves of hope left to draw on.

This is happening, and it's happening now. I can't stop trembling. Ben notices, and gives my back a reassuring rub with the hand that isn't holding my leash.

"It'll all be over before you know it, don't be scared. I'll take care of you afterwards myself."

I nod to show I understand, and then Neville is there, taking my leash and tugging harder than necessary to lead me onstage.

It's clear immediately that this is not a typical party. There's no decoration but the equipment. Dickon didn't adorn the girls and his staff with silk and satin; Robin doesn't sing throatily over the sounds of clinking crystal and laughter.

A number of men, masked as usual, sit in a semi-circle before me. A few small tables hold bottles of a dark brown liquor. Several of the men have already availed themselves of it, a few to excess, I can tell from their slow sway and the undercurrent of darkness. I recall something Martha mentioned once, chattering away to Mrs. Medlock in the kitchen over rising dough. That intoxicated men often have trouble getting hard.

It would be a comfort if these weren't Neville's handpicked men. They'd surely blame me, punish me for any failure on their own part.

"Gentlemen, you remember our virgin Mary. Last time she was up here she was only offering her mouth, hoping God would forgive her. Now she needs to be fucked like the unrepentant whore she is. You can make her remember it for the rest of her life. Who's willing to buy a night she'll never forget?"

He's not even pretending I'm here willingly, though he stops short of admitting I'm his captive. That must turn them on. Hands holding paddles shoot up, eager to offer numbers.

But instead of letting them bid, Neville wags a finger. "Ah, ah, ah. I knew Mary was a rare prize, so I took a few private bids before the auction began. The winner of that round was Mr. Every, so his price will be where we begin this evening. Mr. Every, will you remind us what that was?"

The crowd glances over to a man in a tuxedo. He's handsome, with salt-and-pepper hair and a commanding build, and he holds up his bidding paddle with casual ease. Then he names a number that makes everyone gasp.

"Has she been checked since the last auction?" another man calls from the crowd. I recognize him: he's the one who bought Susan's virginity. Tonight, he's dressed in a simple suit, but he's already lost his tie somewhere; his shirt is open at the collar and his glass is nearly empty. "If we're talking amounts like that, I'd like a guarantee of the merchandise."

Neville leers. "Of course, of course, Mr. Daniels. These religious girls are all the same. Nothing like denying themselves to make them desperate, eh? But we can demonstrate that she's intact. And maybe, once she's been purchased, I'll take her gag off so she can say her Our Fathers while you show her who her daddy is now."

The crowd laughs raucously as the chair is pushed to the center of the stage; I'm strapped in and my legs are spread wide. Between the clamps and the eyes of the crowd on me, I expect to feel turned on—but it's faint, not the helpless, out of control way I often do. I shiver when Ben spreads my cunt open and men come peer into my illuminated core. Each masked face could be the one above me when I'm held down and taken by force.

Ben notices, as he always does, the subtle cues of my body. He brushes his rough finger gently over my clit, overcoming my reluctance and making me wet yet again. I remember wondering how he would be as my first. I wish it could be so, now.

But he won't.

After the men have looked their fill, and everyone agrees that I am, in fact, a virgin, Ben unstraps me and helps me to my feet. My knees are shaky, but there's nothing for me to do except stand there while the bids come rolling in, thick and fast. I don't want to look at them as the numbers rise. But how can I look away?

At first there are so many men bidding I can't keep track of what's coming from who; someone will jump in, raise the number once, twice, a third time, before bowing out. Then another man who thinks we must be close to the cap takes his place.

The only two constant bidders are Mr. Every and Mr. Daniels. They're studied and unhurried, but they check in regularly, letting everyone around them know they mean business. The numbers quickly become incomprehensible to me—the kind of thing that could buy me whatever I wanted, if the things I wanted were possible to buy. For the first time, I begin to grasp the true amount of power assembled in this Garden, and what it would mean to rule over it.

This money didn't come from nowhere; these are the men who make the world that most people just live in.

I have no idea how much time passes before everyone else has dropped out, and it's just Mr. Every and Mr. Daniels trading numbers back and forth with the same casual disinterest they had at the start of the evening. Neville's practically drooling every time they one-up each other, and from the murmurs of the crowd, I can tell I'm not the only one who's impressed by what they're willing to spend tonight.

But then Mr. Daniels calls out a high bid, much, much higher than the numbers we've been discussing so far, and at last, Mr. Every hesitates.

"Any takers?" Neville asks. "No one wants to go even a cent higher?"

Silence.

My heart squeezes. My rapid heartbeat is a clock counting down.

Mr. Every remains silent. I prepare myself for Neville to declare Mr. Daniels the winner.

But then there's a stir in the crowd. Mr. Every is raising his paddle once again, and then he softly calls out a number double Mr. Daniels' last bid.

After that, there's no doubt who the winner will be. At least I knew what I was getting into with Mr. Daniels, having watched the way he methodically rutted Susan. Mr. Every is a wild card. The crowd is roaring, but all I can hear is the blood rushing inside of my own head. My time is up. It's time to face my fate.

I'm wet, the clamps doing their job, keeping me stimulated no matter where my mind is, but...this isn't what I want, and I can't pretend that it is.

But my body is no longer mine to withhold.

"Congratulations, Mr. Every," Neville calls. He can hardly keep the grin from his face. My pussy has just made him richer than even he anticipated. I blink rapidly, not willing to offer him my tears, knowing that would be the cherry on top for him.

"Come collect your prize. We're all eager to enjoy the show."

31

MORE APPLAUSE as the crowd agrees, but Mr. Every hasn't moved from his spot. He checks his watch and stares blandly ahead.

Neville seems as confused as I am. What is he waiting for? He bought me. And for the amount he paid, I can't imagine why he wouldn't be eager to take possession.

Unless he's planning to draw out some kind of emotional pain along with the physical. The pit in my stomach might just swallow me up from the inside if this takes any longer than it has to.

"Now, Mr. Every, Mary's waiting, too." Still nothing. Neville is growing too angry to hide how flustered he is now. His face is turning red under the stage's spotlight, and you can just see him trying to figure out if he's being made a fool of somehow.

If this was any other occasion, I'd be relishing the sight.

I'm so focused on what's happening right in front of me that I miss the beginning of the swell of whispers and murmurs, which picks up near the gates and takes a moment to travel to the stage. But then I realize people aren't looking at me anymore—they're distracted, peering around and over each other, trying to see who's coming in.

The lights are in my eyes, and they're too bright for me to be able to tell anything at first. What I can see is that Mr. Every is smiling now.

Whatever makes a man like him smile and a crowd like this concerned cannot possibly end well for me.

For the first time, I consider the fact that it might not only be my virginity he plans to take, but me altogether.

With the sum Neville will have made on this and the fury that Arch will surely be in if he finds out what happened here without his permission...it would be the best way to keep both secrets by giving Ben a generous severance and simply gifting me to Mr. Every. All he has to do is tell Arch I ran away.

My body is shaking so hard I think I might fall over. The prayers I'm offering up to God are nearly wordless, just *please, please*. I close my eyes, and wait for resolution.

Then the gag is being removed from my mouth and I open my eyes in surprise to see Dickon.

I thought he went away with Arch, or was otherwise occupied. I take in a long, gasping breath. My jaw is sore from being held open; I can still taste the metal of the ball on my tongue, and the corners of my mouth feel cracked and dry. He offers me a wink before slipping away, before my cramped jaw has a chance to loosen enough to form a question for him.

My gaze returns to the crowd and now I can see it's tripled—quadrupled—I can't keep track. More and more people are flowing in, dressed as extravagantly as I've ever seen, more over-the-top than any previous entertainment. Around them, staff are putting out roses and lilies and ivy, so much ivy. Others are passing champagne. I don't understand. Next to me, Neville is slowly backing up, face now drained of its earlier color. He backs right into the wall of Ben's chest. Whatever Ben mutters in his ear is enough to stay his feet, though his eyes are darting back and forth like a caged animal.

Then suddenly, Colin is there, sweet Colin, faithful Colin, who must have gone looking for me, and I'm positive now I won't be able to stand much longer, so great is my relief.

But he's carrying something that Mr. Every stands to help him with, a wooden crate they hoist to the stage next to me before Dickon returns and takes a crowbar to it, prying it open with practiced efficiency. When the wooden slats fall away, there's a collective gasp. The loudest one is from me.

Here on stage, after all this time, is my painting.

My mother's final painting. My first sight of Lily Craven. I study the image hungrily. This was the last woman Arch loved. She's beautiful, of course, with raven-black hair and large brown eyes.

My mother painted her smiling, her plush mouth turned up at the corners. In the picture she's naked, sitting on a swing in her own private garden. Rose bushes have grown up the swing's ropes, and they surround her, their petals almost as delicate as her burnished skin. She doesn't look coy, though: even here, she's looking down from her throne at you, daring you to come closer, to find out if she's as soft as she looks.

You can tell that my mother loved Lily, that she took care to paint her so that she'd be just as magnetic on the canvas as she was in real life. It's maybe five or six feet tall—but even if it were the size of a book you would still feel the force of Lily's personality and the sway of her sensuality radiating from every inch. It's so beautiful, even more gorgeous than the other pieces of her work I've seen. In its presence, I understand, finally, why it's worth so much money. Why everyone considers it her masterpiece.

I see, too, why Arch would have wanted it destroyed. How difficult it would have been to see her, so lifelike the painting practically breathes, and ever recover from the loss of her.

And I know why my mother never painted again. No one could look at anything she produced and want to live in shackles, praying to a silent, withholding god.

Why, then, would she?

It's hard to tear myself away from her—from Lily, and the shadowy image of my mother, whoever she was when she made this painting, but there's a force more powerful than memory sweeping toward me. I feel its pull like gravity, inescapable.

I can't see beyond the staff removing the ring of chairs, but even their faces seem shocked.

Then I hear it.

His voice. Arch's voice, from the back of the crowd, a deep rumble like an earthquake rising, changing everything. It strokes my skin, down my spine, against my nipples, my clit, my mouth. At last, he's here, *here*, behind the walls he swore he'd never enter and saying the words no one ever thought they'd hear:

"Is this any way to greet your Master?"

32

THERE'S a moment of complete and total stillness, where even the birds in the trees seem to hold their breath, and the breeze won't dare rustle the leaves. Every eye in the Garden is fixed on Arch.

He's wearing traveling clothes; he must have rushed straight here from wherever he's been. Even in less-than formal wear, he looks twice as elegant as the men in tuxes. His magnetism and power radiates from the top of his tousled hair to the dust-covered soles of his boots. He's pushed up the sleeves past the corded muscles in his forearms. I'm struck by the way his hands clench and then relax when he sees me standing on the stage, trembling.

I'm rooted to the spot, waiting for him, as he presses through the commotion towards me. His gaze is fixed on me like a spotlight, and I shake in its hot glare.

"Mary Lennox," he says, loud enough for everyone to hear, but his eyes never waver from mine.

Arch Craven.

"I've never claimed to be a good man. But in my own way, I've tried. The mistakes I've made have haunted me more with each passing year. One of them was your mother, Grace. When she found out she was pregnant…I made assumptions. I thought of my business, how an unplanned pregnancy could force a guest into a family, how it would ruin everything that Lily and I had built."

I'd long known I wasn't conceived in love, but this is the first time I've truly thought about the fact that my father could be here, among the men in the Garden. It's an enormous, terrifying thought, but before I have time to chase it, Arch continues.

"I paid him off. He didn't need my money, but he would have benefitted from my connections, so it was a job I offered him, halfway around the world. So far away that he'd never know about Grace. But she knew about *him*. She heard the news before I did, about the accident, and she knew I'd been the one to send him away. It caused a rift between her and my wife, and it turned me into the devil in her eyes." His drift to the painting momentarily, but then return to me.

"When she went to the commune, Lily and I thought it was a self-imposed penance, as though she were also complicit in your father's death. I swore to Lily I'd do right by you if the opportunity ever presented itself. But I didn't. When she died, I ordered the painting I was meant to keep for you destroyed. And rather than admit what I'd done, when you arrived at Misselthwaite, instead of writing a check, I tried to control you the way I'd tried to control Grace. I wanted you, Mary, from the moment I saw you, I wanted you and I was ashamed."

He does move in closer to me, finally, finally. He's so tall and so broad, and the warmth radiating off of him is a shock after so much time naked in the cool night air. I long to touch him, to offer reassurance, but I'm still chained.

"I turned away from so much in these past years that I nearly forgot how deeply I cared. For my son, for this place. And because I wasn't looking, I let my brother grow monstrous. When Mrs. Medlock told me what he was planning, she also told me she betrayed me all those years ago. When I ordered this painting destroyed, she sent it away. She saved it. And me."

Dickon's behind me again, unlocking my cuffs with a key he must have run off to find. When my arms are freed, pain shoots through them from being in the same position for so long.

"It might be too late to save what could have been between us," he says. "But it's not too late for you to save yourself. I'm offering you this painting as an apology," Arch continues. "It will buy you any life you want. The commune would change completely with this investment, and you'd never be the sinful girl to them again. Or you could travel. Study. You can have anything you want now."

He falls silent as I dry my lips with my wrist.

"I want the painting."

It's Arch's turn to be disappointed, and even his carefully practiced stoicism can't hide the pain in his eyes. The pain I needed to see, the guarantee that what I'm about to say is what we both need.

"I want it to hang in Colin's room. He should have a memory of his mother, and I like to think of my mother's work being a part of that. I don't want the money, Arch. I don't want the commune. It's not my home anymore. And nowhere will ever feel like home if you aren't there."

At last, he steps onto the stage and takes my hand. This time, he speaks only to me.

"I love you. Are you certain about this?"

I kiss his palm; I taste his beloved, familiar skin. *He loves me.*

"Yes," I say. "Yes. I'm yours. Show me what that means."

Whatever hesitation has been holding Arch back finally disappears, and I watch his eyes go hooded and dark as they sweep down my body, taking in Lily's clamps around my nipples, the nakedness that feels as comfortable as clothing to me now. How ready I am for him. How ready I've been for weeks.

"Good," he growls, and then turns his attention back beyond the lights.

"Ladies and gentlemen." Arch's voice booms

throughout the Garden. "After tonight, she may have her choice of anything and anyone within these walls, but first, always, and forever, she is mine. Behold—I give you your queen."

The response is instantaneous, this time: hooting and hollering, accompanied by ear-splitting whistles and a crash of applause. Now I understand the party, why Arch brought seemingly everyone who's ever stepped foot here in. Not merely to witness his apology, or to watch him anoint me in his ownership.

This is my coming-out party.

Ben is taking Neville somewhere; I can't bring myself to stop looking at Arch long enough to watch. Dickon has brought a new chair to the stage, and this one looks like a throne.

That surreal feeling is back again, but not because I feel disconnected from myself. It's because all my silent prayers were answered, even the ones I never admitted to myself I was making when I longed for belonging and power.

God gave me Arch, and Arch is giving me a new kingdom. More than that, he's given me, in front of the most powerful people in the country, his heart. For that, I *am* more powerful than them. Their money means nothing to him compared to what I now hold in my hand.

My subjects can see everything: my swollen nipples, the chap of my lips from being stretched around the ball gag, how hungry I am for their attention, and, most of all, for Arch's cock.

The sound of a zipper alerts me that he's pulling it out before he presses the thick, hard length against my ass, a private reminder of what we've already shared.

He tugs me into his lap, and I can feel him behind me: so close. So close.

He lifts me up by my hips, hovering me over him.

And then he sheaths me onto him like it's nothing, his cock opening me up so fast and hard and perfect that my eyes roll back in my head.

For a few long moments, I'm nothing but sensation: Arch's mouth pressed against my shoulder, his teeth digging into the skin; his fingers tweaking my nipples, teasing their soreness; his cock, so big all I can do is pulse around him and squirm. I lift myself up once—twice—riding him in a frenzy, finally taking everything I've ever wanted, letting pleasure swallow me whole.

My orgasm obliterates me. When I come to, I'm still twitching and panting, and Arch is still rock hard inside of me, his fingers toying idly with my clit. I take hitching, gasping breaths, but he doesn't let up; instead, he rocks his hips, snugging his cock even deeper, as far into me as it will go.

I relax into his rhythm as the crowd enjoys our show, begin to touch one another, to enjoy the festivities. The view they're enjoying must be magnificent. His huge cock pistoning in and out of me, his fingers dancing over my engorged clit. The way he tugs on the chain, sending the sharp pain in my nipples into an electric current that makes my eyes roll back.

"With me, now," he murmurs, and we come together, this time, his body held inside of mine, his roar of release and satisfaction making the ground shake underneath our feet.

And then afterwards, it's everything I dreamed of. Susan gives me a glass of champagne and Robin pets my hair while teasing me about being her new favorite slut. Ben offers to massage out the knots I have from being tied up, but there's only one man I want to touch me, now that he has, now that he's mine.

It isn't long before we leave our party, and he runs me a bath in his own tub, which is somehow even more magnificent than the one I'd been using.

Maybe I drift off; because the next thing I know, I'm being cradled in Arch's arms as he lifts me out of the bath. He dries me off carefully, lingering between my legs and smiling smugly when he sees what he did to my pussy. There are finger-shaped bruises on my waist and I'm sure his teeth left an imprint on my shoulder.

"I suppose I'll have to let you rest," he says, picking me up again to carry me to bed. "But in the morning—"

I interrupt him thoughtlessly. "In the morning, you'll fuck me again?"

"Yes," he says, laying me out in bed, his eyes hungry on my skin already. He reaches down to massage my clit, and my legs fall open for him, help-lessly obedient. "In the morning—and as often as you want, for the rest of your life, sweet Mary—I will bring you to heaven and through hell, again and again."

EPILOGUE

THERE'S A RATHER long pause between my first party as Mistress of the Garden—where I was initiated with Arch's cock—and my second.

That's because, for several weeks, I'm too busy with Arch, whose instructions continue to be demanding and delicious, and inevitably end with me impaled on his cock, my body wracked by more sensation than I was ever permitted to think possible.

The Garden is our private paradise, and we try out everything together: the spanking benches and the wheel, which I learn is called a Catherine Wheel. He shackles me to the walls; he spanks me with stinging nettles and even once the rose-thorn whip he had me make with my own hands. I kiss his feet; he ties me in knots; he comes on my face, my tits, my back, and my ass, marking me inside and out. I love all of it, though nothing so much as when he gives me his cock, sinking into the deep wet heat of my pussy with a groan of smug satisfaction.

Fucking Arch is nothing like training with Neville, who's been banished. It's not even like the experiences I had with Colin and Susan. Those were wonderful in their own ways, but this is on another level entirely. It's stunning how well-matched we are, how he rises to meet my intensity every time. Sometimes I wake to find myself tied to the bed with silk ribbons, easy enough to escape though of course I don't want to; sometimes he feeds me nothing but his cock all day. I'm deliriously happy.

Martha is the one who reminds me what my obligations to the estate are. "Of course, you don't have to," she says, getting me up for a late breakfast one morning. "I'm sure Master Craven would be just as happy to stop the parties all together, but—"

"No," I tell her. "I want them to continue. I want other people to get to experience themselves to their fullest here. To find pleasure and satisfaction they can't find anywhere else."

The question is, can I rule their pleasure and satisfaction? Do I have the imagination? I can't possibly have Arch's personal power.

"You're not nervous, are you?" Martha asks.

"It's just that I don't think I'll be as good at it as Lily."

"Well, I disagree." Martha's grin is devilish. "We're all going to help you prove you're as good, or better."

After that I take to spending long afternoons with

her and Ben and Dickon and the girls, Susan and Robin and everyone else who works in the Garden.

Spring has fully given way to summer by the time the appointed night arrives, and you can smell roses in bloom everywhere on the property, their soft floral scent perfuming everything.

I watch from our bedroom window as the servants prepare the grounds, going through their familiar motions: lighting candles, pouring champagne, laughing and teasing and flirting with one another. They're dressed in white.

Everyone will have the chance to feel like a blushing virgin bride tonight.

The door opens, and I don't have to turn my head to know it's him in the room. The powerful shape of his body causes a breeze that shifts the fine silk of my chemise when he crosses the floor and comes up behind me. He presses himself against my back, his chin resting on top of my head and one arm coming around to circle my waist. He presses a flat palm against my belly and my cunt tingles with desire.

"Your bridesmaids are waiting for you," he says, kissing the back of my neck. "And you're up here in your undergarments."

"I was just making sure the flowers were right." I point to one of Dickon's men placing one of the many huge vases of white lilies at the side of the stage. "I want everything to be perfect."

The hand that was on my stomach dips down between my legs, rubbing against me through the folds of my skirt. Dickon made me a new wardrobe at Arch's demand, and now everything I wear is tissue-thin chiffon, or else slippery satin and silk. My skin is always being caressed by something, a reminder of how much Arch loves me, how much he wants me to be and do and feel.

"You are perfect." Arch rumbles.

"You know what I mean." My hips roll into his touch.

"Are you wet already?" he asks softly, mouth almost brushing my ear.

"Y—yes."

"Good." And then he withdraws, leaving me aching and confused. I turn around to see him pulling something from a black leather case. It's gold, glimmering in the fading daylight, the kind of thing I once mistook for a sculpture, but now recognize as a plug. Except this one seems to have two ends on it.

"You are Mistress of the Garden," Arch intones. "You can do whatever you want there. Your desire is the law when you are between those walls. But..." With his pause, I'm ready for him to make a last-minute change to my responsibilities, confirming that I'm not ready. That's not what he does. "No matter where you are, no matter what you are doing or with whom, you are mine," he says.

I nod again, blushing, this time. Every time he says that it feels like fingers on my clit, a smack landing exactly where I need it. Water trickling cold down my throat on a hot, dusty day.

"I'm the only one who gets to be inside you," he says, and it's not a question. "Lie on the bed and lift your skirts up for me."

I do as Master Craven commands, spreading my legs so he can see what he's doing to me.

"You've never taken the power you've earned," he says, slapping me there with an open palm. I struggle to hold still. "Until tonight." He smacks me again before returning to rubbing, spreading my wetness down between my cheeks to the pucker of my other hole. "And you've never opened yourself to me fully." He slides a finger inside, stretching me out. "I've been patient. That ends now."

"Open me," I say. "I'll tell you."

"No." Arch smirks. "I'll tell you." He starts working me open, teasing me for as long as I can bear. "My flower," he says when my legs are shaking. "You're afraid I'll see you commanding the Garden and find you wanting. That I'll wish you were Lily." He slides the plug inside of me, one bulbed end penetrating my cunt while the other presses into my ass. "There's no way I can assure you that won't happen, until you find your footing. And you won't be my first wife." The second bulb enters my ass, and I let out a gasp. "You'll be different. You'll be my Mary. The Queen of the Garden."

When the bulb is fully seated inside of me, the rod connecting the two is a perfect pressure between my legs, and I flex around it experimentally. Fuck. This is going to be torture.

"It's time," Arch holds out his hand to help me up. "Let your subjects help you get dressed."

When I stand, the chemise drops back around me. I feel dressed in his command, and adorned in his power. The metal inside of me is the only ornament I need: a sign of who owns me, who loves me, who cares for me.

And yet, the Garden needs me too, so I go downstairs to get dressed.

My wedding gown is purest white. It has delicate, jeweled lace at the skirt and a silk corset bodice that's tied so tightly, I'm breathless. My veil is a single layer of fishnet, attached to the bottom of a white leather eye mask. It covers my nose and mouth and drapes behind me in a long trail.

It skims my body perfectly, highlighting the peaks of my nipples and the curves of my ass. It's nothing like what I wore on my first day at Misselthwaite, and I smile in the mirror, remembering how I longed for her confidence, her ease in her skin.

My wedding dress is sexy, and virginal, and empowering—Dickon's masterpiece.

Colin stands next to me at the iron gate—the one I was not allowed to enter all those months ago. Now everything on the other side of it is mine.

"You look beautiful," he says, eyes aglow. He's lost the sad hangdog look I thought was a part of him.

"She's going to be your stepmother," Susan turns around to say. She's wearing head to toe white leather, held together with gold buckles. Next to her, our best man Ben shakes his head and chuckles.

"Shoo! You're up!" I tell them.

She and Ben quickly face front to walk down the center aisle and take their place at the stage, where my king awaits. Among similarly dressed men, he stands out as the most confident, the most commanding, the only dominant authority.

Colin and I walk down the aisle. I keep my chin high. Robin plays the piano and sings the most perfectly erotic French song.

Everyone is dressed in white, except the groom and his men. They're all masked, and they all bow when I pass.

Colin gives me away, and I take Arch's arm.

The legalities of the marriage are already complete, and the ceremony is of our making, for our community. Dickon officiates, and it's all pretty straightforward until the vows.

"Master Arch," I begin, looking up into the depth of his eyes. There's still a little sadness at the edges, but they're open to my love in a way that makes them both kinder and crueler. "I give myself to you." I reach back and pull a string at the back of my skirt. "My soul. My heart. My body." The dress comes off. I am naked except for the veiled mask. "I am your property, forever."

Arch looks at me with dark, hungry eyes, and I

know that his hunger is deep, and I'm the only one who can satisfy it.

"Mistress Mary," he says, turning my naked body to the congregation. Their eyes skim my breasts and belly, fondle my legs and worship my bare feet. I have never felt so powerful with so little clothing, while the man I love claims possession of me. "I will treasure every moment that I own your body. Your mouth is mine. Your ass is mine. Your cunt is mine. Do you vow to me your body?"

"I do."

"Then I give you this Garden for your pleasure."

He leads me to a throne next to his. Both are decked in white flowers. I sit, and Arch kneels before me and parts my legs.

"Rule it as you wish," he whispers and moves beside me.

This is the moment, and it's all mine.

I snap my fingers, and through the front gate, a line of people enter, each carrying a cat o' nine tails. I've added strands of something in the garden, so there's both the slap of the fine, white leather and tickle of soft reeds and braided grass.

These are my people. They know their roles and they fulfill them immediately. The last attendant enters with a whip I made especially for my husband. She kneels before him and offers it. He takes it and dismisses her. The handle was braided especially for the size of his hand, and I paid special attention to how much pain and pleasure I can bear—knowing he'd add more of both.

Arch stands before me with my spread legs, the bulge in his trousers already stretching the fabric. A shot of pleasure goes through my body imagining how hard he'll get when he lands his blows, the whip singing through the air and landing on my skin with a satisfying *crack* each time.

"You expect this on your bottom," he says with a mischievous grin.

"I expect it on my body."

He put my legs over the arms of the throne, showing off the metal rod between ass and cunt to the attendees still watching, curious eyes behind their masks.

"Mistress." Arch twists the whip around his hand and lets it go, testing its resilience. "You're going to remember this night for the rest of our lives."

He flicks the whip and jerks his arm forward. It snaps inside my thigh.

"Oh, *God!*" The shocking burn makes me shout in a most unregal manner. He gives me a look that asks if I'm all right, and I respond with a shrug.

"You all," he says to the voyeurs leaning against the stage. "Come up here. Watch how a queen takes her pain and her pleasure."

They scramble up to watch us.

"You ready?" he asks.

"Yes." I spread my legs wider. I trust him.

He brushes the stinging bites with the thong part,

which is mostly soft grass with flower petals braided in. With a loop and a flick, the leather cracks against sensitive skin twice, once inside each thigh. He's skilled, accurate, and fast, hitting a fresh spot each time and coming so close to the tender, soaking wet center I can feel the breeze against my folds. The pain is almost as intense as the hunger for more.

"I asked if you're ready," he says, and I realize my eyes are closed. When I open them, three of the men are actively jerking off. My God, I love it.

"And I said yes," I answer impatiently.

"So you did." His wrist flick seems too casual to be accurate, but it's exactly the right force, hitting its pinpoint target—my swollen, begging clit.

It detonates an explosion it can't finish, leaving me suspended between an orgasm and the need for one.

Arch smiles. It's exactly what he intended.

He throws the whip aside and gets on his knees before my throne. He takes my welted inner thighs and pulls me open, then licks his lips. I look over his head. One woman has her hand under her skirt. Another is riding the arm of her chair. All of the men have their cocks in their hands.

"Finish with me!"

Arch nods approvingly and flicks my clit with his tongue, plays with the bar, then sucks me softly until I'm begging to come. The jerking and rubbing of my guests gets harder and hotter, until I'm brought to a climax worthy of a king.

The night is a blur after that. I suck Arch's cock on stage; we bet on two girls riding rocking horses like the one from the library. I try to oversee scenes between all kinds of different people; everyone wants the Mistress's blessing tonight. I finger myself for them, and Arch lets me come. I make them kiss my feet when I'm done.

Finally, though, Arch tugs me towards him. "How does the bar feel?"

"Like an inadequate replacement for your cock."

"Good girl." He runs the back of his hand across my mouth and down my body, stroking my nipples, my belly, before cupping my pussy.

"We'll have to take care of that now."

That's all it takes; I bury my face in his jacket and come hard, shaking through it. The rush of pleasure and humiliation is the same as ever: that everyone knows how much I want it, and how easy I am for this man. That he'll give me exactly what I need, every single time.

Arch leads me out of the party, into the quiet, starlit night. He put a real door on my garden so no one would wander in there, but he unlocks it now, and sets me on the swing so I can admire his perfection while he undresses in the moonlight.

He takes off the mask and veil so we're both naked together, running our hands over each other's bodies, appreciating the shapes and curves of our new life together.

The noise from the Garden is just a hum, here, the soft clatter of talk and laughter, pleasure and pain as he lays me down on a silky patch of grass and pushes up my knees.

He pulls the front plug out, stretching my cunt for a moment before I'm suddenly empty again.

"Our first fuck as husband and wife," he says, playing with the rear bulb. "Where shall it be?" He takes the plug out partway to stretch me, then lets my body suck it back in.

"Yes. All."

"Cunt first." He slides deep in one push. I cry out in relief and pain, his cock so much bigger than the plug. It rubs against the one still inside me as I urge him to fuck me harder and harder. He slams my clit with his body when he goes deep. I claw at his chest.

"I'm going to come," I groan.

"Do it, you beautiful little whore."

I come like a wild thing, bucking and arching under him. I'm almost done when he pulls out and flips me onto my hands and knees.

"You're everything to me," he says, hitching up my hips. He takes out the plug and with his fingers, he gathers lubrication from my pussy and rubs it to my behind. "And I love you."

I look at him over my shoulder as he's placing his cock at my stretched anus.

"Til death do us part," I say. He thrusts into my ass, and I let out a cry.

"You belong here," he says, pounding me. "With me. Forever."

"Yes." All I can do is agree. His hands are everywhere. His cock is so deep inside me, I forget my name.

"You and me, say it," he demands, breathless.

"You and me."

"Forever."

"Forever. Always. Arch."

When I say his name, he comes inside me with a grunt so loud the ground shakes.

When he's done, I roll over and he falls into my arms with his head between my breasts. We are quiet together. All our promises are made. All our devotions have been said.

The earth moves underneath us, and the air stirs, and I don't know if it's the garden or him or everything...but with him in my arms and the walls of the garden around me, I am truly the ruler of a beautiful, peaceful kingdom of love.

If you loved this erotic fairytale, you'll love Raven Jayne's debut series, **Master Class**.

> Dark, delicious, and damn near addictive! If you like your books scorching, your mysteries sexy, and your men wonderfully, temptingly dangerous, then you need the Master Class series. Right now. Don't keep The Master waiting.

— *USA TODAY BESTSELLING AUTHOR*
SIERRA SIMONE

Master Class: The First Three Lessons

Ten lessons are all that stand between me and my future...
My entire life has been determined for me.
I will be the trophy wife of a powerful man.
But another powerful man stands between us.
The first lesson he teaches me is obedience.
The second, patience.
My third lesson is supposed to be learning to control my mind.
But maybe I'd prefer he do it for me...

ALSO BY RAVEN JAYNE

MASTER CLASS

A collection of dirty, erotic novellas

PAIGE PRESS

Paige Press isn't just Laurelin Paige anymore...

Laurelin Paige has expanded her publishing company
to bring readers even more hot romances.

**Sign up for our newsletter to get the latest news
about our releases and receive a free book from
one of our amazing authors:**

Laurelin Paige
Stella Gray
CD Reiss
Jenna Scott
Raven Jayne
JD Hawkins
Poppy Dunne
Lia Hunt
Sadie Black

ABOUT THE AUTHOR

Two NYT erotica authors got together and thought up a dirty little story. You're welcome.